PROLOGUE

Andrew Whitney, known as the Old Man (sometimes affectionately and sometimes not so much) by the agents of the Goddard Project, perused the data presented to him by one of his top analysts. There was no denying the pattern the data revealed. Military technology that was not supposed to be available to any country in Africa, but especially not these volatile nations, had been leaked.

The question was: What to do about it? Was the technology being stolen, or had it been provided by the U.S. military itself? Very few people realized the all too real presence that the U.S. military had in several African countries, countries few would imagine received proprietary military training from the United States.

But oil wasn't the only commodity of interest on the African continent. Africa was a continent rich with minerals and the necessary labor to extract them. More than fifty percent of the world's cobalt and ninety-eight percent of the chromium reserves could be found in countries located in southern Africa. Most of which were far from stable, both politically and militarily.

So, what was the U.S. military doing training their soldiers? Protecting national interests, or at least that's what the politicians claimed.

Whit wasn't so sure, but his opinion hardly mattered. The only thing he had any influence over was the illegal distribution of proprietary technology. And the only way to find out if the distribution was intentional or not was to send in his own agent. Another memo on his desk gave him the perfect cover too.

The State Department was sending out several auditors to Africa, who were supposed to determine whether human rights violations were happening in the extraction of minerals being purchased by the federal government and American corporations. Whit would send one of his agents, ostensibly to audit the mines, but also to try to gather firsthand intel on whether or not the military technology finding its way into questionable hands had done so in violation of U.S. law.

Bennet Vincent would be just the agent. While the man looked like a mild-mannered accountant, he could kill with his bare hands, handled weapons even better and knew his way around a computer like it was a kiddy maze at the park.

He was also the next on Whit's list of agents who needed to get a life outside of the Goddard Project. Whit couldn't see much opportunity for that on this assignment, but there was always the next one.

Books by Lucy Monroe

The Real Deal
Come Up and See Me Sometime
Goodness Had Nothing To Do With It
3 Brides for 3 Bad Boys
Ready
Willing
And Able
Heatseeker

The Goddard Project series
Satisfaction Guaranteed
Deal With This
The Spy Who Wants Me
Watch Over Me
Close Quarters

Published by Kensington Publishing Corporation

SHE HADN'T BEEN ABLE TO GET ROMAN OUT OF HER HEAD

Despite plentiful evidence to the contrary, the idea that he might share the attraction would not leave her alone.

No doubt it was just wishful thinking, but what a wish.

He and Ben were standing beside a table near the one she and Fleur sat at during mealtimes, and talking to the other men in the security detail.

Despite the fact that he was in active conversation with the soldier who had introduced himself as Neil, Roman's gaze caught hers the minute she entered the hut.

She did her best to give him a casual nod of acknowledgment, but ruined the effect with a blush he no doubt took for some misplaced shyness or embarrassment. It wasn't, though; the heat climbing her neck and into her cheeks was pure, unadulterated arousal.

Was she going through midlife crisis early, or something? She was only twenty-eight, but something had to explain the way her nipples tightened to hard points every time she saw the man.

And that wasn't even taking into consideration the heat between her legs. She'd never had such a physically visceral reaction before. Not to anything. Not fear. Not joy. Definitely not passion.

It was just a little terrifying.

CLOSE QUARTERS

LUCY MONROE

KENSINGTON BOOKS
http://www.kensingtonbooks.com

KENSINGTON BOOKS are published by

Kensington Publishing Corp.
119 West 40th Street
New York, NY 10018

All Kensington titles, imprints, and distributed lines are available at special quantity discounts for bulk purchases for sales promotion, premiums, fund-raising, educational, or institutional use.

Special book excerpts or customized printings can also be created to fit specific needs. For details, write or phone the office of the Kensington Special Sales Manager: Attn.: Special Sales Department. Kensington Publishing Corp., 119 West 40th Street, New York, NY 10018. Phone: 1-800-221-2647.

Kensington and the K logo Reg. U.S. Pat. & TM Off.

ISBN-13: 978-0-7582-4202-0
ISBN-10: 0-7582-4202-6

First Brava Books Trade Paperback Printing: September 2010
First Kensington Books Mass-Market Paperback Printing: July 2012

10 9 8 7 6 5 4 3 2 1

Printed in the United States of America

CHAPTER ONE

Roman Chernichenko pushed open the heavy wooden door without knocking. It swung forward without a sound, revealing an office that would better suit a U.S. senator than the director of a highly classified black-ops unit like the Atrati. Walls covered in floor-to-ceiling bookcases surrounded an imposing, oversized desk and two pairs of armchairs facing it. The dark wood and rich upholstery screamed quality and power, and yet the man behind the desk was not a politician.

Not one elected by the American people anyway. Richard Corbin, retired Air Force Lieutenant General, had left the military despite all signs he would achieve General Air Force Chief of Staff one day in the not too distant future. He'd taken a job that would never get him on the cover of *U.S. News & World Report,* but offered him as much power as any elected official and more than most.

He was also Roman's boss. Well, technically, his boss's boss, but being the team lead for the Atrati's most effective unit, Roman often took his orders directly from Corbin.

"Thank you for joining us, Chernichenko."

Roman inclined his head, taking in the other occupants of the room besides Corbin. Two men sat in the chairs facing the desk, having left two empty chairs between them. Colleagues perhaps, but not friends.

Though he did not recognize them and they both wore suits, there was no doubt they were military. Their haircuts and posture gave them away. Both men flicked him a glance, but the one on the right returned his attention to Corbin almost immediately. The one on the left sized Roman up with an experienced eye.

"Gentlemen," he said, looking at the one on the left as he sat down.

No one spoke for several seconds, but Roman felt no need to break the silence. He settled back into his chair, prepared to wait.

The man on his right fidgeted; the one on his left looked forward, but remained still and silent, and Roman's boss ignored them all as he did something on his computer. After a few clicks and some quick typing, he nodded to himself and finally focused his attention back on the men facing him across his desk.

His gaze zeroed in on Roman. "We've got a situation."

"We generally do"—Roman paused for a beat of silence—"when you call me."

Corbin's head jerked in a short nod of acknowledgment.

"So, this is your guy?" the officer on his left asked.

The man on his right made a disparaging sound. "I still don't see why we can't handle it in-house. From what I understand, this man used to work for us. His training can't be any more specialized than our men's."

So, they were Army. Interesting.

Roman turned and gave the man a cool look. "Wrong."

"Watch your tone, soldier." The Army brass glared with enough heat to singe.

Roman merely lifted his eyebrow.

"What the hell do you mean I'm wrong?" the other man pugnaciously demanded when Roman didn't bother to reply. "What was I wrong about?"

"Everything."

"Explain yourself," the older man demanded in a tone that said he'd have Roman's balls if he didn't like the answer.

Roman wasn't nervous. It would take more than a riled-up officer who had the look of a man who had never served in action to worry him. "If you could handle it internally, you would have. I never worked for *you*. I served my country and I still do. And my training goes well beyond what I went through to become a Ranger."

"He's right, at least about us handling this thing with our own ops," the man on Roman's left said.

Roman turned to face him. "You're Army too?"

"Yes."

"No one's supposed to know," the other man furiously inserted.

"I'm not *no one*," Roman said, without looking at the other man.

The one he was facing was more interesting. He had the haunted edges that indicated he'd seen action, probably more than he wanted to. War did that.

"According to Corbin, you're the only one who can fix this mess."

"Alone?" Roman jerked around to face his boss. Even an assassination required a team of operatives.

"With a truncated team."

So, it *was* an assassination. Roman didn't like it, but then if he did, that would say something about him he wouldn't be happy knowing. It was bad enough that he had no qualms about doing his job. He shouldn't enjoy it . . . and he didn't. Still, his family would never understand the man he had become.

"What's the job?" he asked.

"There's an information leak in our operations in southern Africa. All indications point to the courier being a medical relief worker with Sympa-Med."

The name of the relief agency rang a bell, but Roman couldn't remember why. It would come to him.

"Hell, for all we know, she's the one gathering the intel as well," the Army brass on his right inserted.

"That's highly unlikely," disagreed his fellow officer. "In fact, despite the circumstantial evidence indicating she's the mule, I don't think the relief worker is our spy. She doesn't fit the profile."

"A good spy never does." Roman knew that too well.

"She's a medical relief worker, for shit's sake. She's your typical girl-next-door out to make the world a better place. Tanya Ruston—"

Roman put his hand out and barked, "Let me see the file."

"Wait a minute, we haven't agreed to turn the situation over to your team."

Roman ignored the other man and waited for his boss to hand him the gray folder on his desk, which he did. Roman flipped it open and started reading. They were right. There was definitely an information leak, but what in hell did it have to do with Tanya Ruston? Turning a couple of pages, he found out. All the evidence was circumstantial, but it was also damning. Her movements were linked too closely with the dissemination of the intel for it to be coincidence.

"What about other relief workers on her team?"

"She's the only one who made every single circuit. Dr. Andikan sometimes stays in main compound and the other members of the team fluctuate."

"But Tanya goes every time?" he asked, even as he confirmed it for himself with a list of her assignments from the file.

"Yes."

As he continued flipping through the file, Roman had no problem seeing why Army intelligence needed to pass the job off to someone else. Whoever had compiled the information had done such a piss-poor job that they hadn't even discovered Tanya's link to him, or the fact that her brother was married to a former Goddard Project agent.

He could understand the lack of info on his sister, Elle's, former employers. Even his boss had never heard of the Goddard Project, the black-ops agency responsible for protecting America's proprietary and potentially dangerous technology. However, Roman considered the cursory mention of his sister as wife to Tanya's brother sloppy investigating. Elle's past as a security specialist and current role as chief of security at ETRD wasn't something that should be dismissed in a report like this.

Well, shit. It wasn't exactly fubar, but it wasn't real far from it either.

"Who the hell did you have assigned to this case, a junior gofer?"

"That's none of your business," the brass on his right said.

The man on his left sighed. "You're not far off the mark. Nepotism isn't reserved for politicians; you find it in the Army too."

"And it led to giving a highly sensitive investigation to an idiot?" Roman asked with exasperation.

"You can't possibly draw that conclusion, just from reading the file."

"On the contrary, my agents are trained to see things most miss," Corbin said, entering the conversation for the first time since his announcement they had a situation. He gave Roman a penetrating look. "Do you know her?"

The question proved it wasn't only Corbin's agents that noticed everything and knew how to interpret it all.

"I met her once. At my sister's wedding," he said, only giving part of the story. He lived his life on a need to know basis and his boss didn't need to know everything.

Army guy on the right cursed.

"Is this going to be a problem?" Corbin asked.

"No, sir." Roman couldn't put personal considerations ahead of his duty.

Especially when it came to treason. He'd made that mistake one time. Once was enough to cause devastation he would never forget. He had lost three good men, one the best friend he'd ever had, when he'd allowed sentiment to influence the performance of duty. When it came to serving his country, he would never again let private thoughts or feelings get in the way.

He couldn't.

"You're kidding, right? You expect me to believe you won't have any problem taking out someone you know?" the increasingly annoying officer on his right disparaged.

"The easiest way to kill a target without making it look like a hit is to get close to him, or her. A passing acquaintance with Tanya Ruston will only make my job easier." Roman met his boss's gaze. "It will also make it easier to verify Tanya's guilt."

"The investigation is done. You are being brought in to remove the threat."

Roman gave the Army brass on his right the full weight of his disgusted glare. "You want a kill without even knowing who she's working for?"

"Sometimes, you have to settle for disrupting the pipe-line."

"Bullshit. Your initial investigation was so sloppy, it might have been done by a kid without access to Google even."

"It isn't your job to pass judgment on our efforts."

"*You* don't define my job."

"I do," Corbin said firmly.

Roman inclined his head.

"Time is of the essence. The threat must be neutralized before a specialized JCAT program ends up in the wrong hands."

JCAT was a highly effective, expensive to develop, classified software used to train groups of soldiers in hard-to-recreate real-time battle scenarios. As far as Roman knew, only Nigeria had access to JCAT in Africa. He could think of several politico-military leaders who could cause even more mayhem than they did now with access to that kind of training.

"What the hell are our JCAT programs doing in Africa?" he demanded of no one in particular.

"Officially, this one isn't," the annoying officer admitted.

That went without saying. "Well?"

"Some stateside colonel"—the man on his left gave the one on his right a disgusted frown—"got the bright idea to offer a single seminar of training on this particular JCAT in exchange for first rights to a new naiobium mine."

Roman could understand the temptation to do something that stupid, but not giving in to it. Naiobium was used as a superconductor and had several weapon, anti-weapon and armor uses, but was in short supply worldwide. Still, only an idiot would offer such sensitive military software in exchange for the rights to a new mine. And he guessed he was looking at the idiot responsible on his right.

"So, you want me to kill Tanya Ruston to cover your own stupidity?" Roman asked, his disgust ratcheting up a notch.

"You do your job, soldier, and I'll do mine."

Roman turned to the other man. "You're sure the JCAT is in jeopardy?"

"Chatter about its sale has been picked up. You don't want to know which terrorist groups are celebrating right now."

They were definitely approaching fubar on this

one. "And you're sure the Tanya Ruston connection applies?"

"No."

Colonel Idiot made a sound of disagreement, but his colleague just glared. "We aren't sure of the relief worker's involvement. Our best guess is that the information leak linked to her movements is also responsible for the chatter on the JCAT."

"Tanya Ruston has to be neutralized before that software ends up on the open market."

"You don't even know she has the software," the other man exploded.

"We can't take any chances."

Roman didn't say anything. This was one messed-up situation.

Corbin said, "You and your team are going in as personal guard for a State Department bean counter doing an audit of the mines near Sympa-Med's base camp in Zimbabwe. You'll be staying there with the auditor, Bennet Vincent. The camp is not near Internet access, but Ms. Ruston has her own satellite phone. Per our routine post 9/11, we've been monitoring her calls."

"And?"

"If she's using it to make contact with her buyers or anyone besides her family, we haven't seen the evidence."

"We can't dismiss the possibility though."

Roman refused to give Colonel Idiot the courtesy of responding to him. The man was really getting on his nerves. "What about her Internet use when she gets access?"

"Nothing to raise red flags with our government or that of Zimbabwe."

"So, you are basing her guilt entirely on the fact she's been in the wrong place at the wrong time?"

"Repeatedly," the man on his left said grudgingly.

Roman rifled through the file again until he came to the financial reports. "There's no indication she's been taking payment for espionage."

"She probably has an account in the Caymans. Only a fool would take payment to her personal checking account."

That was the first thing Colonel Idiot had said that Roman agreed with, but he still didn't like the guy. And he had no intention of sticking around to get to know the Army brass any better. He stood up. "I've got a team to prepare."

"Wait, this meeting isn't over," Colonel Idiot spluttered.

Roman looked at Corbin with a raised eyebrow.

His boss shook his head. "I have nothing else."

He'd given Roman his assignment: neutralize the threat. Roman knew what that meant and he wasn't about to stick around gossiping about it like a bunch of teenage girls.

"Well, I do." Colonel Idiot jumped up from his chair, turning to face Roman full on for the first time. "It's my people doing the training over there and I've got some ideas on how to handle this mission."

Roman flicked a glance to the man on his left. His expression was blank, but it wasn't too hard to believe he wasn't any more impressed with Colonel Idiot's posturing than Roman was. "What's your pony in this race?" Roman asked him.

"I consulted on the JCAT, the voice of experience from real battle." He grimaced. "It's a powerful training tool. We'd be royally screwed right up the ass if it landed in certain hands."

Roman nodded. That he understood. Oh, he understood Colonel Idiot too. C.Y.A. was a strong motivator, but it didn't inspire any sort of respect in Roman.

Accordingly, he made no effort to mask his contempt when he replied to the colonel's remarks. "Those ideas would be welcome if your people were doing the mission. They're not. I am and I'm not interested. If your command is responsible for the training going on, then they're also responsible for the compromised intelligence."

"That's not the way it is," the other man spluttered.

But Roman wasn't listening as he headed for the door. The brass never thought they were responsible, but nine times out of ten they were. Roman knew it, being team lead himself. It didn't matter how many bars or stars you wore on your uniform. The fact was, when men or situations under your authority got compromised, you held ultimate responsibility.

And he had no respect for a man who didn't see that.

The buzz of excited chatter outside the medic hut pulled Tanya Ruston's attention from the inventory report she'd been working on in the small office off the main exam room.

"What's going on?" she asked the Tutsi woman sitting at the other desk.

Dr. Fleur Andikan looked up from her own patient reports. "Good question. The man from your country's government is not supposed to arrive for another two days." The sound of jeeps approaching in the distance came in faintly through the open window.

"Surprising the mine owners with an early visit might be his way of attempting to get a truer read of what is going on in the mine."

"Do you believe the man really cares if human rights violations are happening?" Fleur's tone implied she didn't.

Of course, Fleur had more reason than most to doubt the genuine concern of any government official. She'd been an innocent teenage girl during the Tutsi massacres in Rwanda, surviving only through blind luck and ingenuity. She had not come out of it unscathed, though. Her years living with distant family in Nigeria, attending university and medical school, had not undone the trauma of her final months in Rwanda.

No matter how much Fleur wanted others to believe she was untouched by her past and untouchable by the present, Tanya saw the haunted darkness in the doctor's eyes.

"You don't think it's the corporate guys from Sympa-Med, do you?"

Fleur rolled her eyes. "They were quite unhappy your team missed the final stop on your last tour, but I do not think they would show up here to make their displeasure known."

"They take their schedules way too seriously." The powers that be ran the medical relief agency a lot like a corporation, with rigidly scheduled routes for the traveling clinic and mandates regarding what type of medicine she and Fleur were allowed to practice.

Fortunately, Fleur was fully prepared to treat outside their mandate when the case warranted it.

She wasn't as flexible on the schedule and routes for the traveling clinic. "They have their reasons for the schedules and routes we take. If Sympa-Med offends a village elder by not showing up when promised, he might well refuse to allow us access on the next trip through."

"That's so stupid." But Tanya knew Fleur was right. "It couldn't be helped anyway. We got slammed with that outbreak at the last stop we managed. One of our own team came down with it and we were out of medical supplies. If we hadn't returned, we would have lost him."

"I am aware."

"But you still think I should have managed to stop by the village?"

"You could have sent the rest of the team on and made a visit on your own. The jeep could have been sent back for you."

"Travel without security or supplies?" Tanya jerked her head in a negative.

She cared about the people she served, but she wasn't putting herself at that level of risk just to keep some egotistical village official happy. "Maybe it's Ibeamaka, come courting again."

"Speculation, while pleasant, is a waste of time." The regal African woman stood, her expression showing how little true pleasure she felt at the prospect of a visit from the pompous government official. "I suppose we should find out."

"It beats paperwork."

"You and your dislike of paperwork. It is a good

thing you did not go to medical school." Fleur shook her head.

"I didn't want to wait eight years to come back to where I was needed."

Fleur nodded. "And you would have hated all the papers and written tests necessary to pass."

"Two years training as an EMT was bad enough," Tanya had to agree. She had not enjoyed school, which neither of her parents had understood.

Her brother hadn't understood either, but he had supported her choice to enter the Peace Corps right out of high school.

"I have known few others as intelligent as you who had so little use for traditional education."

Tanya shrugged. "What can I say? I live to disappoint my parents."

"I know that is not true."

"Trust me—I'm a complete disappointment to them." They'd been upset when her older brother chose to pursue science rather than a more lucrative career as a professional football player. However, that was nothing in comparison to how ballistic her mom and dad had gone when Tanya decided to forego university altogether.

They hadn't been any happier when she'd returned Stateside to do her EMT training only as preparation for returning to Africa. The soil reclamation project she'd worked on in the Peace Corps was important, but Tanya hadn't been able to get over the desperate need for medical care almost everywhere she went.

So, she'd decided to get EMT training and come back. She'd never regretted that decision. The work they did in Zimbabwe and the surrounding countries was not only rewarding, it was absolutely necessary.

"I do believe they did not approve or understand your choices," Fleur said, "but I do *not* believe you enjoyed disappointing them."

"You know me too well." It still hurt that her parents had never once acknowledged she might be doing something good here.

Fleur looked surprised by the comment. "Yes, I suppose I do."

Tanya knew that a big part of the other woman's reserved nature was due to her Tutsi heritage. She'd been raised to always comport herself with dignity, to express very little emotion, and to believe she had a responsibility not to squander the privilege she'd been born to. The fact that her heritage had caused her to be the target of a vicious genocidal force had not erased her sense of duty.

She was an amazing doctor and could have worked in any of the big hospitals, or even left Africa for more stable and profitable climes. Instead, she'd taken the directing doctor's position for Sympa-Med's southern Africa medical relief team.

Fleur was one of the few people in Tanya's life who actually understood her reasons for coming back to Africa as a medical relief worker after her stint in the Peace Corps was through.

They were two women from very different backgrounds who were very alike. Tanya had been raised to stifle her emotions as well, though the lessons had not taken like they had with Fleur. Though she hadn't been raised to believe she had a responsibility to those less fortunate, she had been taught to appreciate the opportunities offered to her.

The fact that that appreciation had led her to want to use those opportunities to better the lives of people half a world away hadn't gone over well with her parents. She imagined that Fleur's parents would not have liked her career path any more, had they survived the Tutsi slaughter in Rwanda.

Ultimately, Fleur and Tanya had made the same choices. And from what Tanya could tell, Fleur did not regret hers either.

When they came out of the medical hut, there were two unfamiliar, military-looking jeeps parked in front. There were eight men, six clearly military, one just as obviously the State Department auditor and the other a not unfamiliar local government official.

Tanya couldn't help grimacing as her eyes fell on the local official. If anyone had an interest in glossing over human rights violations in the local mines, it was Ibeamaka. Unlike Fleur, Tanya did not believe that all government officials were corrupt, but this one certainly was. And he had an over-the-top, if unrequited, crush on Fleur.

With the self-important walk of a man who craved power, but really wasn't all that important, he approached Fleur. "Dr. Andikan, these men are from the United States government."

Tanya noticed the official's use of the less polite *men* rather than *gentlemen*. In addition, the man spoke Shona rather than English. Petty. She rolled her eyes, and then had to stifle a smile as Fleur neatly avoided shaking hands with the political wannabe.

As she nodded in her usual dignified manner, the blue-and-white turban she wore moved just enough to signify respect, but not enough to imply obeisance. "Mr. Ibeamaka. It was good of you to escort them to our compound. We were told to expect them in two days."

"Yes, well, they were on a military flight and arrived early." He didn't sound any happier about it than he looked. "This is Bennet Vincent, an official from the State Department and his personal security team."

Ibeamaka didn't look any more pleased that the man had arrived with his own security than he did that Bennet Vincent had arrived early.

"Call me Ben," the investigator said as he put his hand out to Fleur.

She shook it while Ibeamaka looked on with a disapproving frown. "Dr. Andikan."

"It's a pleasure to meet you. I enjoy your blog." Tanya was happy to see that Ben wasn't put off by Fleur's reserve, his mouth curving into a warm smile. "I'm impressed with what you are doing here."

Fleur jolted as if startled. Whether it was from the man's hand, which had yet to let go of hers, or his words, Tanya could not tell. "I can only update the blog infrequently."

"I know. I'm a subscriber so I get notified whenever you make a new post."

"Oh, well . . . that's nice to know." Fleur didn't sound like she was sure she meant it and she tugged her hand out of Ben's. "Let me introduce my colleague, Tanya Ruston."

"It's a pleasure." He put his hand out to Tanya, squeezing her fingers in a friendly gesture rather than shaking her hand. "Dr. Andikan has written glowingly about you on her blog."

"I didn't know that." Tanya had never read the blog that Fleur updated whenever she had Internet access, usually only when she was in Harare on a supply pickup.

Fleur said it was important that the news out of Africa was not limited to official government channels.

"She's very impressed with you."

Tanya stared at her boss. "Thank you. The feeling is mutual."

Fleur nodded, giving Ben a disgruntled look. "Tanya does not read my blog."

"She should."

Fleur frowned. "Mr. Vincent."

"Ben, please."

"Ben . . ." Fleur paused, as if trying to gather her thoughts. Finally, she shook her head and said, "You and your security force will be staying in an empty chalet on the east side of the compound."

Tanya let her gaze travel over the American soldiers while Fleur pointed out the three-room hut that they often used to house Zimbabweans displaced by the eighty-percent unemployment rate and the recent, government-sponsored deurbanization programs.

While two of the men looked younger than the others, not one of the soldiers appeared fresh faced or anything approaching naïve. These were seasoned warriors, even now hyper aware of their environment and any trouble they might find there. The two youngest soldiers had Marine uniforms. The others wore state-of-the-art camouflage, but no badges or epaulettes had been sewn onto their clothes to indicate which branch of the military they hailed from, or their rank. One sported a Marine high-and-tight, but the others had the short buzz cuts usually found in the other branches of the armed services.

As her gaze landed on the man to the farthest left, the one who wore the mantle of leadership, if not the insignia, her breath escaped in a loud gasp.

"Tanna?" Fleur asked, slipping into the local pronunciation of Tanya's name, concern evident in the doctor's voice, if not her carefully neutral expression.

Tanya could not answer. She was too busy staring. "Roman?" The question came out in an embarrassingly squeaky croak. "Is that you?"

"You know the civilian, Geronimo?" the big soldier with the high-and-tight asked.

Roman . . . Geronimo nodded.

So, it *was* Roman. Here. In southern Zimbabwe, as far out of the lab as a man could get. Leading a team of soldiers providing security for a State Department official. It didn't make any sense. He'd run the security at Elle and Beau's wedding, but it had been Tanya's understanding that the Special Forces soldiers Beau had pulled in to help had been friends, not colleagues.

Unless his family had been lying to her, that was their understanding too.

"I thought you were an Army scientist." According to Elle, he was every bit as brilliant as Tanya's brother, Beau. Why would Roman Chernichenko be in Africa on a security detail? When he didn't reply, simply staring at her, she turned to the other man who had spoken. "Why did you call him Geronimo? He's Ukrainian, not Native American."

He might have black hair and chiseled features that could possibly be mistaken for those of certain tribes found in North America, but his perpetual five o'clock shadow, gray eyes and six-foot-five frame were far more Eastern European. All fingers to press every one of her personal hot buttons.

Not that she'd acted on the nearly debilitating attraction she'd felt when they'd met. What would be the point when she had only been in the States for a couple of weeks and their worlds had no chance of colliding again?

Or so she'd thought.

"Geronimo was a warrior who led other warriors and he preferred counting casualties to counting coup."

"Are you saying Roman . . ." Her voice trailed off as everything she thought she knew about this man rushed to realign itself in her brain.

He was not a scientist. According to his fellow soldier, Roman Chernichenko was not only their leader, but he didn't balk at killing for his country either.

And even knowing that, the attraction that had hit her harder than a semitruck on a downhill runaway the first time she'd seen him came roaring back with no safe uphill grade in sight.

She swallowed against her dry throat and put her hand out to the man with the high-and-tight. "I'm Tanya Ruston. Roman's sister, Elle, is married to my brother."

"I heard your name when that pretty doctor said

it, but I gotta tell you this is the first we heard you were related to our chief." He shook her hand, his big paw gentle. "Nice to meet you. I'm Kadin Marks. The boys call me Trigger."

"Do I want to know?"

"Probably not."

She nodded in acknowledgment and turned to the next man, who introduced himself, but didn't share a nickname. The others all followed suit until she had a name to go with every face. "You're all here to keep Mr. Vincent safe?"

Kadin said, "That's the plan."

"Ben, please," insisted the bald man, who didn't look more than thirty-five.

She smiled at him. "Ben."

"Do you prefer Tanya or Tanna?"

"I'm used to Tanna. It's what everyone around here calls me and well, I like who I am here. So, it sounds good to my ears."

Ben looked at her as if he were trying to read her mind. "That's good to know. I didn't realize you were acquainted with one of my guards."

"I don't think any of us did."

"Except him."

"Did you know I was here?" Tanya asked Roman, not one to suffer assumptions when the source for facts was at hand.

"Yes."

The one-word answer almost shocked her after the way he'd ignored her other question. "Did you tell Beau you were coming?"

"No."

"Oh." Man, the attraction was so *not* mutual. And so not going away. She wasn't sure if that was good or bad. The fact it wasn't mutual kept her safe from doing something stupid, but then safe wasn't all it was cracked up to be either. Safe could be really, really lonely. "Well, when you get home, you can call him and tell him I'm healthy and happy. He doesn't always believe me."

Roman didn't reply.

She didn't remember his being this rude at the wedding, but then she'd barely worked up the nerve to say, "Hello," much less open a conversation. She'd been avoiding him and her shocking, thigh-clenching desire to experience him naked. She'd had relationships, but she had never reacted to a man the way she did Roman. Not even Quinton, the man she'd thought she would one day marry.

He turned to Kadin. "We need to get the chalet ready."

Fleur called the buildings "chalets." Tanya preferred huts, but the fact was, whatever you called them, they were simple dwellings built from local materials. None of the structures had glass in the windows, just screens and shutters for the rainy season. Not all of the buildings even had electricity. The medical hut did, as did her and Fleur's quarters, and luckily for Ben and the soldiers, the chalet they would be staying in did as well.

"I'll have Mabu stop by your hut in an hour. He can give you a tour of the compound," Fleur said, speaking of one of the non-medical Sympa-Med staff members.

"I would prefer to have Tanya do it."

Roman's request shocked her, coming as it did after his nonreaction to pretty much everything she said.

Fleur looked at Roman coolly. "Mabu is in charge

of the compound security. I am sure he will be able
to answer any questions you might have."

"I will talk to Mabu, but I want Tanya to show
me around."

"I assure you Mabu's English is quite up to the
task."

Roman gave Tanya an inquiring look. "Do you
mind showing me around?"

"Of course not."

"Is that the building you work in?" he asked, indicating the medical hut.

Naturally, he'd noticed her coming out of it
when he arrived, the super-observant soldier that
he was. "Yes."

"I'll find you there when I'm ready for the tour."

And then he walked away, dismissing her pretty
darn effectively.

CHAPTER TWO

"So, this soldier is related to you in some way?" Fleur asked as she walked back into the office they shared, twenty minutes after Tanya had returned to the despised paperwork.

"Technically he's related by marriage to my brother." She certainly never thought of Roman as family. When she thought of him at all (which was more often than she was comfortable with since the wedding), she thought of Roman as the sexy embodiment of feminine dreams she preferred to think she'd outgrown. Tall, dark and uber-gorgeous. Not to mention scary smart and mysterious in the way only a top military scientist could be.

She wasn't sure what she thought of him now that she knew he wasn't the man his family had told her he was. He was still plenty mysterious. This Roman Chernichenko was a true soldier and, in a totally unforeseen turn of events, that made him even more attractive to her.

Africa was rampant with the best and the worst that the military had to offer. She was far more likely to look at a soldier with wariness than desire.

But she definitely wanted Roman and the man was every inch the warrior he'd been nicknamed for.

He had too much knowledge in his eyes to have spent the last few years in a lab. "I don't know how I missed it."

"Missed what?"

"The look in his eyes. His family told me he was an Army scientist and I took him at face value."

"Why should you not, if his family said it?"

"Because one thing I've learned during my years in Africa is that people are not always what they seem, or what others say they are."

"Is that not the truth?"

"Speaking of, did you feed our local government official tea?"

"Hospitality demanded I do so."

"You kept it short."

"I had to offer him refreshment." Fleur's lips twisted in distaste. "I did not have to offer him my afternoon."

"I bet he was disappointed."

"I fear Mr. Ibeamaka is destined always to be disappointed where I am concerned," Fleur said dryly.

"I don't understand why he's fixated on you. He so obviously wants a traditional wife who will follow her husband's lead in all things, which would make her the direct opposite of you."

"He believes he can train me." The disgust in Fleur's voice when she said the word *train* left no doubt what she thought of that possibility. "You know I do not intend to marry."

Tanya understood her friend's decision, even if it saddened her to think of Fleur going through her life alone. Should she choose to marry, her husband would have the power to stop her from pursuing her work for Sympa-Med. He would control their finances and most Zimbabweans still saw no problem with that reality, or the country's archaic land rights and inheritance laws.

Perhaps that was one of the reasons Fleur had taken in Johari when the young girl managed to survive the Congolese Wars, but her parents didn't. Johari was Fleur's chance at a family without the complication of a husband.

"So, has Ibeamaka left the compound?"

"Yes. I do not believe he likes the Americans. He thinks he has shown them some sort of petty slight by not offering to stay and take the evening meal with them."

Tanya laughed. "I'm sure they'll be horribly disappointed."

"Without doubt." Fleur's voice dripped with a sarcasm that more than matched Tanya's.

Both women smiled in understanding.

"Disappointed is not the word I would use," a deep male voice said from the doorway.

Tanya jerked her head around to look. "I didn't hear you come in." The wood floor in the medical hut did not make for silent entry into the building.

"I walk quietly."

"Don't tell me, you're not just a soldier, you're some kind of dark-ops-trained assassin," she joked.

For a fraction of a second, a strange expression showed on Roman's face before his features slipped back into impassivity. "Soldiers are all trained for a certain level of stealth."

Maybe he'd been offended by her little tease. His words were right, but she felt something was missing from his explanation. No surprise there, not with Mr. Congenial Communication.

"Even lab rats?"

"I think it's obvious I don't spend all my time in a lab." He stepped back into the hall. "The tour?"

Arrogant, much?

"Sure." She turned to Fleur. "I'll finish this up later."

"I will have our newest med-tech finish them for you, but you'll have to check them over for accuracy."

Sympa-Med sent them new interns every six months to be trained before being assigned elsewhere. Fleur wasn't just the compound director and lead doctor, she also ran the training program for workers stationed all over Africa and the Middle East.

"No problem."

"Don't look so pleased with yourself. We all know how much you hate paperwork. Maybe Mr. Taylor will turn out to enjoy the chore."

The trainees never got on a first-name basis with Fleur. Tanya hadn't either, until a good three months after she'd been assigned permanently to the Zimbabwe team.

"Sounds like a plan." Six months with truncated amounts of paperwork sounded more like heaven than a plan, but Fleur would understand that without Tanya having to say it.

"Go on, show the soldier around." Fleur waved her hand in dismissal.

Tanya smirked at Fleur's less than awed description of Roman as she led him out of the medical hut. "I'm sure you've figured it out, but this is the main building in the compound. It houses our exam rooms, the clean room for procedures, the office Fleur and I share and inventory storage for medical supplies."

"I did not notice a guard on the premises."

"He must be on his meal break. We do keep a guard on the premises at all times, and Mabu sleeps in a room beside the storage area."

"He does not have anyone cover the guard's meal breaks?"

"No."

"That is sloppy security."

"We're safer here than we are on most of our routes."

"That isn't saying much."

She agreed, but you either learned to live with that condition, or you gave up and went home. She wasn't leaving the people who needed her, so that left learning to live with the constant danger from thieves, human traffickers and the violence always on the verge of erupting in some of the places their traveling clinic took them.

"I find it hard to believe you spend any time at all in a lab." It didn't make sense for a scientist to be called in on a protection detail. Nor did his attitude about and knowledge of security protocols coincide with that of a man who worked as a scientist, even part-time.

Roman shrugged. "It pleases my family to believe that is where I spend my time."

So, at least her new sister-in-law hadn't lied to Tanya. Unfortunately, for their family anyway, Roman was clearly lying to the other Chernichenkos.

"Do any of your siblings know what you really do?"

"Myk."

"He's the only one?" she asked as they walked by the hut that housed the rest of Mabu's staff and his office.

"Yes, and I would prefer it stay that way."

She pointed out the security hut before asking, "Is that why you didn't tell Elle you were going to be seeing me?"

"What is that building?" he asked, pointing to one of the larger structures in the compound. Once again he was asking a question rather than answering hers.

That could get really annoying after a while. "Do you always ignore questions you don't want to answer?"

"Yes."

"That's rude."

"Yes."

And clearly he didn't care.

"All right then. This building was the original clinic. We now use it as sort of a long-stay building for people who cannot make it to the hospital in Harare, but who absolutely require supervised care."

"Is there anyone in there now?"

"The better question would be if it is ever empty. Most of the beds are full, which is pretty common despite Sympa-Med's policy on the matter." Which wasn't all that tolerant of long-term treatment of the locals. "It's less crowded than last week when we had a local village chieftain staying with his entourage."

"He couldn't go to Harare?"

"More like he refused."

"What was wrong with him?"

"Migraines. He feared he had a brain tumor, but it turned out he was allergic to expensive French cologne a trader had given as a thank-you gift for being allowed to peddle his wares in the village."

"I bet he doesn't get that opportunity again."

"If he shows up in the village again, he'll be lucky to leave with his life."

"Harsh justice." Roman gave her a cynical smile. "The government doesn't mention that in their tourism brochures."

"They do their best to keep information about the rampant human trafficking going on in Zimbabwe out of the media as well, but it's a big and growing problem in this part of Africa despite what P.R. people for tourism want you to believe."

"I'm surprised you'd be willing to work in such a risky location."

Sympa-Med took measures to protect their employees, but it wasn't something she was supposed to talk about. "Medical workers aren't as at risk as the tens of thousands of displaced and poverty-stricken Zimbabweans."

"Being less at risk is not the same as not being at risk at all."

"Some things are worth it."

"Things like?"

"Helping people who need it."

"There are plenty of people who need help in the U.S."

"Yes, there are, but there are also a lot more people trained to do the helping back home."

"So, you're here because you think the Zimbabweans need you more than anyone back in the States?"

"There's that, and then there's having half a world between me and my parents."

"Ouch."

It was her turn to shrug. "They're not bad people. They just define success and happiness really differently than either Beau or I do."

"I bet they just love your current occupation."

"Is that sarcasm, Roman?"

"Could be. Is that the mess hall?"

"Yes. Meals are served twice a day, but there is always something in the pot for people who can't make it to official mealtimes and who get hungry in between them." Positions within the compound were highly coveted because living conditions were so much better than outside. "Come on, I'll introduce you to the cook and her helper."

They spent a short time in the dining hall introducing Roman to the kitchen staff, who did most of their cooking in an open-air lean-to situated behind the one-room hut where everyone in the compound took their meals. The rest of the cooking happened in and on fire pits situated far enough from the buildings to minimize the risk of an errant spark sending the compound up in flames.

"The fence does not look too hard to breach," Roman said as they walked past the staff living quarters, where Tanya made no effort to point out where she slept.

No matter how she was tempted by the thought of his joining her there.

"It's meant to discourage small animals and petty thieves. Serious threats wouldn't be deterred by anything less than an electric fence with barbed wire. We can't afford the power to run one, much less get Sympa-Med to fund the cost."

"Where do you and Dr. Andikan sleep?"

"We share that hut with her daughter, Johari."

"She has a daughter?" he asked, sounding both annoyed and suprised.

"Yes."

"There is no record of that."

"You read our personnel records?" Tanya asked, taking her own turn to be shocked.

"Bennet Vincent's safety is in our hands. His job is not popular with the Zimbabwean government, no matter how much they pretend to be glad he is here. Assessing any potential threats in his domicile is standard procedure."

"Oh. Well, Johari isn't Fleur's natural child. She adopted the girl when she was orphaned in the Congolese Wars."

"That is commendable."

"Yes, it is. And Johari is a wonderful child."

"You sound wistful."

"Part of me longs to do the same thing."

"But you haven't."

"I'm on the road a lot more than Fleur. Since my arrival, she's pretty much limited herself to running the stationary clinic."

"I imagine it's a big enough job."

"Yes, and I don't mind taking team lead with the traveling clinic, but being gone for weeks at a time doesn't lend itself to good parenting."

"No, it doesn't."

She stopped outside the medical hut as they finished their tour. "You sound like it's something you've thought about too."

"Not being a parent, but relationships require time that constant and prolonged travel does not allow."

"Is that why you're single? You travel too much for your job, the one that isn't in a lab?" As the words left her mouth, she felt heat climb her skin, unable to believe she'd asked something so personal of the standoffish man.

"Yes."

"Wow, you actually answered."

He gave her a look that probably should have chastised her, but instead just made her toes curl.

"You're certainly not single because you're ugly."

"You sound like Myk's new wife."

"She thinks you're hot too?" She couldn't see that going over well with a Chernichenko male.

"No. She doesn't have any filters between her brain and her mouth either."

"Oh, I have filters. I just don't choose to exercise them all the time. I don't see a reason to pretend an indifference I'll never be able to sustain for the length of your stay."

"We're only supposed to be here a couple of weeks."

"Exactly."

"I was wrong. You're not like Lana, you're a lot like your brother, Beau. Very forthright."

"Yep." She blew out a noisy breath. "Most of the time, I don't see a reason for being any other way."

"But you do make exceptions."

"Of course. I'm not about to tell Mr. Ibeamaka I think he's a slimy toad and that he has more chance with Paris Hilton than he does with Fleur."

"He did seem taken with her."

"Much to her disgust."

"What about you?"

"Me and Ibeamaka?"

"You and anyone."

"There's no one." And hadn't been since before she started working with Sympa-Med.

When Roman returned to his team's quarters, he found Lieutenant Neil Kennedy, otherwise known as Spazz, installing technical security measures in the communal room. "Where is everyone?"

Neil finished securing a micro-cam in one corner. "Trigger is walking the perimeter." The camera was so tiny that unless someone knew to look, it would be virtually undetectable.

"I didn't see him."

Neil squatted down and tucked unused equipment into the black duffel at his feet. "He'd be embarrassed if you had."

True. Of all the members on their team, Kadin's training and skill set most closely matched Roman's. "The others?"

"One of the baby grunts is getting some shuteye before his patrol duty tonight. The other is with Vincent at the mess."

"Good." They'd brought two Marine privates to work the majority of the actual physical security detail with Vincent.

"Face is in our room getting his beauty rest."

Captain Drew Peterson came from Army Special Forces Psych Operations. His official title had been Social Engineer. Unofficially, he was the ultimate con man with government sanction. Despite being African-American, his teammates had dubbed him "Face," from a character in an old eighties sitcom who had the reputation for being able to lie his way into or out of any situation.

Spazz was their computer and communications expert. He'd been turned down for the SEALs, but the Atrati didn't limit themselves to super-soldiers. They simply looked for the best of the best. Neil was no wimp, but he wasn't your typical Special Forces soldier either.

His IQ? Off the charts, but he wasn't the type of guy to be happy in a lab any more than Roman was. And when it came to computers, Neil *was* the best of the best. He could hack into Microsoft, never mind the Pentagon, and if there was a communications product on the market, he knew specs, availability and limitations.

The sound of soft footfalls had Roman turning.

Trigger pulled the door shut behind him. "So, what did you think, chief?"

"Security isn't anything to write home about. I'm surprised Sympa-Med doesn't do more to protect their investment here. The medical supplies alone would bring in top dollar on the black market, not to mention the trained medical personnel."

"I wasn't talking about the compound," Kadin said with a verbal eye roll. "I meant the target. She seem like a spy to you?"

Roman looked toward the bedroom that housed the sleeping Marine, but the door was closed. He flicked a glance out the screen-covered window for signs of anyone near enough to overhear them, but all was clear. Not that he would expect anything else. His men knew better than to compromise their assignment with loose lips.

Roman hadn't survived this long being sloppy, though. "She's a hell of an actress."

"Or she's not guilty. The Army brass want to cover their asses a little too much on this one," Kadin replied.

Roman leaned back against the wall with a peripheral view out the window. "You think they ordered the assassination of an innocent woman to cover their own mistakes?"

"Don't you?"

"It doesn't matter."

"Like hell. We don't kill innocents."

"That we know of."

"So, we better make damn sure before you kill your sister-in-law."

"She's not. Technically."

"What-the hell-ever."

"Our orders are to neutralize the threat," Neil asserted.

Roman frowned at his subordinate. "I know what our orders are."

Unaffected by Roman's ire, Spazz continued. "They're not to kill the woman per se."

"No." Kadin crossed his arms and glared. "According to what you told us, that's what the Army brass wants."

Shit, he did not need this. "We're under orders from our government."

"Exactly," Neil said.

Kadin nodded firmly. "Not the Army."

The tension in Roman ratcheted several notches higher. "You let your personal feelings get in the way of doing your duty and good men die."

"If we don't, a good woman is going to," Kadin growled, clearly unimpressed with Roman's logic.

Roman knew what his gut was telling him, but he didn't know if the message was coming from his libido or his instincts as a soldier. He'd wanted Tanya Ruston the first time he saw her and that desire had not gone away. Spending time with her touring the compound had only made it worse.

He liked her. Damn it. Wanting her was bad enough. How many layers of complications did he need on this assignment?

"So, what are we going to do, chief?" Trigger demanded. "We going to serve our country or some idiot Army officer who should never have okayed a copy of the JCAT coming to Africa in the first place?"

"We're going to find the threat and neutralize it."

"Well, that's a relief," Face said from the open doorway to their room. "I thought for a minute I was going to have to go on the run with the babe."

Roman's head snapped up with a sharp jerk. "Hands off, Drew."

"Oooh, he means business, he used your real name," Neil said before jumping out of reach of Roman's smack to the back of his head.

"You think our Geronimo is actually human?" Kadin demanded, his voice laced with mocking amazement.

"Whatever the hell I am, I know how to handle insubordination. You want to keep pushing it?"

The former MARSOC sergeant just laughed and shook his head. Definitely too much like Roman. "So, what's the plan?"

"First, we figure out if she has a copy of the program," Roman said. "Hiding it is going to be a lot harder here than someplace where technology already has a foothold. The closest Internet access is Harare and as impressive as their cell phone network is for an African nation, they don't have ready access to mobile browsing either."

"So, it has to be on a storage device of some kind."

"Exactly and since these buildings have simplified construction, it shouldn't be too hard to find."

"I'll start with a search on her laptop," Neil said.

Roman nodded once. "But you're going to need to search all the computers in the compound. Security is too loose; she could have it stored somewhere else for safekeeping until she can transport it."

"Finding it won't mean she's the leak," Kadin pointed out.

"It could be someone else in the compound," Neil agreed.

"Or no one here at all," Drew said. "Just because her movements coincide with the transfer of information, doesn't mean she's not being set up."

"That's for damn sure," Kadin grumbled.

Goddard Project Agent Bennet Vincent drank a cup of surprisingly good coffee as he sat at a table in the dining hall and watched.

Medical relief workers, security personnel and other non-medical staff came and went in a trickling stream that never seemed to end. None of them looked like spies, but then he didn't expect them to. He wouldn't mind if the spy turned out to be Ibeamaka, though.

The man was smarmy, and his obvious feelings

for Dr. Fleur Andikan did not sit well with Ben. No doubt because she so clearly did not return them. She was too lovely and too *good* to be smarmed by the minor government official.

Regardless of Ibeamaka's guilt or innocence, someone here was connected to the leak of proprietary military technology. He just wasn't sure how or who.

The data pointed to an inescapable connection between this Sympa-Med compound and the disturbing pattern of technological leakage. There was even circumstantial evidence that indicated Tanya Ruston might well be the leak, but none of the confirmation indicators in her background were there.

She didn't live above her means and showed no particular desire for monetary wealth. She'd spent eight of the last ten years living in what would be considered poverty to most Americans, in order to help those she saw in need. She was fiercely loyal to her family, even the parents who disapproved of her career. Her colleagues liked and admired her.

Besides all that, if Tanna wanted to sell secrets, she'd have easier access and a much safer life doing so back in California. She was related to a brilliant scientist working on cutting-edge technology, who trusted her implicitly.

In addition to that, his own research indicated the espionage may have started before Tanna had come to work for Sympa-Med. Unfortunately, the data set was too small to make a definitive determination, but his instincts told him that the sister-in-law to his former co-worker was *not* an international spy.

And there was still the very real possibility that

no spy existed at all, but that American military technology was being traded for access to African oil and minerals. If the leaks were sanctioned by military authorities, heads were going to roll at the Pentagon. Hell, they were going to explode, because once the press got wind of what TGP had discovered, it was going to be a media bloodbath of epic proportions.

Perhaps because his own father had been both an Army general and a bastard, Ben had an inherent distrust of the military. He wasn't sure what to make of the fact that Elle's brother was in his protection detail. Tanna had made it clear she and Roman's family believed he was a military scientist.

One thing Ben knew about the Army: They did not send their scientists out into the field to protect State Department bureaucrats. So, Roman was not a scientist. Why lie to his family about it? Maybe he wanted to avoid disappointing them, but what was the man doing leading a security detail? He was higher up in the food chain than that. At his age, with his education and obvious skills, he had to be.

As far as anyone else knew, Ben was just one of the many bureaucratic cogs in the over-spoked wheel that was Washington, certainly not someone who warranted high-ranking military personnel for his protection detail. The two Marine privates made sense, the other four did not. The privates did not seem to connect with the other four as they did with each other either.

Add that to the fact that while their camouflage matched the Marines', the four older soldiers wore no branch insignia or rank indicators. While they all obviously deferred to Roman, there was no way to tell where the others fell in the ranks and that went extremely counter to military culture.

In addition, Roman had not told his family he would be seeing Beau's sister. That set off an alarm klaxon in Ben's mind. No way had Roman not realized he would be seeing Tanna, so what did his oversight mean?

Ben didn't believe in coincidences when the data suggested something else entirely. The data undeniably indicated that Roman Chernichenko was not all that he appeared, and most likely his three "unmarked" colleagues were not either.

With his own experience in covert operations, and with the way the military worked, Ben had no choice but to entertain certain unpleasant possibilities. It was more than a little likely he was not the only member of their party working under cover. If he'd seen the circumstantial evidence against Tanna, others could have too and drawn their own conclusions. Speculation on what the four-man team was doing in Zimbabwe led down a less than pleasant path.

Ben had never been on an assassination squad, but he had an ugly feeling he'd just found out what one looked like up close and personal.

Damn, this was a definite wrinkle. He needed to contact the Old Man.

Elle's sister-in-law might very well have a military target painted on her forehead.

CHAPTER THREE

For the first time since arriving at the Sympa-Med compound, Tanya's heart raced at the idea of entering the dining hut. And it wasn't the prospect of eating that was doing it either, but the man she would see.

She hadn't been able to get Roman out of her head since he'd left her earlier. Despite plentiful evidence to the contrary, the idea that he might share the attraction would not leave her alone.

No doubt it was just wishful thinking, but what a wish.

He and Ben were standing beside a table near the one she and Fleur sat at during mealtimes, and talking to the other men in the security detail.

Despite the fact that he was in active conversation with the soldier who had introduced himself as Neil, Roman's gaze caught hers the minute she entered the hut.

She did her best to give him a casual nod of acknowledgment, but ruined the effect with a blush he no doubt took for some misplaced shyness or embarrassment. It wasn't, though; the heat climb-

ing her neck and into her cheeks was pure, unadulterated arousal.

Was she going through midlife crisis early, or
something? She was only twenty-eight, but something had to explain the way her nipples tightened
to hard points every time she saw the man.

And that wasn't even taking into consideration
the heat between her legs. She'd never had such a
physically visceral reaction before. Not to anything. Not fear. Not joy. Definitely not passion.

It was just a little terrifying.

Forcing her eyes away from him, she heard
Fleur invite Ben to join them at their table for dinner. Roman didn't wait for an invitation to sit beside Tanya on the bench at the long table. The
other men all sat at the table they'd been standing
by, seemingly unaffected by their colleague's de-
sertion.

Okay, if looking at him affected her, sitting next
to him was a stimulation overload. Not only could
she smell his subtle masculine scent, but his heat
reached out and touched her like a caress to every
nerve ending along the side facing him.

She found herself inhaling deeply to more
firmly imprint his scent into her olfactory memory. It was such a primal reaction and she couldn't
help it any more than she could the need to
breathe.

"Are you okay?" he asked, sounding like he knew
exactly what was wrong with her.

She was not a mare in heat, controlled by her
body's urges, no matter how much she might se-
cretly want to be.

Taking a deep breath, she then let it out slowly,
concentrating on getting her voice under control

before she spoke. "Of course. Are you settling in all right?"

He certainly didn't look like he was suffering jet lag, or culture shock as so many newbies did when arriving in Africa for the first time.

"No problem."

One of the kitchen helpers delivered food to their table.

Tanya waited until everyone had been served before asking him, "Is this your first trip to Africa?"

"No."

He took a bite of food, showing neither pleasure nor distaste for the traditional local fare.

It had taken her a while to get used to the lack of spices, or the different spices in most African cooking when she'd first arrived with the Peace Corps.

When he didn't clarify his one-word response, she asked, "To Zimbabwe?"

"Yes."

"It's an amazing country."

"If you say so."

"Don't you think so?" No matter the drawbacks to life on the original continent, Tanya loved so much about the different African cultures she had experienced. And the ability to experience nature at its most pristine was unparalled. "There is so much unspoiled beauty here, both in the people and the land they inhabit."

"And a human-trafficking industry that rivals any other location on earth."

She couldn't deny that, but it was only part of the picture. "The U.S. has its own severe problems with gang-related crime and violent crime overall, not to mention its own human-trafficking issues."

"True."

"No country is perfect, but the people here are resilient. They live and persist in hoping for the future, despite their troubled political past and present, and a terribly debilitating near eighty percent unemployment rate."

"And Victoria Falls is supposed to be one of the most beautiful spots in the world." The words were right, but the subtle sarcasm lacing them belied his sincerity.

She shot him a disgruntled frown. "It is, in fact."

"You've been?"

"Naturally." Did he seriously believe she would have lived here for nearly two years and never made the trek? She couldn't imagine that level of indifference to the beauty the world had to offer.

It would be one thing if she had no way to travel, but she had both sufficient time and money.

"I thought you were too busy providing medical help to the needy." Again with the sarcasm.

She would have been offended if she didn't suspect he wasn't trying to annoy her, but simply reacting as per usual for him. "Even relief workers get personal time."

"And you use yours to visit Zimbabwe's top tourist spots instead of going home to family?" he asked, not sounding condemning, just curious.

"I do both."

"How much longer do you plan to stay in Africa?"

"My contract with Sympa-Med is up in six months." She'd thought about taking a year to travel, then going home for an extended visit. "I haven't decided if I will renew it."

"You know I hope you will," Fleur inserted from across the table.

Tanya smiled and nodded. "I want to stay in Africa, keep doing what we do, but I think a sabbatical is in order."

"Sabbatical?" Roman asked.

"We can never help everyone who needs us. The AIDS epidemic has a huge hold on the African continent. Children die daily from it, and from malnutrition and malaria, just to name a few of the big diseases. If you have any kind of heart at all, it gets to you. It has to. I want a break, not to leave permanently. But if I don't take that break, I'll probably burn out. I've seen it before. So, yes, a sabbatical."

"I'm surprised you haven't taken one before," Ben said, his voice warm with admiration and understanding.

Roman stiffened beside her and gave Ben an impenetrable look. "She spent almost two years Stateside training for her EMT certification."

"That was hardly a sabbatical," Ben said.

Tanya found herself laughing. "If you knew how much I dislike formal education and sitting in a classroom, you'd realize it was more a test of my endurance."

"You passed the test," Fleur said with approval and a little humor.

"I did." Tanya turned to Roman. "Considering the fact you chose a career path that took you out of the lab and into the *field*," she said, for lack of a better description, "you probably have more in common with me than either of us know."

He looked down at her, his steel-gray eyes trapping her gaze until everyone around them fell away. "We definitely have a few things in common."

Oh, man, he didn't mean that the way it sounded, did he? All that wishful thinking came back with a vengeance. He didn't want her, not like she wanted him. His every action had made that clear. But the heat burning from his eyes to hers said differently. She felt it all the way to the molten core of herself.

She barely noticed when Ben left the table to chat for a moment with a couple of the other soldiers on his security team. She was too busy trying not to act on the desire bubbling through her blood like champagne. Delicious and way too heady for a woman used to chemically treated water with her dinner.

If she didn't get a handle on these feelings, she was going to make a fool of herself. And though Roman would be gone a few weeks from now, the other Sympa-Med workers would not.

Ben came back and struck up a conversation that brought forth laughter from both Fleur and her daughter, Johari, who had returned from her schooling an hour before dinner. Conversations ebbed and flowed around Tanya, but she was hard-pressed to join in.

She reeled from that sexually charged moment with Roman and what it could mean. If he returned her attraction, what did she want to do about that?

She'd regretted not at least attempting to get to know him better at the wedding. She was not into casual sex, but he had fascinated her and she'd allowed a whole host of fears to stop her from even pursuing a friendship. She hated the fact that she was so unwilling to put the most innocuous of her emotions out there. Her fear of rejection made her a coward and that shamed her.

Her parents' repudiation of Tanya's life choices had damaged her deep inside. She felt that she should be able to just ignore the fact she disappointed them so deeply, but she'd never been able to. She could not change who she was, and heaven alone knew she'd tried.

Tanya had never told anyone, but when she'd gone back to the States to take her EMT training, she'd considered staying. Then the offer from Sympa-Med had come and she'd known she could not deny the part of her that most defined her relationship with the world. Her need was to make a difference for the people who had so little offered to them.

Her parents weren't the only ones who did not understand what made Tanya tick. The other Peace Corps volunteers on the soil reclamation project had looked askance at her when she talked about staying in Africa long-term. Especially Quinton. He'd done his stint in the Peace Corps with every intention of returning home to pursue the whole American dream.

And he'd made it clear he didn't think she'd fit the other half of the perfect marriage that was supposed to result in the white picket fence and two-point-five children.

She mentally shook off the harsh memories and focused on her current dilemma. What did a woman who abhorred casual sex do when she was desperately attracted to a man who was only a temporary fixture in her world?

She hadn't had sex in so long she almost wondered if casual wasn't better than nothing. It wasn't that she needed the sexual release, like that mare in heat she so did not want to emulate. But she missed touching. She craved the intimacy of skin against skin. Of course, her job required she touch her patients, but she always did it through a layer of latex. Policy dictated she not even take a child's temperature without donning gloves. Though the locals might be affectionate with each other, they maintained a certain distance from her. Not because they rejected her, but out of respect.

One of the things she missed the most about home was her brother's hugs. He always made her feel safe and that was not a sensation she'd been accustomed to since reaching adulthood.

There was no guarantee that sex with Roman would include affection, but she had a feeling he would be so good at the sex part, she wouldn't mind. He exuded masculine sexual magnetism and primal aggression, an irresistible package wrapped in darn near irresistible pheromones.

Besides, holding out for a relationship had only left her alone . . . and lonely. Chances were, she'd spend her life as alone as Fleur and maybe it was time to face up to that reality.

Why shouldn't Tanya take comfort and human connection where she could get it? It wasn't as if she was going to start sleeping with any man who would have her.

She still didn't like the idea of casual copulation, but sharing her body with Roman wouldn't be casual. Just because he had no feelings for her didn't mean she couldn't indulge in the feelings that had been growing inside her since their first meeting. After all, Quinton had not loved her either, but she'd loved him.

Okay, she'd believed he loved her, but that only made her a fool, not a moral paragon. Knowing Roman's feelings for her extended only to the physical had to be better than the self-delusion she'd lived under with Quinton.

If there was a chance of sharing intimacy with Roman, she owed it to herself to pursue it, for the short time it could last.

Didn't she?

Wasn't a slice of happiness, no matter how temporary, better than none at all?

Ben thought nothing of dosing the dinner of the Marine sharing his room that night with a compound that would induce heavy sleep. The private would wake the next morning feeling refreshed and no worse for wear. The other young Marine sharing the room was on guard duty and would actually be easier to slip by than a well-trained soldier sleeping lightly in the same room.

Keeping to the darkest shadows, Ben made his way silently to the far side of the compound. He used his satellite phone to connect to TGP's server and made a text call to Whit.

He had to wait about ten minutes for the Old Man to answer.

They exchanged pass codes.

Whitney texted, "What is your status?"

"In the compound. Think four of the guards in my 'security' detail may be undercover military black ops," Ben sent back.

"Hell."

"Answers one question, sir." Ben typed. "The military has not approved the technology leaks."

"At least whoever ordered these agents didn't approve them. We know damn well one arm of the military doesn't always speak to the other."

"Just like the government."

"Exactly." The one-word text managed to convey both disgust and cynicism.

"Proceed as you think best."

"Permission to reveal my own assignment?"

"If necessary, but under no circumstances reveal your agency."

Ben smirked as he typed, "I'm just a drone for the State Department."

"Precisely."

"One last thing . . ." He wasn't sure exactly how he wanted to break this news, but with the Old Man direct was usually better.

"What?"

"One of my guards is Elle's brother."

It took a few seconds to receive an answer, which said more than any texted words could have. "Our Elle?"

"Yes."

"That could complicate things."

Ya think? Ben shook his head even as he texted back. Complicated was a simple word for a very complex situation. "Yes. He didn't tell his family he would be seeing Tanya Ruston."

"Shit." So, his boss had drawn the same conclusion Ben had.

Ben typed, "I concur."

"I met her at the wedding. She's a good person." Despite the silent nature of their communication,

Ben could "hear" the frustration and concern in his boss's words.

"Agreed." He liked Tanya Ruston, in a very different way than he did Fleur Andikan, but no less significant for a man who was used to solitude and trusting almost no one.

"I don't want her disappearing."

Neither did Ben. "I'll do my best to head off that possibility."

"See that you do."

"Disclosure may have to come sooner than later, sir."

"Follow your instincts. They haven't steered you wrong yet."

"Will do. Out."

He disconnected the satellite transmission and carefully made his way back toward his room.

As he passed behind Fleur and Tanya's hut, he noticed a movement. The shadows resolved themselves into the shape of Fleur sitting on a board swing hanging from the baobab tree behind her hut. The gentle sway back and forth ruffled her sari skirt.

He came out of the shadows before he'd made any conscious decision to do so. "Dr. Andikan. It's a lovely night to gaze at the stars."

She turned her head slowly, as if his presence did not surprise her at all. The kind of trauma she'd experienced in the Rawandan genocide of the Tutsi often left survivors with a heightened sense of their surroundings, coupled with varying levels of paranoia that never went away completely. "Mr. Vincent, are you finding it difficult to adjust to the time change?"

"Ben, please." Drawn by an invisible, but irresistible force, he stepped closer. "I was in the mood for a walk."

"Without your guards?"

"Yes."

Her lovely face creased in a frown. "This compound is secure, but you are here for reasons that will not make you popular with those in power. You should consider asking for company on your evening strolls."

"They were all sleeping, except the guard with night duty."

"Not all. One of them, that big one, was patrolling the grounds not too long ago."

Ben filed that information away with his other knowledge of his security detail. "Perhaps Kadin found it as difficult to sleep as I did."

"Perhaps."

"What about you? I would think *you* would be exhausted after the kind of days you put in."

"Sleep is sometimes an elusive guest."

More likely she was haunted by past ghosts, but he did not call her on it. "I am sorry."

"Do not be. I find the quiet soothing and there is too little of that during the day."

"I am interrupting your solitude. I should go." There was no question whether he wanted to; he didn't.

"Peaceful company is not an interruption."

"And you are so sure mine is peaceful?" He didn't feel peaceful. At thirty-five, he was long past the time when his hormones controlled him, but around Fleur, Ben's libido became youthful, overwhelming again.

She looked at him for several moments before answering. "Yes, I think you know how to be peaceful. I think you also know how to make war, which does not fit your role here."

"I look dangerous to you?" Now that was a first. Part of the continued success of Ben's cover was how innocuous he appeared—the mild-mannered accountant, who was neither an accountant, nor mild mannered.

"You look like you *could be* dangerous."

"I can be," he found himself admitting. "But you never have to fear that."

"So, tonight, you are not dangerous."

"No."

"Then you are welcome to share my view of the night sky."

Her acceptance shocked him, but he wasn't about to reject it.

He settled against the tree trunk. "There are the same number of stars in the sky wherever you are in the world, but our ability to see them is limited by our environment. Here you can see millions."

"Their beauty reminds us that life is not all sorrow."

"Johari reminds you of that as well, doesn't she?"

"Yes. She reminds me that life is precious and surviving violence is a blessing, not the curse it sometimes feels like."

"Does she have nightmares?"

"No. She smiles. She laughs. She lives." The satisfaction Fleur felt at that was clear in her voice.

"And you? Do you do those things?"

"Sometimes."

"She helps."

"Yes, she does."

"And Tanna, does she help you?"

"She is so pure of heart. Innocent in ways I will never be again. She's lived on this violence-ridden continent for eight of the last ten years, but she remains optimistic and trusting of the nature of others."

"You are not."

"No."

He wasn't offended. "I am not either."

"We need people like Tanna in our lives to remind us."

"Yes, we do."

"Do you have someone like that, back in the States?"

Ben thought of the other TGP agents and the cynicism that came with their job. "No," he said with regret.

"I am sorry."

"Me too."

Silence reigned while she swung for a few long minutes before she asked, "Are you really going to report human rights violations?"

"If I find evidence of them, yes."

She nodded. "The pity is, you probably won't. The mine you are auditing is run by the government and they are mindful of regulations, but other human rights atrocities happen all around us. Young boys stolen from their villages and sold to work farms in South Africa, only to be turned in as illegal immigrants a couple of years later and sent back with no hope of finding a job to support themselves, much less a family."

"But none of the mine workers are slaves?"

"Not that I am aware of, though the possibility cannot be dismissed entirely. And how does one define slavery? Being forced to work long days under dangerous conditions for no more than a place to sleep and one, maybe two meals a day?"

"That's what I'm here to look into." And he would. It wouldn't be the first time Ben had needed to fulfill the requirement of his cover while resolving his assignment for TGP at the same time.

The fact that he now had three objectives did not escape him. He needed to audit the mine labor practices, find the source of the technology leakage and shut it down, and possibly protect Tanya from an assassination team.

No problem.

The jeep carrying Bennet Vincent, the two Marine privates and Face to the first meeting with the mine directors had become a distant rumble when Roman turned to find both Neil and Kadin waiting to talk to him.

He opened his mouth to ask Neil for a status report from the night before, but Kadin didn't give him a chance. "Our State Department official has some pretty strange nocturnal habits."

Roman jerked, not expecting that conversational direction at all. "Don't be cryptic, Trigger. It only pisses me off."

"Yeah, maybe I like pissing you off."

Roman just shook his head. "Maybe you do. Now tell me what the hell you're talking about."

"He left quarters last night."

"The latrine is fifty feet behind the chalet."

"He wasn't using it and he was alone." Kadin's brows rose. "At least in the beginning."

"Who did he meet?"

"Dr. Andikan, but it wasn't planned."

"You're sure about that, are you?"

"I eavesdropped."

"Good man."

"I live for your approval, chief."

"You know Geronimo wasn't a chief."

"Might as well have been."

"You're a smart ass, Kadin."

"So?"

Neil gave his fellow Atrati team member a mild frown. "He got out of his room without waking his guard?"

"Oh, yeah." Kadin's eyes gleamed with undisguised approval. "He got to the other side of the compound without any of us noticing."

"You noticed," Roman pointed out.

"I was walking the perimeter. I would have missed him if I wasn't feeling jumpy and checking every shadow."

Roman said, "You're always jumpy."

"You always check every shadow," Neil added.

Kadin smirked. "Maybe. Doesn't change the fact the D.C. suit got out of his room without waking his Marine-trained guard."

"I know you think Marines are superhuman, but they sleep like anyone else," Neil jibed.

"Like hell." Now that was a real Kadin glare, the kind you took note of or paid the consequences for later. Roman's team wasn't known for bothering themselves about a little consequence or two. "Marines sleep with one eye open and that private is no exception."

Neil gave a fair impression of a man who was bored, rather than impressed.

Heading off the explosion he knew Spazz was

angling for, Roman said, "So, Bennet Vincent knows how to move with stealth."

"Super-stealth," Kadin insisted.

"Super-stealth." Roman rolled his eyes. "What was he doing on the other side of the compound?"

"Texting, using a satellite hookup."

"So, he was checking in with his superiors." Right. That kind of communication was hinky any way you looked at it. Vincent could have made the satellite text call in his room, unless he was feeling extremely cautious about being interrupted.

Damn.

Kadin's expression said he smelled the hinky too. "In the dead of the night, having snuck past his guards and us."

Neil's brows drew together, but he didn't say anything.

"Yeah." Not likely. Shit on a shingle.

"This might explain something I found," Neil said then.

"What did you find on Bennet Vincent?" And why hadn't Neil brought it forward before?

"Nothing."

He just gave Neil the "do you want to live to see lunch?" look.

"I mean it. I did a routine background search on Vincent and found nothing. He's so clean, he could do an infomercial."

"So?"

"So, I dug a little, wanted to know what part of the State Department signs his paycheck, that kind of thing."

"Not exactly public record."

"And that matters to me?" Neil's sarcasm was justified.

"Of course not."

"So?" Kadin prompted, showing he was as impatient as Roman to find out what Neil had uncovered.

"So, I couldn't find it."

Had he heard right? Neil admitted he hadn't been able to find information on a computer network he'd hacked more times than Roman even wanted to think about. "*You* couldn't find it?"

"The closest I got to the account was the Presidential office umbrella."

"So? He's here on behalf of the President," Kadin pointed out.

"Not exactly. While the audit was a Presidential mandate, the other human rights auditors came from the regular bureaucratic pools. This guy works for somebody, or *something* as deeply buried as the Atrati."

Roman got that feeling in his gut that he'd learned a long time ago he couldn't ignore. "TGP."

"Say what?" Kadin demanded.

"The Goddard Project."

Neil frowned. "Never heard of it."

"Very few have. It's an agency with the mandate to protect America's technological integrity." And Roman still wouldn't know anything about it if his sister hadn't gotten herself fired and Myk hadn't gotten himself hired not long after.

"Sounds exciting," Kadin said dryly.

Neil's frown moved one degree toward real. "Hey, don't knock my obsession."

"You aren't like other techies, Spazz," Kadin assured the other Atrati agent.

"Neither are these agents," Roman said. "My sis-

ter, Elle, worked for them until her cover was compromised."

"Your *sister*?" Kadin asked.

"Yes."

Shaking his head, Neil laughed. "Hell, is your
whole family made up of secret agents?"

"Nah. Matej is a scientist to his fingertips and
Myk has never been secretive about working for
the government." He'd been an agent though.
Maybe it *was* in their DNA.

"So, you think this guy is a Goddard Project
agent?"

"It's a distinct possibility." He didn't know of another agency buried that deeply, but then, that
would be the point, wouldn't it? "One thing I do
know is that when we tried to get intel on Elle, all
we could find out was that she was being paid
through the State Department."

"You investigated your sister?" Kadin asked with
curiosity, but no shock.

"We knew she was federal, but she wasn't telling
us anything."

"And you hit a wall?"

"The same one you did, except we didn't get as
far as the Presidential umbrella."

Neil shrugged. "Yeah, well, you're not me."

"Neither was the agent I asked to help."

"Why didn't you ask me?"

"You were on assignment under no-contact orders."

"That's okay then."

"If you ladies are done working out your emotional shit . . ." Kadin let his voice trail off.

Neil told him to do something anatomically impossible before asking, "You think Ben's here investigating the same thing we are?"

"Technically, we are not investigating."

"To neutralize the real threat, we have to investigate."

Roman didn't bother arguing. Truth was, his men were right, but he wasn't going to let their obvious liking for Tanya Ruston compromise their objective either.

"Considering the directive of TGP, it's almost a certainty that if one of their agents is here, he's investigating the leak in military technology."

"So, what do we do?"

"We talk to him," Neil said before Roman could answer. "What? If the guy is as good at his job as you implied these TGP agents should be, he might have information that will help us identify the threat to the JCAT."

"What about Tanya?" Kadin asked.

Here they went again. "What about her?"

"Her computer was clean. So were all the computers in the medical center," Neil supplied.

"Can you get in the security center?" Roman asked.

"Do they even have a computer?" Kadin wondered.

Neil said, "I'll find out."

"Okay, so we talk to Vincent?" Kadin asked, looking for confirmation. "You think he'll tell us the truth?"

"Yes, we talk to Vincent, but no, I doubt he'll reveal himself. However, we're trained to read the truth on a man's face and in the way he uses his body."

Neil sat down at the small square table in the community room and started doing something on his computer. Without looking up, he said, "Maybe he's trained to lie without tells."

"Even the best liars have tells," Kadin asserted.

"Besides, I don't think we should wait for him to tell us the truth," Roman said. "I plan to tell him."

That had Neil looking up from his computer. "Blow our cover?"

"No, blow his."

Kadin looked unhappy despite Roman's assurance. "If he is a trained agent, he's got his doubts about us too."

Neil asked, "Why would he?" And then immediately he looked mad at himself for having done so. Roman gave him the benefit of the doubt—he'd been focusing on whatever hare he'd been chasing on his computer.

"The fact we don't wear military insignia?" Kadin asked with all the sarcasm the question warranted.

Roman added, "The distance between us and the baby grunts." Plus a hell of a lot of other tells that wouldn't matter at all if Bennet Vincent was who he was supposed to be.

"Stuff that a normal bureaucrat wouldn't think twice about," Neil said, reflecting Roman's thoughts.

Kadin was looking more and more cranky by the minute. He didn't like surprises. "Right, but if Geronimo here knows what he's talking about, and even I got to admit, he usually does, Vincent's no ordinary bureaucrat."

"This is all speculation," Roman felt he had to say. "He might just be a government suit with an uncanny ability to get past his guards to make nocturnal calls back home."

"Right." Kadin didn't even pretend to be convinced.

Roman sighed. *"Right."*

"Now is the time to do a search of Tanya's quarters, since she's working in the clinic," Neil said.

Roman nodded. "I'll search the doctor's rooms."

"I'll take the dorms." Kadin looked entirely too happy at the prospect that the dorms might not be empty. The man thrived on adrenaline.

Two hours later, they were all back with not a single thing to show for their time. Kadin hadn't even gotten a chance to put anyone in a sleeper hold.

Roman was not in a happy place as he finished off a protein bar while he and the others determined their next move. He was willing to figure out where the threat originated, but he hated like hell not to have made a single move forward in that direction. Nothing pointed toward Tanya, but nothing pointed away from her either. Their discussion devolved into snark more than once, but none of them took the negative tones seriously. They were all equally frustrated and used to working together.

The sound of approaching footsteps had them all switching the topic with seamless ease.

Roman was only mildly surprised when he found Tanya on the other side of the door to their chalet.

She smiled in that warm, friendly way she had that went straight to his dick. "Hi. Fleur told me you didn't all accompany Ben on his trip to the mine."

"No."

"Why not?"

"Did you have a reason for stopping by?"

"You're doing that 'avoid the answer with rudeness' thing again."

"You're surprised?"

"No. I'm getting used to you."

He wasn't sure that was a good thing. "So?"

She grinned again. "I've got to make a call on a local village and I thought you might want to come along, experience one aspect of the true Zimbabwe."

"I have a job here."

She looked less than impressed by that claim. "And he's at a mine more than thirty miles away."

He couldn't argue with that logic. Not when all he was supposed to be doing was supervising a bureaucrat's security detail. And strangely enough, he discovered that he wanted to go to the village with Tanya. And not because it would be an opportunity to observe her and try to get her to spill where she was keeping the JCAT software. Not good. Not even close.

"Who else is going?" he asked.

"One of Mabu's men and an intern in training." She looked regretfully at Kadin and Neil. "I'd invite you two, but there's not room in the Rover. Unless you want to pile in the back with all the medical supplies?"

"Thanks for the offer, but I'll take a rain check," Neil said.

What the hell? The man wasn't getting any rain checks with Tanya and Roman gave him a look saying so.

"I'd come, but I want to talk security with Mabu," Kadin said with a straight face.

Tanya smiled and nodded. "Okay then, are you in?" she asked with a pointed look at Roman.

"That's not much security for venturing outside the compound," he said, instead of answering, knowing it would annoy her and not sure why he wanted to.

Tanya's eyes tightened, but she shrugged. "Can't be helped. Sympa-Med won't spring for a bigger security staff and we're down two right now."

"Why?" He couldn't tell if she was irritated with him, or the insufficient security.

"One man has returned to his village to marry. He won't be back for a month, but Mabu is doing his best to hold his position open for him."

"He's coming back without his wife?" Kadin asked, sounding scandalized in a way Roman had never heard him.

Tanya didn't look happy about it either, but she sounded resigned. "It's the way of life for too many here."

"And the other missing man?" Roman asked.

"His HIV status went to full-blown AIDS. He returned to his village too, but he won't be back."

Roman said, "I'd think men would be lining up to take the job he left open."

"Definitely, but Mabu handles hiring security staff and Fleur leaves him to it. He'll find the right person."

"I see." Though truthfully, Roman didn't. He couldn't understand Mabu's willingness to leave the security of the compound at risk while he took his time finding the perfect man to guard Sympa-Med's assets.

"So, are you coming?" Tanya asked again.

"Yes." Hell, even if he hadn't been inclined to already, the minute she'd told him there was only one security man assigned to her trip, Roman knew he had no choice.

They were in the aged Rover, bouncing over something that might have resembled a road when the intern turned around from the front seat and said, "Weren't you supposed to go to Tikikima? I thought I'd be making this trip on my own."

Tanya shook her head decisively, a frown giving her sweet features an unaccustomed fierceness. "It's not fair to send a trainee for a village visit alone."

"But Sympa-Med—"

"Is too worried about offending the powers that be to see a situation for what it is sometimes. Going to Tikikima would be a waste of resources right now. I can reverse the circuit on the next traveling clinic and go there first if it's so important, but I'm not putting off an acute situation for a bit of political maneuvering."

"Oh, that will go over well with Sympa-Med." The intern turned around to face the front again, shaking his head.

"What did he mean?" Roman asked.

She grimaced. "Sympa-Med has a strict schedule and route the traveling clinic is supposed to follow. On my last circuit, I had to skip the final stop because one of my team was seriously ill and I had run out of supplies in the last village because of a disease breakout."

"And the suits back in the States are complaining you didn't follow their plan?" Typical bureaucrats.

"Actually Sympa-Med's suits are in France and yep, they've e-mailed Fleur twice and called her once to demand I take the traveling clinic to Tikikima."

"Why don't you just do it?" From what he could tell, Tanya was all about helping people. He didn't see her refusing to go somewhere she was needed.

"Because we have lots of other people who actually need our medical services and that particular village is within walking distance of a stationary indigenous clinic. As far as I can tell, they're only on our circuit because the village officials have ties with Sympa-Med's main office. It's all a power game to them, but we're treating live people who would go without medical help otherwise." The passionate belief in her voice was only matched by her clear frustration.

"Fleur's okay with you ignoring directions from the home office?"

Tanya's expression revealed that the opposite was true, and it didn't make her happy. "She's annoyed with me, but no one's threatened to terminate my contract."

"And if they did?"

"Then, I'd have to look for another relief organization that could use my training and expertise." Tanya's voice rang with both certainty and sincerity, the tones of an idealist still convinced in her ability to do right.

He had a very hard time reconciling this woman, one who would risk her position and the anger of a doctor she clearly admired, in order to do what she thought was right, with a woman who would sell her country's secrets. Not only that, but if her espionage required the cover of traveling relief worker, she wouldn't risk losing that position. If she was the information leak.

Maybe it wasn't just his libido telling him Tanya was innocent. Maybe his gut was saying the same thing. And maybe it was time he started listening.

He'd screwed up badly once before, allowing personal feelings to blind him to the truth until it was too late. He'd vowed never to do that again.

If he ignored Tanya's innocence because of his feelings for her, he would be doing the same thing. That would be stupid. Monumentally so. And Roman was not a stupid man.

"So, why *this* village?"

"It has a large population of children, and the mothers are more open to modern medicine than in other villages. We'll be doing a wellness check, weighing children, checking for disease, treating what we can." Her hazel eyes sparkled with enthusiasm.

If it wasn't genuine, he could not see it, which would make her more than an expert liar. It would make her a master at the craft. And that? He did not buy it.

"Sounds like you'll be busy."

"I will, but it's worth it. So many villages continue to rely on the old ways. If a child gets sick, the village shaman or a medium will be called in and asked to intercede with the ancestors on their behalf." She bit her lip, her expression turning troubled. "They reject modern medicine, but going to the ancestors is not going to cure malaria, or AIDS. Not that we've got enough of the antivirals to touch that epidemic, even today."

"That doesn't discourage you?"

"It hurts that so many children die, but we make

a difference. If only a dozen children live that
would not have, isn't it worth everything we do?
And we treat way more than a dozen."

"I like your attitude," he admitted.

She cocked her head to one side, looking at him
as if trying to decide his sincerity. "I thought you
didn't like me at all."

"I like you too much," he said, with more hon-
esty than he'd intended.

He didn't know what it was about this woman
that made him admit something he would normally keep under wraps.

"Really?" she asked, the shock in her voice bely-
ing any thought she was flirting, or coyly fishing
for compliments.

Without conscious volition, he ran his fingertip
down her smooth cheek. She was just so damn
sweet. "Yes, really."

Her eyes widened, the pupils expanding.

"So, what else happens at the village? Will you
treat adults?"

"Some, but most will hold off in favor of having
the children seen. When we're all done, we'll
share in the evening meal. There will be music,
traditional dance, storytelling." The soft breathi-
ness of her voice did not match the mundane nature of her words.

He reached out and ran his fingers through her
golden-brown hair, the silky strands sensually caressing his hand. "That sounds like a party." He
could so do this woman.

"It is." She grinned, her gaze both heated
and teasing. "Why do you think I wasn't willing to
miss it?"

Dropping his hand, he shook his head. "Somehow, I think the work actually takes precedence over the entertainment in your mind."

"Don't be fooled. They're both important." Her tone was as serious as he'd heard it to date. "That's one of the things I've learned living here; don't dismiss the chance to enjoy life trying too hard to make someone else's better."

"That's a pretty important lesson."

"I thought so. In America, we're raised with a results-oriented mentality that doesn't work for every situation. It's way too easy to get discouraged trying to apply that attitude to relief work."

"Because no matter how much you do, there's always more to do so the results are always skewed."

She gave him a surprised look from her hazel eyes. "You sound like you've got some experience."

"Fighting the good fight has a lot of the same drawbacks."

"There's always someone out there ready to threaten our nation's security," she guessed accurately.

"Yeah."

"Is that why you left the lab? You felt like you could make a bigger difference to the American people protecting them than trying to develop new weapons or anti-weapon technology?"

She understood his former job better than he would have expected her to. "I'm a damn good scientist, but when it comes to being a soldier, I'm the best."

"No false modesty there."

"Waste of breath."

She laughed. "I see." She gave him another probing look. "I'm still trying to work out what you are doing here with Ben. Is he somebody special, traveling incognito? One of the President's advisors maybe?"

"You're assuming *I'm* something special."

"You just got through telling me you're the best. That usually implies Special Forces. Maybe I'm naïve, but I wouldn't expect an average bureaucrat to have a security detail made up of Special Forces soldiers."

"Actually, depending on the level of threat, it's not unheard of."

"So, you're not going to tell me?"

"There's nothing to tell."

"Right." The look she gave him dared him to stick with that particular party line.

"Elle says your brother is stubborn as a mule with an attitude problem."

"Your point?"

"I think it might run in the family."

A grin flirted at the corners of her mouth. "You can count on it. My grandmother locked herself into the local library and went on a hunger strike until the city council agreed to leave *Catcher in the Rye* and other supposedly subversive books in the stacks. She was seriously opposed to censorship, but she didn't limit her opposition to rhetoric."

No more than the woman in front of him was content to take a passive stance in regard to the needs she identified here in Zimbabwe.

"Let me guess, she was the librarian?"

"Yep."

"I wasn't talking about ancestors."

"Ancestors are a big thing among the Zimbabweans."

"So you said. Not only are you stubborn, but you're not bad at misdirection."

"If you say so."

"I do." And why did that knowledge make him smile?

She gasped.

He did a quick inventory of their surroundings, but there was no threat he could see. "What?"

"You smiled."

"So?"

"I never saw you do that before. Not even at Elle and Beau's wedding."

"You find that odd?"

"You don't?"

"No."

She shook her head. "Wow. You're so serious."

"Isn't that a redundant observation when you reacted with such shock to my smile?"

"Are you teasing me, Mr. 'I don't show frivolous emotion'?"

"Could be."

"Well."

"Well?" he prompted.

"I think I like it."

"I think you're flirting." And he was damn sure he liked it despite the fact he should not. He muttered a Ukrainian curse.

"Oh," she gasped.

"Now what?"

"Elle said that, when the zipper on her wedding dress got caught. Your mother and grandmother started yelling at her to beat the band."

"I'm not surprised."

"Neither was I once I convinced Mat to tell me what it meant."

"I'm surprised my brother told you."

"I tricked him into it." Tanya smiled smugly. "He

might be a brilliant scientist, but he's kind of hopeless at male-female interaction. Chantal has her work cut out for her with that one."

"So she has said more than once."

"Smart woman."

"You would think so."

"Don't you?" Tanya asked.

"I have only met my sister-in-law a couple of times, but yes, I found her intelligent."

"She's also sweet."

"Yes."

Tanya studied him for several silent seconds before asking, "Do you like sweet?"

"I prefer stubborn." Damn it, why had he said that?

Again with the admitting stuff he would never say to another woman, much less a mark. He was no longer convinced she was guilty of being the information leak, but that didn't mean he should allow himself to start thinking of her in his bed.

He never screwed around on a job. Not unless sex was required to meet his objective.

Her pretty hazel eyes went dark green with an emotion that caused a corresponding reaction in his pants. "That's good to know."

"Is it?" He leaned toward her, invading her personal space and considering the best way to touch her without drawing the attention of the two men in the front of the truck.

"Yes," she said in a husky voice that went straight to his cock.

Excited voices filled with agitation broke the spell their proximity was casting in the back of the ancient Land Rover.

Tanya's head snapped forward. "What's going on?"

"There is a military blockade on the road ahead," the interning medical worker said in a stress-filled voice.

Other than a slight tensing of her shoulders, Tanya did not show any concern over the news. It pissed Roman off though, that he'd been so wrapped up in her, he hadn't seen the roadblock before the others pointed it out. She was too much of a distraction. Damn it.

"We'll be fine." Tanya patted the intern's shoulder. "Calm down. We've got our papers and Sympa-Med is well known."

The driver said something in Shona and Tanya just shook her head. "Getting worked up isn't going to help anything."

"What did he say?" Roman asked.

"He doesn't trust government soldiers."

Roman got the feeling the local security man had said something just a little earthier than that, but with the same meaning. "Does that mean he *does* trust mercenaries?"

"I don't know."

Both men in the front seat emanated stress. The driver's was tinged with anger, while the intern practically vibrated with fear, but calm determination filled Roman.

He didn't know what in the hell was going on, but no local military flexing their bully muscles was going to compromise his objective.

As the driver pulled to a stop at the roadblock, Roman saw four soldiers. They were all the dark espresso brown of Zimbabweans, but he recognized U.S. military when he saw them, and two of the men had been trained by Uncle Sam's Army. Little tells indicated they weren't at home in the Zimbabwean uniform.

Roman watched with interest as one of the American soldiers masquerading as Zimbabwe military, approached the driver's door.

The driver lowered his window, but did not unlock the door, or make any move to step out of the Rover.

The pseudo Zimbabwean soldier demanded in American-accented English to see papers for the Rover's occupants and medical supplies.

Roman saw the U.S. soldiers giving particular attention to Tanya's papers.

They conferred with the Zimbabwean soldiers, and then the leader said something in Shona to their driver, who immediately started yelling and gesturing with his hands.

"What's going on?" Roman asked Tanya in an undertone.

"They want to search the Rover and they want to search us." She let out a trembling breath. "They want to *strip-search* us." Tanya's voice shook, but he wasn't sure if it was from anger or fear.

"No way in hell." Roman dialed a familiar number on his satellite phone as he swung out of the Rover. The first mistake they had made was ignoring his exit from the SUV, thinking that the driver posed more of a threat. The second mistake was remaining preoccupied with the arguing driver while Roman made his way to within striking distance of them.

CHAPTER FOUR

There were only four, and one of them was un-armed. Whether he'd left his weapon in their jeep, or somewhere else, it was not near at hand.

The other genuine Zimbabwean had a pistol in a snapped holster on his utility belt, and an AK-74U within reaching distance, but the safety was on. The American soldiers had newer weapons, but wore them holstered as if they were not expecting real trouble.

In other words, no one knew he would be with Tanya today. Because there was no doubt in his mind that this little roadblock was targeted at her.

Whether that was because she was a woman, or others suspected her of having important military intel, he refused to guess.

Roman went straight for the American soldier who spoke with more authority than the other one. He grabbed the man, flipped him in front and took the soldier's weapon from its holster, swinging it up to point at the other men. The American cursed and went rigid, his hand coming back to strike Roman. Roman blocked the hit and pressed his thumb into a particularly vulnerable pressure point on the man's neck. "Stand down, soldier," Roman said as he knew the other man's vision headed toward black.

The soldier stopped fighting and allowed him to cuff his hands behind his back with a zip-tie. All of this took less than a minute.

Once again, Roman held the soldier in front of him, with his gun pointed at the others. "Step back from the Rover."

When they didn't move fast enough, he said, "Now," in a tone even Kadin knew not to mess with.

The soldiers stepped back. The unarmed one tried to angle toward their jeeps.

Roman let off a single shot that kicked up dirt at the man's feet. "Stay."

The soldier stopped.

"Down on the ground, hands on the back of your heads."

One of the Zimbabwean soldiers spat something at him in Shona. Roman didn't ask Tanya for a translation. That kind of talk was universal.

He waited until they'd obeyed his directions before stepping back from the man he'd been using as a shield. Grabbing his satellite phone, he was glad to hear the active air sound that indicated a connection.

Before he got a chance to speak into the phone, the soldier still standing demanded, "Who the hell are you?"

"A man with a hell of a lot higher pay grade than you and that's all you need to know, soldier."

"Like hell, sir. We've got our orders."

Roman ignored him and lifted the phone to his ear. "Sir?"

"Chernichenko?"

"Yes."

"What's going on?"

"I'm at a roadblock and two of our own are here with a couple of Zimbabwe nationals. They want to perform a strip search."

"You're with Ms. Ruston."

"That would be an affirmative, sir."

"Let them do the search. We'll find out if she's carrying the software on her."

"That's a negative, sir."

"Excuse me?"

"This is my operation."

"Agreed."

"Do you want the intel to fall into Zimbabwean hands if she does have it?" he asked in Russian.

"Shit. No."

"There will be no strip search, at least not by these men."

"You plan to conduct your own strip search?" his boss asked, sounding almost amused.

He hadn't considered it, but the prospect was a good one. If he was going to get busy on a job, he needed more than the objective of comparing the softness of Tanya's cheek to her inner thigh. "That would be the plan, sir."

"Get to it."

"Some things need to be finessed."

His boss snorted. "Whatever you say. You're the best operative we've got. If you want me to call in favors and prevent an international incident, I need names."

Roman stepped toward the Rover and indicated that Tanya should roll down her window, which she did. He handed her the phone and reverted to English. "Hold this please."

She took it without comment.

He spun on his heel, toward the soldier still standing and yanked his dog tags out from beneath his borrowed uniform's shirt collar.

"Tanya, repeat what I say to the person on the phone."

Her eyes widened, but she put the phone to her ear. "Ready."

He recited the information off the dog tag.

She repeated it into the phone.

Roman told the security guard to get out of the truck. "Get the other soldiers' identifications."

The driver did not argue and went for the second American soldier without being directed. He took time to secure the man's hands with a zip-tie before he dug out the dog tag and read the information off it for Tanya to repeat into the phone. He then secured the other soldiers with zip-ties before searching them for dog tags, which he did not find.

"Look for paper identification," Roman instructed.

"There is nothing," the driver said in heavily accented English after searching all the pockets. "I will look in their vehicles."

One of the Zimbabwean men stiffened at that assertion, growling something in Shona that made the security guard glare.

He didn't bother responding, but went to the jeeps.

A couple of minutes later, he was standing in front of Roman with a small hand-held electronic device. "All I found was this."

It wasn't a PDA, or a phone. In fact, it didn't have any kind of display screen at all. "What is it?"

Roman's brows drew together as he studied the small black device. "I don't know."

He turned to the men. "What is this for?"

His question was met with stony silence.

"You all won't mind my keeping it then, will you?"

"That is mine. You cannot take it. I will have you arrested," one of the men said from the ground.

"Really?" Roman asked.

"You are already in grave trouble for treating us thus."

"Am I? Funny, somehow I doubt the local base is going to come out en masse to protect your dignity."

He ignored the further spluttering and said to Tanya, "Tell the person on the phone that I don't think this roadblock is a government-sanctioned military activity."

The small flinch on one of the Zimbabwean soldier's faces confirmed Roman's guess. Interesting. "In fact, I don't think a single one of these four men are Zimbabwean military."

Tanya relayed his supposition while Roman watched the reactions of his captives carefully. A minuscule grimace, a jerking shoulder, a stony expression with partially parted lips and Roman knew he was right.

The soldiers started cursing and yelling at him, demanding he let them go.

"Shut it," he said in the voice he used when he expected to be obeyed, which was pretty much always he had to admit. If only to himself.

Quiet fell.

"As you may have figured out, I called my superior. He'll be contacting your superiors, or at least whoever is responsible for Uncle Sam's military parading in Zimbabwean uniforms today. There will be no strip search of American citizens on my watch."

The soldier standing said, "You don't know what this is about."

"Are you sure of that?"

"Who are you?" he asked again, this time sounding worried rather than belligerent.

"That's not something you need to worry about. I would be worried about pissing me off more than I already am."

"How long until your boss gets through?" the other man asked, showing enough intelligence to be nervous.

"Don't know."

It was ten very tense minutes later when the radio on the standing soldier's utility belt buzzed to life. Roman unclipped the GMRS unit from the man's utility belt and held it so the soldier could speak into it. First, he listened to a staccato burst of speech before giving an affirmative.

The soldier had been ordered to stand down. The other American soldier looked resigned, but not overly worried. The two Zimbabwean men grew even more agitated, demanding of the other men to continue with the plan.

"We obey orders and they're clear. No one is

supposed to get in this man's way," the standing
soldier said, indicating Roman with a jerk of his
shoulder.

"I will undo your cuffs, but do not release the
other men until we are thirty minutes out. Understand?"

"Understood, sir."

Roman was confident the soldier would follow
orders, but just as certain the Zimbabwean men
were not about to let the situation go.

He took the small electronic device with him as
he returned to the truck. Neil should be able to
figure out what it was.

Tanya concentrated very hard on not hyper-
ventilating as Roman gave instructions to their security driver. Her over-the-top stress levels were the
only excuse she could give herself for not realizing
what those instructions were until the Rover was
facing in the other direction.

"What are we doing? The village is that way." She
pointed out the back window, the exact opposite
way from the one the Rover was now headed in.

Roman gave her a look that doubted her intelligence. "And that roadblock may not be the only
one between here and there. We're not risking
getting pulled over again."

It was the same look her parents had given her
when she'd told them she was joining the Peace
Corps, and then again later when she'd told them
she was returning to Africa.

"This is the first time this has ever happened to
me." Though not the first time she'd ever heard of
such a thing, or worse, happening to others. "I'm

sure it's an isolated incident. Besides, you did your super-soldier mojo with that phone call and got them to back down. You could do it again. We can't miss our trip to the village."

"You can and you will." His expression was so intense, it was almost scary. "We can't rely on my super-soldier mojo to work a second time."

"But—"

"Look, Tanya, you might be willing to risk another brush with power-hungry soldiers, but I'm not," the intern said, interrupting her.

She glared at him, but her lower lip trembled infinitesimally. "Risk is part and parcel of what we do."

She was hiding her fear behind bravado. In her mind, they had to continue on to keep things sane. Roman had seen it before with soldiers facing combat. He wasn't going to give in, but he understood why she was being so unreasonable.

"But we don't have to be stupid about it," the other medical worker said impatiently.

"I'm not stupid."

"No, you are not," Roman said firmly, giving the intern a look that had the younger man facing front in a hurry. Roman laid his hand over one of Tanya's clenched fists. "Which is why you are going to stop arguing about this. Those soldiers had a hard-on for you, and I don't mean the ones in their jockey shorts."

"That's ridiculous. I was just part of the car."

"Well, they didn't start demanding searches, strip or otherwise, until they saw your paperwork," he pointed out, watching her closely as if expecting something.

She felt the blood drain from her face as her throat constricted, making it hard to breathe. "I . . ."

"What?" he demanded with an air of expectation she did not understand.

"I . . . they . . . wouldn't . . ."

"Wouldn't what, Tanya?"

"Rape me," she whispered, sick to her stomach. But the possibility was all too real. How many horror stories had she heard, and not old ones?

Some soldiers believed their uniforms gave them power over life, death and any woman's body they wanted to use.

Roman's expression turned deadly. "No one is going to rape you while I'm here."

"There were four of them and only one of you."

He gave her a look that said, "So?" and she almost smiled, but she couldn't quite make her facial muscles work in that direction. And it wasn't as if his attitude was unjustified. He'd gotten the drop on the soldiers and incapacitated them so quickly, she hadn't even realized what was happening until three of the men were on the ground and their security driver was praising Roman's machismo in Shona.

"Sometimes, your arrogance is borderline comforting." She bit her lip, not really regretting admitting that, but feeling even more vulnerable with the knowledge.

"It's only arrogance when the confidence isn't justified. Mine is."

"Who are you that your boss has influence over the Zimbabwean army?"

A strange expression flitted over his features before he shrugged. "Believe it or not Uncle Sam has influence in a lot of places you wouldn't expect."

And then she remembered his assertion that the roadblock had not been sanctioned by the Zimbabwean military. "I still don't—"

"Don't overanalyze it. Your specialty is saving people, mine is protecting our country's interests. Let's leave it at that."

"Does protecting U.S. interests include protecting its citizens?" She couldn't believe that was the case, but she certainly wouldn't mind if he'd taken a personal interest in her safety.

"In your case it does."

Warmth suffused her as the implications of his statement sank in. He wanted to protect her. Coupled with his behavior in the car before they came onto the roadblock, indications were good that her aching attraction wasn't in fact one sided. She almost smiled. "That's good to know."

"I'm glad you think so."

She took a deep breath and let it out, trying again for a smile and almost making it. She should not be so freaked. After all, nothing had actually happened to her, but that didn't seem to count for much with her emotional equilibrium. She forced the fear aside and said, "I think you're flirting again."

"Maybe I am."

"Good, because I'm definitely flirting."

"I noticed."

She felt her face twist in a grimace as a thought occurred to her. "Fleur is going to be angry."

"That we ran into a roadblock?"

"That I insisted on going to Kimambizi when Sympa-Med wanted me to go to Tikikima."

"And the trip ended up wasted."

"Exactly."

"Is she really that unreasonable?"

"She's pragmatic. Fleur thinks I'm an idealist, and a somewhat naïve one at that. She doesn't like it when I buck the system."

"She doesn't strike me as a traditionalist."

"It's that pragmatism. Sympa-Med makes it possible for us to do what we do. She doesn't want to alienate them."

"Sounds reasonable."

"It is, but sometimes, they're wrong."

He laughed and Tanya felt the sound all the way through her. "You have a wonderful laugh."

"And you *are* an idealist."

"That's not a bad thing."

"No, but I think you and Dr. Andikan are probably a good balance for each other."

Tanya felt a real smile curve her lips. "We are. She's a good friend."

"I'm sure she feels the same."

"More than I realized, considering what Ben said she writes about me on her blog."

Roman frowned at the mention of the other man.

She found that curious. "Don't you like Ben?"

"He's an unknown quantity."

"I thought he was just a government bureaucrat?" she mocked.

"I'm not saying he's anything else. I'm simply saying he seems to have hidden depths." And Roman really did not sound happy about that fact, or maybe it was the fact he'd admitted it to her that bugged him so much. He looked a little surprised by his own words.

*   *   *

"You think they were there for Tanya?" Kadin asked after Roman gave them the sit-rep upon returning early from the aborted trip to the village.

Once again, they were talking in the communal room of their hut. Drew had not returned from his trip to the mine with Vincent and his Marine guards, but they were expected back soon.

Roman's jaw went tight. "You know I'm not a fan of coincidences. Here are two Army recruits dressed as members of the Zimbabwe military working a roadblock. And this roadblock just happens to stop Tanya on her trip out of the compound? I wouldn't buy that story with counterfeit two-dollar bills."

Kadin looked equally unwilling to buy the coincidence theory. He spat out a curse.

"Exactly."

"But how did they know she would be on that road?" Neil asked, his brain clearly spinning as he worked this whole snafu out.

"That's a good question. If she didn't tell them—" Roman started to say.

But Kadin interrupted with biting frustration, "Come on, chief, you're not still playing that tired record."

"Tell me why I shouldn't? She's the most likely person to divulge her own movements." He didn't fully believe it, but he wasn't going to dismiss the possibility out of hand either. "She was damn calm when we realized there was a roadblock; the other two Sympa-Med people were not nearly as sanguine in the face of being detained by local military."

At the time, he'd assumed she was braver than your average person. It hadn't been a stretch, since he'd pretty much determined that already. But now he had to at least consider the other possible reasons for her being so stoic.

"That's the kind of person she is." Kadin gave him a look, the one that said he thought Roman should already get this. "You've already seen that. Hell, the woman runs a traveling clinic in an area rife with human trafficking."

"Yeah." He sighed. "She was terrified at the prospect of a strip search, though."

"What woman in her right mind wouldn't be?" Neil asked.

And frankly, Roman agreed with him, so he said nothing. Though there could have been other reasons for her to be afraid. No matter what Hollywood would have people believe, there was no honor among thieves. Especially the variety that blithely stole and sold countries' secrets.

Kadin gave him a look that said he was reading Roman's thoughts. "So, you *don't* think it was her?" he prompted with evident doubt.

They stood for several seconds, staring each other down.

"No, I don't," Roman finally said, going with his gut rather than the rationale that didn't even carry a lot of weight in his own brain.

Neil asked in his matter-of-fact way, "So, who?"

"How public is the schedule for the traveling clinic?" Roman asked, assuming his communications expert would have an answer.

He wasn't disappointed. "Pretty public. They like to get the word out in advance, so people can travel from the surrounding villages to attend the clinics."

"Anyone could have known she would be on that trip then?" That didn't give them squat.

"Well, as to that, the team originally assigned did not include her," Neil put in, reminding Roman of what Tanya had told him in the Rover. Neil must have found out after they'd left. He was the information king and for that, Roman was always grateful. "She decided to go and Fleur did not overrule her."

"That's interesting," Kadin mused.

Roman pulled the odd electronic device he'd taken off the Zimbabwean soldiers out of his pocket. "So is this. Any clue as to what it does?" he asked Neil.

Neil put his hand out and Roman gave him the device.

The other man turned it over and examined it closely. "It has a nonstandard outgoing USB port, but nothing for input. This looks like an on-off button," he said, pressing part of the shell. "I'm going to have to take it apart to figure it out for sure, but my guess would be it is some kind of hand-held, wireless transfer device. The fact that it doesn't have any input mechanism implies it is storage only."

"Considering the miniaturization of storage devices, it could hold a hell of a lot, right?" Roman asked, his gut twisting at the implications.

Neil nodded. "Unless it's old technology, which it doesn't look like, it could easily hold the JCAT software."

"Well, damn," Kadin grumbled.

Roman agreed. Nothing about this assignment, or the woman who was supposed to be their target, was simple and straightforward. Not one damn thing. "If it was meant to make the transfer, Tanya had to have the program on her in the Rover."

And what were the chances she had and didn't know it? Zilch, right? Damn. Shit. Piss. He released a frustrated growl as Kadin started glaring again. Not that the man's usual expression was all that pleasant, but he looked ready to kill someone and Roman didn't have a death wish. Or the desire to hurt his friend protecting himself.

"She might not have been the one with the JCAT software, even if the roadblock was put in place to make the transfer." Neil didn't look like it mattered much to him either way. He had that "lost in thought" expression on his face that he got when faced with a unique computer problem.

"Right," Kadin said. "It could have been one of the other two."

"It could, but I have to make sure it wasn't Tanya." Roman sighed, and debated not telling them his plan, then decided they'd figure it out once he started it anyway. "I told Corbin I would perform my own strip search."

Kadin opened his mouth, but Roman forestalled him. "Don't. First, I've done worse and so have you to protect our country's interests. Second, Corbin wanted me to let the soldiers do the search. I convinced him it was my operation and that a public strip search wasn't in our country's best interests."

"You've ignored Corbin before," Kadin accused.

"When I thought he was wrong, yes. But I don't think he is. We need to know and we've already searched her domicile and workplace."

"There are still the other computers in the compound."

"Yeah, but that little gizmo implies that if she is the target, she had the plans with her today." He rolled his shoulders, trying to release tension that did not want to let go. "Look, she's attracted to me. I'll seduce her and she'll never even know I did the search."

Neil frowned. "Unless she has the JCAT, and then the leak has to be plugged."

"Bullshit, she's not the leak and saving some Army brass's ass is no reason to take out a sweet woman like Tanna," Kadin said.

For some reason, Kadin's use of Tanya's preferred nickname pissed Roman off. "I didn't say I was going to eliminate her, but if she's been selling secrets, she has to face the consequences."

"You don't think having sex with you is punishment enough?" Kadin demanded with pure aggression.

Roman swatted at his head, but Kadin moved and swept at Roman's ankle with a low kick. Within seconds, they were in a sparring session more intense than anything they'd ever done before. The sound of sliding furniture told Roman that Neil was giving them a cleared area for their fight.

Neil wasn't foolish enough to try to stop it. Even friendly sparring between Roman and Kadin was dangerous to interrupt.

Kadin got Roman temporarily pinned. "She's not the information leak in this assignment. Open your damn eyes."

His own inexplicable anger coming to the fore, Roman flipped Kadin and ground out, "They are open and they see you taking entirely too much interest in our target."

"I'm not the one threatening to screw her." With

a powerful full-body heave, Kadin threw Roman off.

Roman used the momentum to roll into a backward somersault and come up on his feet in a crouch. "It's not a threat. I'll give her more pleasure than she knows what to do with."

"And then break her heart," Kadin practically shouted.

Roman stopped fighting and stared at his team member. "What the hell? Do you have a thing for this woman?" If the answer was yes, Roman did not know if he could back off and allow the other man to do the seducing. Shit. Could this situation get any more screwed up?

"Yeah, I've got a thing for her."

Roman felt his insides twist to the point of pain. "You—"

"I've got a thing for you not breaking her heart."

"Since when do we let hearts get involved with what we do?"

"You can't control what *she* feels."

"What she feels is a physical reaction to my body, asswipe. She's not in love with me. She barely knows me, damn it." And he wasn't the lovable type. He was too hard, inside and out. He looked around the room, but Neil wasn't in it. "Where's Spazz?"

"He's probably working on the new toy you brought him." Kadin glared. "Don't try to change the subject."

"Drop it, Trigger. We all have our jobs to do and they rarely fall in the without-consequences category. You of all my team should understand that."

Kadin's expression turned to stone. "Maybe I should, but I don't. There's something there, between you and her. You send it fubar and that's your chance gone."

"A thing between me and Tanya?" This wasn't about Kadin's feelings for the much too appealing woman. "What are you talking about?"

"She's your chance."

"My chance?" He felt like an idiot repeating everything Kadin said, but none of it was computing in the world they inhabited.

"At normal. At life outside what we do. At love."

"You're serious."

"Yes."

Roman shook his head. "You're talking about fairytales and sunshine up my ass. No matter what you think, neither one of those things are going to come true in this lifetime."

"Just because you're a soldier doesn't mean you have to be alone."

"Maybe if we weren't Atrati assassins. But Kadin, you and I, we're not like other men." That chance Kadin was talking about, it had passed Roman by the day he'd walked out of the lab and started training to kill men with his bare hands.

"No, we're not." Kadin looked tired all of a sudden. "Try not to break her heart, Roman. She's still so damn innocent."

"It's just sex, Kadin. I'm not going to make promises."

"If you say so." But the other man did not appear convinced.

Roman ignored the small voice deep inside himself that said he wasn't either.

CHAPTER FIVE

That night at dinner, the whole security team and Ben squeezed around the table where Tanya and Fleur sat, forcing others who usually sat with them to eat elsewhere. Tanya found herself squished between Roman and Kadin. And rather than feeling overwhelmed by the men's size and presence, she felt safe.

After the day she'd had, safe was good. Very good.

Fleur had surprised Tanya by responding with preoccupied silence when told about the road-block, rather than anger or frustration at the waste of scheduling resources. She still looked less than immediately present in her seat across the table from Tanya.

Johari sat beside the Tutsi woman, regaling her with a steady stream of school news and chatter about her friends. Fleur nodded in all the right places, but if she heard half of what her daughter said, Tanya would be shocked to know it. Johari finally wound down and started eating her dinner, leaving the adults at the table to carry the conversation.

Fleur turned to face Roman, her expression too odd to read. "I want to thank you, for saving Tanya."

Roman shrugged. "I wasn't about to tolerate a strip search of myself."

"I think we all know that if Tanya had not been in the Rover," Fleur said, her voice laced with disgust, "no one would have insisted on anything of that nature."

"What do you mean?" Roman asked with a quality of stillness that Tanya did not understand.

"Tanya was at risk for something far worse than the humiliation of a strip search."

"You think they intended to rape her?" Kadin asked with a growl.

If Roman was right in his belief that the Zimbabwe soldiers had been there without official sanction, then the only scenario that made sense was that the roadblock had been a trap. A trap designed by predators who wanted to get their jollies hurting others. If not Tanya, then some other hapless woman. She could only hope that Roman's call to his superiors would force the horrible men to give up their plans rather than be caught committing human rights violations that could leave at least the Americans in prison.

"Soldiers believe they can hurt women that way if they want to," Johari said in her near fluent English. "Girls too."

Tanya's stomach tightened at the reminder that Johari had seen and experienced things no child should ever be forced to.

"It is a soldier's job to protect. If someone forgets that around Roman, or any of us, we don't have a problem reminding them," Kadin said in a deadly voice.

Johari smiled at the big warrior. "Good. Maybe there are more soldiers like you somewhere."

Tanya sighed. "There are good soldiers in Zimbabwe's army too."

"But not the ones who ran the roadblock today."

"No, those ones were not good men." She couldn't stop the shudder that went through her at the thought of what those men could have done. A strip search would have been humiliating and traumatizing enough, but the idea of rape left her nauseated and shaken.

She felt Roman's hand on the small of her back, a steady, sure presence that comforted her more than it should have. "You are okay."

She glanced sideways at him, making no move to shift away from his touch, wanting very much to lean into it. "Thanks to you."

"I'm glad I was there." Honest certainty laced his tone, melting barriers she'd erected around her heart when Quinton had dumped her and their relationship.

Despite tendrils of concern at how deeply Roman's words had affected her, she allowed herself to relax against his hand and revel in the small connection to his heat and strength. "Me too."

"We missed out on the village party." His thumb moved up and down her spine in an unconsciously possessive gesture that did nothing to shore up the walls tumbling from around her heart at a terrifyingly rapid rate.

"Maybe we can reschedule the visit before you leave."

"There will be no travel for the next few days."
Fleur's voice brooked no argument.

Despite the intransigent tone of the doctor's
voice, Tanya couldn't help asking in shock, "What?
Why?" The traveling clinic never was put on hold.
It was every bit as important as the stationary clinic
to Sympa-Med's directive for the Zimbabwe team.

"Sympa-Med is sending representatives from the
home office for a supervisory visit." Fleur smoothed
her blouse in a move Tanya recognized as sup-
pressed agitation. "No one is to be away from the
compound when they arrive."

"That's ridiculous. When are they supposed to
arrive? We can't stop our work just because they
don't want to be inconvenienced waiting to meet
members of the staff."

"Sympa-Med pays our wages, they provide our
supplies. If they want us to hold off travel for the
next few days, we'll do it." The ice Fleur usually reserved for people like Ibeamaka chilled her voice.

It bothered Tanya to have Fleur so clearly upset
with her, but she couldn't leave it there. "How long
is a few days?"

"I don't know."

"Did you ask for a more specific schedule?"
Tanya tried very hard not to sound like she was
grilling her boss, but she needed answers. This situation simply didn't make any sense.

"I did."

"And?"

"The director said he was surprised I was so
keen to have a set schedule considering how little
regard we show for the traveling clinic schedule."
Fleur's dark eyes radiated disapproval, directed
right at Tanya.

Tanya felt her eyes widen, even as her mouth flatlined in a frown, more than a little irritated herself now. "That's stupid. We had good reason for putting off the last stop on our schedule." Sheesh. How many times were they going to go back over the same thing? Talk about beating an issue to death. No one was going to convince her that putting Sympa-Med's schedule ahead of the health of her co-worker or the people they treated was the right thing to do, not even Fleur. "Sympa-Med's director is a control freak."

"He is your boss."

Tanya opened her mouth and then thought better of what she was about to say. She loved her position with Sympa-Med, even if the home office sometimes drove her nuts. Offering to quit in the heat of the moment was neither rational, nor mature. "I still think it's beyond unreasonable to expect us to stop all travel until they deign to show up," she grumbled.

Fleur thawed a little, giving Tanya a commiserating glance. "To be fair, the director didn't put the hold on travel in place until after I told him about today's roadblock."

"You called the home office on the sat-phone? I thought your weekly check-in wasn't until tomorrow."

Fleur gave her a quizzical look as if not understanding Tanya's surprise. "We often speak between our scheduled calls."

"I didn't realize that." Of course, Tanya was busy with her own responsibilities, and usually spent a minimum of two weeks out of every month on the road with the traveling clinic.

"Their willingness to cover the cost of the calls

shows how important our work here is to Sympa-Med."

Personally, Tanya thought it showed a need to control. That money could be used more effectively elsewhere. However, it wasn't her call to make. Literally. "So, the traveling clinic is on hiatus for the next few days." She couldn't make herself sound anything but grumpy about that fact.

"It will give us a chance to run an extra wellness clinic for the area children," Fleur said. "Mabu can send his nephews as runners to the area villages letting them know about it."

"Do we have enough vaccines to do the wellness clinic now instead of in the spring?"

"We should have enough for the number of children that will show up." Fleur turned to Ben. "How did your meeting at the mine go today?"

The older woman's intention to change the subject was clear and Tanya had no desire to make her angrier by trying to pursue discussion of what was just as clearly a done deal.

"I didn't make any friends." Ben sounded self-deprecating, but unworried by his claim.

"What happened?" Tanya asked.

Ben's eyes glinted with amusement. "I informed them that I would be interviewing the workers as well as going over all the books, comparing the compensation they claim to give their employees against their actual expenses."

His gaze shifted to Fleur, asking a question that her own seemed to answer for him because he looked satisfied. When the African woman asked the next question, Ben actually glowed.

Oh, wow . . . her boss and the bureaucrat? Tanya would never have guessed it. She wasn't about to warn him off, even if she'd never seen Fleur respond positively to a man's interest.

There was a first time for everything and there was something special about Ben Vincent—she only hoped Fleur saw it too.

Tanya was relieved when the rest of the dinner talk centered around Ben's audit of the mine. She wasn't keen on rehashing the clipping of her wings by the head office, or thinking about the roadblock, or the aborted plans to strip-search her.

She'd never been so scared. And she didn't like the feeling. Not one bit.

Roman's hand on her back was incredibly comforting, but safe wasn't the only way he made her feel. If she'd wanted him before, it was nothing compared to the positive craving she felt now. She wanted to share with him the deepest moment of connection two people could make. When he asked her if she wanted to take a walk after dinner, she didn't hesitate.

Not even when Kadin gave them a look that could have singed rock. If he didn't think she was right for his friend, the man was going to have to get over it. Because Tanya had every intention of drowning the emotions that had been trying to choke her all day.

The only thing she could imagine being strong enough to obliterate them, or at least her awareness of them, was the tsunami of desire the earthquake that was Roman Chernichenko caused inside her.

"I think your friend is falling hard for the leader of my security team," Ben said to Fleur as they played an after-dinner game of *mancala* with Johari before she had to go to bed.

"She is not one for casual encounters," Fleur said dismissively.

Johari took her turn, laughing in glee when she got one over both the adults. Fleur gave her daughter an indulgent smile. To see the girl enjoy life in such an innocent manner after all she had been through gave Fleur all the joy she would ever ask of life.

"Are you sure it would be casual?" Ben asked, apparently unwilling to drop the topic of a possible connection between the American soldier and Tanna.

Fleur felt a flutter of fear at the words. "You think she's really falling for him?"

"It looks that way to me." Ben shrugged, as if his answer was of little import.

He was wrong. It was very important. "He will leave with you. He will not look back. It is the way of men like that. I will not see Tanya hurt."

"Even men like him meet their personal Armageddons at some point."

True, but more likely, he would use Tanna for his sexual pleasure and leave her behind. Fleur knew Tanna had already had her heart shattered by one selfish man, she did not want to see it happen again. "You think he wants her?" Just to be sure.

"That goes without saying. I think he wants her more than he is aware and that what he wants will surprise him."

"You are a serious observer of human nature?" she asked, not at all convinced of the accuracy of this particular observation.

Ben's expression closed off. "It's part of my job."

"What is your job?" Johari asked, her intelligent gaze trained on the American.

"I am here doing an audit of the local mine."

"An audit, like to see if they are cheating on their taxes?" her daughter asked in confusion.

"No, an audit on human rights violations. The U.S. prefers not to do business with mines who use slave labor and other heinous practices."

"Really?" Johari sounded highly skeptical.

Ben gave her a wry smile, acknowledging her attitude without denying or agreeing with what it implied. "That's the party line, anyway."

"But you do not believe the government is sincere?" Johari once again showed more wisdom than typical of a girl her age.

"I think expediency often gets in the way of humanity when a lot of money is at stake," Ben said, with what sounded like genuine regret.

"But you are going to try to protect the workers?" Johari demanded demonstrating a surprising idealism for a girl who had lived through the ravages of war.

Fleur loved hearing that innocence in her daughter's voice.

Ben met and held Johari's gaze. "Yes."

"He will try." Fleur did not believe in making, or implying promises one could not be sure of keeping.

But Ben shook his head. " 'There is no try'."

" 'There is only do,' " Johari said with a laugh.

"What?" Fleur asked, looking between the identical smiles on the man and the child's faces.

Ben reached out and tugged one of Johari's many small braids. "It's a quote from *Star Wars*."

"An American movie. We watched it at school," Johari explained for her mother's benefit. "I want to be Princess Leia."

"She's a fighter all right," Ben agreed with obvious approval in his tone.

Fleur assured her daughter, "Then you have much in common with her already."

Johari dropped her eyes in embarrassment at the praise, but she was smiling. A half hour later, she went to bed, leaving Fleur alone with Ben.

He looked at her in a way no man ever had before. She had had eyes of lust on her. She had been looked at with possession. Anger. Contempt. Respect. The whole gamut, but never with this combination of tenderness and desire.

It scared her to death.

"I was raped," she blurted out. "By many men, soldiers of the Rwandan government who murdered my friends and family all because we were born Tutsi. I cannot . . . do physical things."

Then she sat there, breathing as if she'd been running from the sadistic men who had hurt her when she was still a teen. How could she have told Ben her secret shame?

And how could he sit there looking at her as if nothing had changed? As if he did not think any less of her. As if he felt nothing but compassion. Not even pity.

Her throat went tight as emotion choked and threatened to overwhelm her, a woman who prided herself on control.

"Can you put your hand in mine?" he asked in a voice so gentle he almost shattered her.

She was no weakling. She did not need to be babied. "I . . . yes, of course."

"Then do it." This time his voice carried a command, even as it was overlaid with that same consuming gentleness. He put his hand out.

She looked at it, the fingers square and masculine, marked with small scars that said he had experienced more violence than others would expect from his mild-mannered appearance. But she already knew that. His hand looked strong. It looked safe, and yet reaching out to connect with him was hard. Harder than she thought it would be, but after several long seconds, she laid her hand in his.

He closed his fingers around hers, not tightly, but softly as if she was fragile. "Come."

She allowed him to tug her out of her chair at the table where they'd played *mancala*. He led her to the small benchlike sofa in the communal area of her and Tanya's chalet. Sitting down, he pulled her to the spot beside him. Their bodies were touching from shoulder to knee. It was closer to a man than she had been in a social setting since the horrors of her youth. Yet, she felt no fear, or even discomfort at Ben's nearness.

"May I?" he asked as the hand not holding hers hovered above her shoulder.

She nodded.

He smiled, dropped the arm around her and said, "Now, tell me about your parents. I bet your mother was beautiful."

And for the first time since escaping Rwanda with her life, if not her innocence, she talked about her life before the Tutsi massacre. She told Ben about her mother, who had been beautiful, and her older sister, who had been pregnant when she bled her life out on the floor of their family home.

But she didn't think about that. She thought about the future her sister had hoped for. "They would have loved Johari."

"I'm sure they would. Johari's a wonderful child any mother would be proud of."

Fleur nodded, her rigid emotional suppression nowhere in evidence. His kindness infiltrated her heart as no other man had even tried to do in almost fifteen years.

She hadn't known her father as well as she wanted to, and she shared that with Ben too. "He was an important man, with little free time for his family. They killed him first."

"I'm sorry."

"I believe you." How could she not when sincerity shone from his pale blue eyes. Eyes that continued to look at her with that tender desire she found so disconcerting.

"Did you have any other siblings?" he asked.

Pain she had never been able to let go sent its jagged edges through her heart. "A brother. I never knew what happened to him."

"Was he older? Younger?" More than curiosity laced his voice. As difficult as she found it to understand, he genuinely cared.

"Younger. He was an unexpected baby, almost ten years younger than me."

Horror reflected in his compassionate gaze. "He was just a little boy when you fled Rwanda."

"Yes. I searched for him, but could not find him." It was a failure she could never forgive herself for. "Then after the soldiers hurt me, I was in a delirium. When I woke, hidden in the storage room of a family my father had helped, my brother was gone. They sent me to family in Nigeria, but I live in hope my brother still lives *somewhere*."

"That is a good hope to have."

She heard his words through a tunnel as she gave into the tears she hadn't shed since man's evil had destroyed her life and those she loved.

After a quick stop at her hut and another at the medical building, Tanya led Roman out of the compound. She didn't normally leave the compound after dark, but she felt safe with her super-soldier. Wild animals and wild men had no chance against the danger that lurked inside this man.

She wasn't sure she did either, but she was taking the chance.

The guard nodded at them as they exited through the gate he'd opened for them.

"He didn't even ask why we are leaving," Roman commented with an irritated scowl.

The sun had not set, though the sky was heading toward twilight. It was one of her favorite times of day in the African savannah. "I imagine he was showing discretion," she said mildly.

"Screw discretion. That's sloppy security."

"It's a medical compound, not a prison, or a military base either. We don't have to account for every minute of our day"—she paused—"or night."

No matter how Sympa-Med might prefer it otherwise. She'd often wondered if the board of directors had served in the French Foreign Legion or something, with their militarylike need for control.

Of course, they had a significant capital investment to protect, not to mention the fact they saw her and the other medical professionals as assets needing their own protection as well. Their attitude was understandable, if annoying.

"Do you go walking like this a lot?" he asked.

She shrugged. "When I need to clear my head. Sometimes, when I get homesick."

"You get homesick?"

"Don't sound so surprised. I love my family, even if I get along with my parents better with thousands of miles between us. I miss them. I miss Beau." Despite Roman's presence at her side, or maybe because of it and the reminder of home, melancholy swept over her for a second. "Sometimes, it just hurts that I'm not there to get to know Elle better."

"It's only going to get worse when they have kids," he said with a clear tinge of regret, sounding like he knew exactly what she went through.

Considering his career and how it kept him away from his family, he probably did.

"I know." The thought of not being there to get to know her nieces and/or nephews hurt on a level she'd never once considered when making her life choices.

"It's hard." For that flash of moment in time, super-soldier Roman Chernichenko sounded borderline vulnerable.

"It is." She reached out and took his hand, surprised by both her daring and the fact that he curled his strong fingers around hers. "You miss your family."

"I do. My *baba*, I mean grandmother, she's not getting any younger."

"She and your mom are good at playing the age card, from what I've seen." Those two knew exactly what to say for maximum emotional impact from the Chernichenko siblings.

"You've got that right. Whoever thinks Jewish mothers have a corner on the guilt market has never met a Ukrainian *baba*."

She laughed softly. "I'll concede that point. My own parents are good at lecturing, but if they had your mother or grandmother's knack for zeroing in on emotional weakness, I doubt I'd have made it back to Africa the second time."

He snorted. "Hell, if you had my *baba*, you wouldn't have made it the first time."

"She's a scary lady."

"You won't get any arguments from me."

"Is she why your family doesn't know what you really do?"

"No one knows what I really do."

"I do."

"Do you?"

"I know enough."

"And?" he asked.

"What?"

"Does it bother you?"

"That you're some kind of mysterious super-soldier? No, I don't think it does. Especially after today. I keep thinking about what would have happened if you hadn't been there." Images she desperately wanted out of her head played like a disgusting video set on repeat. And she couldn't find the off button.

"Don't."

"I can't help it."

He stopped and pulled her to face him. "I'll help you forget."

"I'm counting on it." Her certainty that sex with

Roman would be enough to dominate her thoughts, to keep them away from the ugliness of what had almost happened at that roadblock, fed her determination to act on her desire for him.

In case he needed more invitation than the meaning behind her words to start something, she tilted her head in blatant provocation.

Showing he could take a hint, he lowered his head until their lips almost touched. "I'm leaving in weeks, if not days." His breath teased across her lips in small, warm gusts as his words took anchor in her mind.

His stillness demanded acknowledgment of the warning.

"I know."

"I won't be back."

"I had that figured out."

"Good."

"Your lips against mine would be better." And then, because she was done talking, even if he wasn't, she moved the minute distance necessary to bring their mouths together.

His lips were firm and soft at the same time, responding instantly to the pressure of hers. He wasn't a passive man and he didn't simply accept her kiss, but immediately pulled her body into his, crushing the blanket she had grabbed from her room between them. His mouth molded to hers, and then shaped the caress of their lips into something hot and carnal. Something unlike any kiss she'd ever before experienced. She'd never felt a kiss as if the connection of lips was the epicenter for a Richter-ten quake that shook her whole body.

Every single one of her nerve endings buzzed with sexual tremors that rolled through her body, only to crash against each other in the heated flesh between her thighs. Never had she been so ready for intercourse with so little provocation. She didn't know what was making her respond this way to him and she did not care.

She craved him with a hunger so intense, she felt the cramp of need deep in her womb. It was so primal, it scared her, but the fear only fed the need instead of checking it.

Sounds came out of her, whimpers and moans that she'd never before made. Roman liked them too. Every time she made one, he did something to intensify the kiss. Thrusting his tongue between her lips and taking possession of her mouth's interior, then tightening his hold on her until there wasn't even air between their bodies, he growled against her lips with his own sexual gratification. Rubbing his hand over her bottom, he kneaded curves firmed by all the walking her life with the traveling clinic required. Finally, burying his other hand in her hair, he held her head in place for an increasingly ardent lip-lock.

Their bodies rocked together and she yanked at his shirt, desperately needing to touch bare skin. When her fingers pressed into rock-hard abs, he yanked his mouth from hers to suck in a deep breath and let out a dark curse in what she was pretty sure was Ukrainian. Though it wasn't one she'd heard before from his siblings.

Mewling like a needy cat, she chased his mouth, but had to settle for his neck, kissing and nuzzling him as she took in his scent on a primitive level she couldn't begin to explain. Had her years in Africa brought her closer to the primal woman at her core? She'd never thought so, but what else could explain the way she responded to him on such an atavistic level?

"Damn, this is going too fast." The chagrin in his tone was tempered by an endearing confusion. Roman Chernichenko was not used to being out of control.

She was glad she was not the only one reacting so strongly.

"No." She fiercely shook her head. "Not fast enough."

But he was pushing her away from him. "It's too open here."

She looked around them. Typical of the savannah, there was nothing but long grass between them and the compound. In the slowly falling twilight, anyone with decent eyesight could be watching. This time of year, full dark came late, which was why she'd been leading him someplace they could be alone, away from interested eyes *and* ears. Living in the compound was like living in a small village and gossip was just as rife.

She had no desire to be the subject of it.

"You're right." She turned and started walking again. If she didn't, she was going to throw herself back into his arms. "Let's go."

CHAPTER SIX

They'd been walking about five minutes in what she hoped was mutual impatient-to-get-there silence, when he asked, "So, where are we going?"

"My favorite thinking spot. It's a good place for solitude, away from people anyway." There was a stand of baobab trees about twenty minutes' walk from the compound, their huge multilayered trunks creating the closest thing to real privacy she'd been able to find.

"You aren't alone right now," he pointed out, as if she could miss his six feet, five inches of walking musclebound sex.

"I don't want to be." What she wanted was to be alone with *him*.

"I'm glad to hear that. If you did, it would put a serious cramp in my plans for the evening." His deep voice was laced with sexy humor.

She doubted he needed the affirmation, but she gave it to him anyway. "Mine too." And how.

When they reached the trees, she didn't pretend a shyness she was not feeling. She quickly laid the blanket over a soft spot of ground where she'd taken a nap more than once. Dropping the condoms she'd gotten from the clinic on one corner, she turned to face Roman.

His steel-gray gaze devoured her with tactile intensity. "I want you."

"Yes."

"You want me too."

She nodded, her throat suddenly too tight to speak.

He shrugged out of his shoulder holster and carefully laid it near the small pile of condoms. He made no comment about the fact she'd grabbed more than one. So, she'd been thinking ambitiously. She didn't think that with Roman Chernichenko she would be disappointed.

She started to unbutton her top, but he shook his head. She gave him a questioning look.

"I want to do it."

That sounded really, really good. She let her fingers fall away from the button.

He smiled, his expression all too easy to read for once. For the next few hours, she was his.

She'd show him it went both ways, but she wasn't about to reject his desire to undress her. The very thought added to the moisture in her panties and that was a good thing as far as she was concerned.

He peeled off his T-shirt and dropped it on the corner of the blanket opposite the condoms and his weapon. He unbuckled his utility belt and removed it, once again putting it in easy reach near his shoulder holster.

He unbuttoned and unzipped his camo fatigues, but did not push them down his hips. "Come here."

"You're going to leave your pants on?"

"As isolated as this spot may feel, we are not in a secure location. I cannot undress completely in case I have to protect you." He said it as if thinking of their safety first came naturally, which she was sure it did. The idea that he'd played out possible scenarios in his head and determined staying partially dressed was the best course of action was a little disconcerting though.

They were so different, but that wasn't even what had her most concerned right now.

"But, how?" She couldn't wrap her mind around the logistics. She hoped he had, because she was not giving in to her desire for a temporary connection for nothing more than mutual masturbation.

He smiled, the expression so darn sensual, her knees about buckled. "Don't worry, *liúba*, we'll use those condoms, every last one of them, but I won't be naked."

She'd heard Mat call Chantal that once. Tanya hadn't asked what it meant; it had been obvious. It was some kind of Ukrainian endearment. It didn't really matter if it was closer to *sweetheart* than *honey*. The point was, Roman had just used it on Tanya.

And her stupid heart clutched at his doing so. She could not afford to forget this was just sex. Nothing lasting. He'd made sure she knew that, even if part of her wished it could be more.

"What about me?" she asked to get her mind off that particular scary amusement park ride.

"Oh, you'll be nude, all right." He was clearly deeply satisfied by that fact.

She cocked her head, giving him a frown she wasn't sure she really felt, but she felt like she had to give at least a token protest. "That's not fair."

"I'll change your mind."

"You're arrogant," she said, but she was smiling.

"Nope."

"Let me guess, it's not arrogance because your confidence is justified." She waited for him to say something cocky like he'd never had any complaints, but he didn't.

He just smiled again. And darned if it didn't work.

She crossed the distance between them without feeling the ground beneath her feet or hearing her own footsteps. She felt as if she was in an altered state of reality and yet, she was wholly there. With him. But only him. Nothing else registered to her senses. Only his presence. The tall, muscular strength of him, the subtle masculine scent that was his alone, the dark predator that lay beneath his gorgeous masculinity.

He removed her blouse first, his eyes dilating with lust at the sight of her simple cotton bra holding in curves that she'd never considered much to write home about. He traced the edges of the undergarment, raising gooseflesh wherever his fingertips went. "Sexy."

"Don't make fun."

He cupped her chin and met her gaze, his oh-so-intense. "Do I look like I'm kidding?"

"No."

"You don't need barely there lace to tantalize a man. Right now, I'm so turned on, I could pound nails with my dick at the thought of seeing your hard little nipples for the first time."

"How do you know they're small?" she challenged, wondering if it made a difference to him. Though her breasts were not large, her nipples weren't proportionate, the areolas the size of silver dollars. She'd always felt funny about that, like she was not as feminine as she could be. It had made her modest in the girls' locker room at school.

Quinton had never commented one way or another, but he hadn't been all that interested in foreplay. Their life in the Peace Corps had not lent itself to lots of private free time together for prolonged lovemaking.

"Are they?"

"Take off my bra and find out." After her years providing medical care to people of all shapes and sizes, she'd outgrown any serious self-consciousness she had about her anomaly.

It seemed silly to worry about not looking like a centerfold model when she'd treated children born with deformed limbs and adults left horrifically scarred by violence.

A sexy laugh accompanied the flick of knowing fingers that unhooked her bra faster than she had ever done. Grasping her straps in each hand, he tugged, peeling the cotton away from her B-cups.

His smile grew when he saw her already erect peaks. More like frozen raspberries than eraser nubs, they tightened almost painfully under his heated gaze. Would he touch them? Sometimes she did, when she was self-pleasuring in her bed at night. It always made her climax faster. But the other couple of men she'd tried to have relationships with hadn't been any more interested in exploring her breasts than Quinton had.

"Delicious." Roman's deep voice made the word sound dirty.

Chills shivered through her and, despite her more mature view of her own body, she had to concentrate on keeping her arms at her sides and not hiding her breasts like a shy virgin.

"I bet they're sensitive too." He didn't wait to test his theory, immediately brushing his knuckles over the very tips.

Moaning, she swayed forward. It was so different having someone else touching them, even that brief a caress.

"Sukin sin," he growled.

Breathless from the touch, she forced out a whispered, "What?"

"Son of a bitch."

"Not a son."

"I know. Damn, don't I know?" He sounded as affected as she felt.

And she liked it. She wanted to affect him as deeply as he did her. She wanted to smile, but licked her suddenly dry lips instead.

Without warning, he swept her up in his arms and carried her to the blanket. With an animalistic sound from deep in his throat, he laid her down on the side with the condoms and his weapons.

"You are so damn sexy." It sounded like more an accusation than a compliment as he leaned down to crash his lips to hers.

The feel of his hard chest against her already sensitized nipples wrenched a cry from her that the kiss could not quite stifle. She grabbed his shoulders, rubbing herself back and forth, almost crying with delight at the sensation of his silky chest hair abrading her hard peaks. The abundant dark curls felt so good against her body.

He slid his mouth from hers, brushing along her cheek and down her nape. "You're something else."

"Something good?"

"Something *fantastic*."

"I'm glad." Her breath caught as his mouth did something incredible right where her neck and shoulder joined. Oh, man, that was going to leave a mark. And she didn't mind. She might never admit it, but the idea added another layer to the out-of-control desire bombarding her every sense. "You are too," she gasped. More than fantastic. "There are no words."

He tipped his head up and grinned at her, his expression not making any sense in her over-heated brain. "Told you."

"What?"

"You aren't going to mind me keeping my fatigues and boots on."

Heck, he was so amazing, she didn't think she'd notice if he painted his face black and put his gun back on, but she wasn't about to admit that. "I've still got my pants on. We'll see when I'm naked," she taunted.

"Oh, yes, we will, *moyá prekrásnyy liúba*."

"What does that mean?"

He shook his head, looking like he'd rather not say.

She just waited, not moving, now more interested than she thought possible in the translation.

"'My beautiful sweetheart,'" he gritted out finally. "Happy?" He said something else in Ukrainian, but she didn't ask him what *that* meant. She had a feeling she did not want to know.

She did smile, however, figuring it was safe because he was now focused on divesting her of her walking shoes and the rest of her clothes as efficiently as possible. The efficient movements, if not the sense of urgency, stalled once she was bared to his gaze. He rocked back on his heels and just looked. He didn't say anything, but his heated gaze said enough to have her breath growing shallow and the moisture between her legs increasing.

Finally, he reached out and ruffled the curls over her mound. "So pretty."

"Yes?" She'd read lots of women shaved or waxed nowadays. That wasn't practical when water restrictions limited her showers to single-digit minutes in the morning.

"Oh, yeah. *Vrodlývyy*," he said in a guttural tone, deep with need. "That means 'beautiful' by the way, *Miss Curiosity*."

His obvious and declared admiration made it easy for her to acquiesce when he pushed her thighs apart to reveal her most private flesh to his gaze. She shivered when he cursed reverently.

She would have said something, she wasn't sure what, but all the air in her lungs deserted her. She didn't know men could find that part of her body exciting to look at as well as touch.

Only he touched too, gently rubbing her labia with his thumbs. "You're nice and wet."

"You're hard." There was no missing the oversized beefstick pushing against the front of his camos. "We're even."

One finger slipped inside her, curving up and rubbing a rich bundle of nerve endings he seemed to find by divine instinct. "Are we?"

She yelped and arched upward, hoping he took that as the encouragement it was and not a sign to stop. She hadn't known that spot was there. Oh, she'd heard about the female G-spot, who hadn't? She'd thought she didn't have one though, but she'd been wrong. So gloriously wrong. He seemed just as adept at reading her reactions as he was at touching her body because he did it again. And again . . . *and again.* Afraid to lose the oh-so-perfect stimulation, she tried to hold her body still, even though her muscles wanted to jerk in response to the sharp pleasure.

Warm wetness spread from his finger down his hand and he used it to lubricate her nether lips and the pleasure spot at the top. She sighed with luxurious delight, her body tipping toward the touch, no matter how much she tried not to move.

"Like that?" he asked, no doubt in his voice about her answer.

She garbled out something that should have been "yes," but sounded more like a yowl as his thumb slid over her clitoris once again. She was more than a little glad they hadn't tried to do this on the down-low in one of the medical exam rooms, or something. She'd never been a screamer, but she sensed that was about to change. She'd already made more noise than during any other sexual experience she'd had before.

"I want to touch you," she panted out between moans and other sounds she wasn't sure how to translate.

He pushed his pants down just far enough to free his massive erection. "Touch away."

She had to look first. She reached out without quite connecting. "It's darker than the rest of you." Quinton hadn't been. "I didn't know it could be."

He shrugged. "It's the way I am made. You are darker there too, your intimate lips a pretty dark raspberry that matches your succulent nipples."

Heat filled her face. "Stop it."

"What? Telling you how beautiful you are?"

"You're . . . I . . . men don't talk about that, do they?"

"I don't know what other men do." And his tone said he didn't care either.

"It's embarrassing."

"It's hot."

"Yes," she had to agree with a soft breath.

"You said you wanted to touch?"

She nodded, her heart hammering.

"Then do it, sweetheart."

She nodded again, this time her hand reaching out, her fingertips just barely brushing him. The brief feel of the heated silk over steel drove her need higher and she wrapped her hand around his hard flesh. They both groaned. That was going to feel so good inside of her. He was big, but not so huge it was going to hurt. He was thick, but not too thick. Some latent feminine instinct told her that despite the fact she'd never been made love to by a man of his size, it was going to feel absolutely wonderful.

Rubbing up and down in slow strokes, her fingers not quite meeting around the circumference of his hard sex, she reveled in the heat emanating from him. "Very nice." Her voice came out low and harsh, as if she had a cold, but she was anything but ill right now.

In fact, she'd never felt so vibrantly alive.

He just made an inarticulate sound and threw his head back as she continued to caress him. His fingers were still busy between her legs. He'd slid a second one inside her as his thumb continued ministering to her clitoris, but the jerky circles he made with it gave testament to the effect her hand on his penis had on him.

"Want to be in you," he ground out, thrusting into her hand.

She'd been ready since their first kiss. "So, do it."

"Yes." He reached for the condom and donned it with practiced ease, despite the tension holding his body rigid. Then he got his forearms under each of her thighs, lifting up until her bottom rested above his knees as he knelt between her obscenely spread legs. She couldn't keep her hold on his erection in this position and she had to let it slip from her hand.

She didn't have time to lament the loss as his blunt head pressed against her core. Showing no strain in his muscles, he pulled her body to meet his, sliding her farther up his thighs. It was not a position where she could move much, but she didn't mind.

Every centimeter he slid in deeper was an excruciating parade of pleasure along her senses. Pushing inexorably forward, he continued to pull her toward him until her bottom was flush with his body. She was filled with him, surrounded by him, and nothing else could exist for her at that moment. It felt almost spiritual.

"Don't move," she pleaded. She needed to experience this moment fully, to wallow in a sense of connection unlike anything she had ever even dreamed of.

"You're tight," he said with a grimace.

"No." She shook her head, looking for the necessary words. "It's right."

His eyes closed for a long second and when they opened again, the heat in them would have burned her if she was not living, breathing flame already.

Their gazes locked and he pulled back, leaving her feeling empty, the firestorm of need inside her demanding more, demanding him. She made a sound of protest, the insistence of her need lacing her voice and bringing a wince of near pain to her face.

He understood though, that he wasn't hurting, just testing her ability to wait. That rare smile that only seemed to show up when he was planning to, or having sex, creased his features again. "Want more, Tanna?"

The sound of her African name on his lips sent shivers of delight through her. *"Yes."*

"Good." He rocked forward again, filling her completely in one long, unbroken thrust, stretching tender flesh to capacity but bringing more pleasure than she had thought possible from this intimate act. He held her like that, seated as deeply as she could go, her insides molten lava. "Touch yourself."

She gasped at the shock of his command. She'd never been willing to do that with other lovers, always embarrassed by the intimacy of it. But despite her shock and lack of experience, she did not hesitate to bring her middle finger into contact with her swollen clitoris.

The initial touch sent arrows of sensation zinging from her womb outward.

"Make little circles, keep the pressure light. I don't want you coming yet."

She stared up at him and found she had no desire to argue. She did as he instructed, her breath coming out in shallow pants as he moved in and out of her while she touched the nerve-rich flesh.

"We are going to come together, sweetheart."

"We are?" He'd better come soon then, because she felt like she was on the edge.

"Oh, yes. But not yet."

She gave him a look that expressed the words she didn't have the breath to say. He just smiled that sexy, arrogant, carnal smile again.

Her body tensed in preparation to orgasm and he shook his head. "Stop moving, just let your finger rest against your clit." She was sure her expression doubted his sanity, but he didn't look offended. Just very sure. "Do it."

Against all she thought she'd be able to do, she stopped the dedicated rubbing and let her finger rest against the small, but powerful nub. Every movement of his hips caused small shifts in her hand, maintaining a light stimulation over which she had no control. It was a surprisingly erotic sensation.

"Good." His thumbs brushed along her skin where his hands held her tightly for his thrusts.

The approving tone of his voice went through her like a touch. What was going on? She'd never thought she wanted a lover to exert so much control, much less tell her what to do. Before tonight, she would have laughed at the thought she would listen and obey. But here she was doing everything he said, letting him dictate not only the pace of their pleasure, but the depth and everything in between. Her attempts to analyze what was happening shattered at his next instruction.

"Now, use your other hand and play with your nipples."

"No." But her hand followed his direction without permission from her brain. She lightly touched first one nipple, then the other, circling each areola and sending tingles of pleasure from her breasts to her groin.

"Pinch them. Lightly."

She first pressed one hard, swollen nub between her thumb and forefinger, and then the other, and felt the intense sensation travel straight to her vaginal core, causing it to contract around him and bringing her another wave of unexpected pleasure. She wasn't going to survive this, it was too much. . . .

"So good," he praised. "So beautiful."

She licked her lips, gasping with delight at the overwhelming sensations. He made love to her with powerful thrusts and it was only his hold on her legs that kept her from sliding up the blanket. Even though she knew it was her own hands on her body, it felt like he was touching her breasts and clitoris too, because he was dictating every movement, from the duration of the touches to the intensity of them.

Her climax started spiraling toward its inevitable conclusion again, but this time, instead of having her back off, he told her to pinch her nipples harder, to rub her clitoris and then do it faster, and faster until she screamed herself hoarse through an orgasm more powerful than anything she had ever felt. Her body wracked with muscle contractions that seemed like they were never going to end.

His own shout of triumph mingled with her cries and she could feel his penis swell and pulse as he released inside the condom.

He panted above her, his arms bulging as he held her in place while the last vestiges of their orgasms shuddered through them. After what felt

like an eternity of floating afterglow that could
have been seconds, minutes, or hours, he gently
lowered her legs and pulled his still semi-erect sex
from her body. She collapsed into a boneless heap
as he tied off the condom.

Afterward, he didn't let her go down completely, but seemed intent on kissing, licking and
nibbling every single inch of her skin. He paid particular homage to her large nipples, tasting them
for long sensation-filled minutes before moving to
lick the line of her collar bone and eventually
turning her over.

He started at the bottom of her feet and made
his way upward, pulling a slow-burn response from
her body that got hotter and hotter the higher he
went. He kissed each curve of her backside before
gently biting her right cheek, making her squirm.

"Mine," he growled against her flesh.

She had no thought to deny him. Tonight, she
was his. "Yours."

He moved up to the small of her back, licking
and teasing flesh she'd never known was so erogenous.

When he reached the almost invisible scar on
her shoulder blade, he stopped. "What's this?"

"Not supposed to say." Sympa-Med preferred
that the extra security measures they took on behalf of their traveling workers did not become
public knowledge.

He leaned down and kissed the spot. "Tell me."

"Why?"

"It's part of you. I want to know."

"Sympa-Med." She never even considered denying him. He might not be staying in her life, but
she trusted him while he was there.

She gasped as his lips traveled to her nape and settled on the top vertebrae of her spine.

"What about Sympa-Med?" he asked against her skin.

"They put GPS chips in us."

He sat back, the loss of heat from his body making her feel cold, even in the warm African night. "What?"

She rolled onto her back and smiled up at him, amused by what she read as shock in his eyes. "They don't want us lost to human trafficking."

"So, they embed a GPS chip in you?"

"Yes."

"Do you all have one?"

"Only the ones who work the traveling clinic." She frowned and sighed, admitting something that had always really bothered her. "Only the medical personnel actually."

"Does the chip have a storage capacity?"

Her brows drew together. "How did you know?" She didn't ask why he wanted to know. That was just Roman. Tonight she was his and everything related to her was his. "They keep our medical information on it."

She'd really never seen the benefit of that since most Western hospitals weren't equipped to retrieve the information, much less African ones.

He said something that sounded suspiciously like an act that was anatomically impossible, no matter how big his dick was.

"Roman?"

It was as if he turned off one light and turned on another. All the tension and what had seemed like anger left as if it had never been there. He gave her that sexy grin of his again and leaned down, covering her mouth with his, cutting off any question she wanted to ask and sending her into another sensual haze from which she was in no rush to return.

They did use all the condoms and stayed in their private grotto until the stars had come out and then started to fade from the sky again. He walked her back to the compound, an arm around her waist supporting her tired body.

She didn't care if she was exhausted the next day; the night had been worth it. She'd never been so consumed by a lover, not that she'd had a lot of them. But she had been in love with Quinton. Or at least she'd believed she was.

Now, she wasn't so sure. Because the feelings growing in her heart for Roman felt deeper and way more permanent. That knowledge terrified her. In a few days, weeks maximum, he was walking out of her life and she didn't know when she would see him again. If ever. The man was an active super-soldier of some kind, which in her world meant a dangerous, life-threatening job.

Which meant that as much as she wanted what her brother had with Elle, Tanya had to accept that chances were *she* would never have it. It wasn't as if she hadn't already reached much that same conclusion before Roman had come to Zimbabwe. It just seemed that she and the life she led were not compatible with the fairytale ending. She needed to accept that the best she could do for herself was to experience everything Roman was willing to give her to the utmost until life took him away just as it had Quinton.

*   *   *

Ben tucked a now sleeping Fleur into her bed without waking her. She'd cried herself into an exhausted, deep slumber. Because he'd wanted to, because she'd seemed so at peace while he did, he'd held her close to his body until his inner clock told him dawn was coming.

He had to get back to his own bed. He would not allow her to become the topic of speculation among her fellow Sympa-Med workers. It would hurt her and he could not stand the thought of the beautiful African woman being hurt again.

She'd suffered enough in her life.

The sound of soft footfalls approaching the chalet had Ben hanging back in the shadows as two people came into view. The man was walking with his arm possessively around the woman's waist. Ben could tell it was Roman and Tanya, despite the lack of light from an already set moon. Roman was a head taller than any of the African men in the compound and none of his fellow soldiers would risk his wrath to pursue Tanya.

He knew it was Tanya because she had not yet returned that night. Even in the fading starlight, he could see her skin tone, which was paler than the other women's in the compound.

Roman's hold on her surprised Ben. He'd assumed the soldier had taken advantage of the attraction between the two of them to further his objective, whatever that was. This act of affection didn't fit, nor did the tender way Roman kissed Tanya before she slipped inside the hut.

As Roman drew even with Ben, he asked, "Enjoy the show?"

CHAPTER SEVEN

"Found it interesting anyway," Ben said in a soft voice as he moved to join the other man, unsurprised that Roman had realized he was there. "I'm glad Tanya made it back to the compound without having an accident."

The reality that Roman could have taken that evening as an opportunity to get rid of Tanya, if he was indeed on an assassination team, hit Ben and he cursed himself. He'd been so preoccupied by Fleur, he hadn't thought to stop the other man from going for a walk with Tanya. He'd actually been amused by the growing attraction between them. To give himself credit, his instincts had told him that Roman would not harm her tonight, but that did not make him feel any better.

Remembering the way Tanya had looked at the taller man before going inside, Ben reminded himself that there was more than one way to hurt someone.

"What do you mean by that, Vincent?" Roman demanded as they started walking back toward their temporary abode.

"I notice that you and your three colleagues don't wear identifying insignia."

"Our names are on our uniforms." But Roman's tone said he knew Ben was going somewhere with this.

"But not the branch of military you serve."

"We serve our country, not the military."

"Point taken, but it's one I don't think your average soldier would make."

"No one said we're average."

"Nor are you military precisely, I think."

"What are you saying, Vincent? Spit it out."

"I'm saying that the two Marine privates watching me are probably my real security team and the other four of you are here for another reason entirely."

"You think so?"

"I'm sure of it." As good as Roman might be at his job, he wasn't better than Ben.

"And what do you think that reason is?"

Crunch time, but Ben had made his decision about how much to share already. "There's been a disturbing pattern of military technology leaks the past few years."

"You are TGP."

Ben jolted in true shock for the first time in longer than he could recall, until he remembered who Roman's sister was. "So, Elle finally told her family."

"Not until that bastard you work for fired her."

"He didn't fire her; he offered her a desk job when her cover was hopelessly compromised." Not that anyone in TGP had expected her to take it. Elle did not have the makings of a desk jockey, even one charged with the nation's security.

"Hopelessly, my ass."

"We operate in total secret."

"So do we, but we don't dump our agents when someone figures out they aren't who they say they are."

"And who are your agents?" Whoever Roman worked for did an even better job of maintaining a no-profile in Washington than TGP.

They weren't simply Special Forces, because as secret as some of their assignments might be, their existence wasn't.

The silence that met Ben's question didn't surprise him. "Tanya is not the leak," he said.

"She is." Roman's tone was absolutely sure.

Even so, Ben argued, "No, she's not. It doesn't fit."

"It does if she doesn't know she's the carrier."

Ben swore.

"Yeah," Roman agreed.

Roman had refused to say any more until they returned to their quarters. Unsurprisingly, Kadin was waiting for him in the main room. His brows rose when Roman and Ben came in together.

Roman didn't bother explaining, just said, "Get Drew and Niel. We've got a problem."

"You saw them too?" Kadin asked.

"Saw who?" Damn it, no matter how incredible sex with Tanya had been, Roman had kept his senses alert for threats. He hadn't seen or heard anyone.

Kadin shook his head. "I'll tell you when we get Spazz and Face out here."

When all five men had crowded around the table in the communal area, Roman said, "Trigger, you said you saw someone tonight?" An immediate threat took precedence over his news.

"When I was walking the perimeter, after night-fall. I saw the reflection of binoculars in the moon-light."

"You track whoever it was?"

Kadin shook his head. "They were gone by the time I made it to the spot. The savannah does not lend itself to tracking in the dark, even with night vision goggles."

Roman nodded in acknowledgment, but he still taunted, "You getting old? Your eyesight's going."

Kadin just flipped him off.

"Special Forces?" Roman asked.

"I don't know, but someone is casing the com-pound. Could be S.F. Whoever it was didn't leave anything but bent grass behind them."

Roman summed it up succinctly. "Shit."

"Agreed," Ben said, looking every bit annoyed as Roman.

Roman gave him a glare.

"What? I came here aware I might not be the only person interested in the probable espionage happening. That doesn't mean I have to like it when more uninvited guests show up to my party."

"Define espionage," Neil said.

Ben outlined a pattern of information leakage well beyond what the file compiled by the military held. "My agency sent me to determine if the leaks were in fact espionage."

"As opposed to?"

"Someone in the military thinking they were being smart, trading military technology in ex-change for access to petroleum or minerals."

"It wouldn't be the first time," Roman admitted.

In fact, the JCAT being in Africa at all was the result of something pretty much just like that.

"No, it wouldn't." Ben gave Roman and his team measured looks. "So, you're here to stop the leak."

"Before a high-level JCAT ends up in enemy hands."

"How do they know the software has been stolen?"

"The security protocol on the computer holding it was compromised, but the culprit was not caught."

Ben's face turned grim. "There's chatter, really quiet, but there nonetheless, about a JCAT program going to auction. I discovered it just before leaving the States, but wasn't sure I was interpreting the identified key words correctly."

Roman ran his hand down his face. "You were right."

"Where is the software?"

"On Tanya."

"No way in hell," Kadin exploded.

Neil and Drew looked just as shocked, but remained silent. Ben merely watched him with an unreadable expression, clearly waiting for more.

Roman sighed, suddenly tired. "She doesn't know it's there."

"How in the hell—" Kadin started to ask.

"An embedded chip," Neil and Ben said at the same time.

"It's in her back, at the bottom of her right shoulder blade. Sympa-Med has GPS chips put in all their traveling medical personnel. The chips have storage capacity because she's been told hers holds her personal medical information."

Kadin said an ugly word that Drew echoed. This time, both Neil and Ben remained silent, lost in contemplation of the technological ramifications of what Roman had revealed.

"Right. She's got no clue they've been using her." The thought of the risk she'd been in all this time, not even counting the fact that the Army wanted him and his team to eliminate her, sent a rare shiver of fear right down Roman's spine. "And I'm guessing whoever was supposed to retrieve the JCAT had one of those scanner things at that village she missed on her last traveling clinic circuit."

"Probably something a lot more sophisticated than the hand-held one you found on the soldiers at the roadblock," Neil mused.

Ben asked, "You found a hand-held scanner?"

Roman nodded, but left it to Neil to fill in his fellow techno-geek on the details.

"So, you think Sympa-Med is involved?" Kadin asked when the other men fell silent.

Roman nodded. "What I don't know is whether anyone local is in on it too."

Ben gave an almost not there flinch and grimace.

Roman sighed again. "Right. Dr. Andikan might be the local contact."

He waited for Ben to refute him, but the other man just tightened his jaw.

"What do you think?" Roman asked him, pushing for an answer.

"I think she's been through hell and back and would do almost anything to ensure stability and safety for her adopted daughter, Johari."

"That's the way I read it too." Unfortunately. Tanya considered the doctor her friend.

"So, what do we do?" Kadin asked, always more interested in action than talking.

Roman met his gaze squarely. "We find out who the hell is casing the compound."

"Those U.S. soldiers in the roadblock yesterday worry me," Drew said with a frown.

Roman agreed and it pissed him off no end. "Me too. Colonel Idiot may have decided to handle his problem in-house after all." If that had happened, Roman would deal with the man when he got back Stateside. No one messed with his operation, not even the men who ordered it into existence.

Ben's mouth curved with dry amusement as he asked, "Colonel Idiot?"

"The Army brass that requested our presence," Kadin clarified. "He wanted us to kill Tanya."

All amusement drained from Ben's expression. "I was afraid of that."

Roman was impressed with the other man's ability to read the situation as well as he had. He'd make a good Atrati agent. Of course, he didn't know if he could handle more than one Spazz on his team.

"But our actual directive is to plug the leak," Neil reminded everyone.

"Which killing her would only do in the short term," Roman said.

Kadin glared at him, while Neil just shook his head. Ben gave Roman a probing look, but it held no judgment. Drew sat there blinking as if he was still taking everything in. Roman knew it was just a front. The man was no doubt plotting at light-speed times ten. He thrived in complicated situations like this one, which made him good for the Atrati. Roman had yet to be on a simple mission.

"We need to get the JCAT software off the chip,

if it's there," Neil said, giving a sop to the remote possibility they were on the wrong track. But the expression on his face and everyone else's said that they were as convinced as Roman that Tanya had been made an unwitting mule. "We can use the hand-held scanner you took from the soldiers and see if it works."

"Right." Ben frowned. "Unfortunately, we can't assume the data transfer will erase the chip."

Which meant that until the chip was destroyed, the JCAT was at risk. "So, we have to get the chip out of her."

Roman gave Face a pointed look. Face's Ph.D. was in psychology, but he'd trained in emergency field medicine and could dig out a bullet or administer an I.V. when the need arose. Their team's usual field medic had not been assigned to this operation. She'd been on leave and Roman hadn't thought he needed to recall her.

Face shrugged. "I'll do it if I have to, Geronimo, but I've got a better idea."

"What?"

"We want to know if the lovely Dr. Andikan is in on the espionage, right?"

"It would help my case, yes," Ben said mildly enough, but irritation had flashed when Drew called the doctor *lovely*.

Roman said, "If she's part of the leak, she's under our purview as well."

"Right." Drew smiled that smile he got which *should* put fear in grown men, but usually just put others at ease. "We ask her to remove it."

Roman tried to figure it out but, not for the first time, he had no idea where Drew was going with this idea. "On what grounds?"

"We tell her the truth." Drew spoke as if that should be the most obvious conclusion to draw.

"And tip our hand if she is in on it?" Kadin demanded, not even pretending to think it was a good idea.

"Watching her afterward will tell us all we need to know about her," Drew assured them. "We're good at that, spying on people who don't suspect us. She'll assume we don't suspect her because we took her into our confidence. She'll act accordingly."

"Sometimes, I think you overmanipulate, Face."

Drew shook his head. "Nah, this is *my* specialty. I've been watching everyone, including the beautiful doctor, since we arrived. This plan will work."

Ben went still at Drew's second compliment to Dr. Andikan's looks. The quality of that stillness was similar to that of a predator waiting to strike. Drew should recognize it. Roman didn't know if his friend was deliberately egging the other man on, or had not yet recognized the danger to himself. He had a hard time believing either, no matter how many times he'd seen Drew skirt the line of death in the past.

"And if she's innocent?" Ben asked, his voice showing no sign of the predatory danger now lurking inside him.

"She's going to suspect Sympa-Med," Drew postulated.

"Then what?"

"She'll start looking for a way out of the program." Drew met Ben's gaze with assurance. "You said her driving motivation is to keep her daughter safe. She'll want to get out before Sympa-Med goes down."

"So, she won't tell us of her suspicions?" Roman asked.

"The woman is more than passin' smart, chief. She'll have figured out we suspect them already."

Okay. Drew's plan was starting to make sense, but Roman required proof the JCAT was on the chip before putting it into action. "First things first. We get the scanner near Tanya's chip."

"Another sex-for-the-job moment?" Kadin sneered.

"It's the job, damn it. Besides, she knows I'm going to be gone soon. She's not looking for commitment or love everlasting," Roman ground out between clenched teeth.

"Yeah, well maybe you should be."

Ah, shit, not this again. "Drop it."

"Consider it dropped." Yeah, like Roman believed him. Kadin was nothing if not stubborn.

Damn it.

Drew was looking at them both speculatively. Roman scowled at him. "You got something to say?"

"Not a word. Well, maybe just one. The sooner you activate that scanner, the better."

"I'm aware of that."

Drew went on as if Roman hadn't spoken. "If whoever is casing the compound kills Tanya, I think our Kadin is going to go AWOL to track them down and wreak his vengeance."

Kadin wouldn't be alone, but Roman knew better than to say so. Hell, he could barely believe he'd thought it. Shit. Piss. Damn. If he didn't watch himself, this assignment was going fubar and he wasn't going to let that happen.

Kadin let out a heavy sigh. "She reminds me of my little sister."

"You got a kid sister?" Neil asked with justifiable shock.

Kadin had never mentioned her before.

"She was killed. I didn't keep her safe." The former MARSOC assassin turned away and headed for the bedroom. "I'm going to get some shuteye."

Neil said a word Roman echoed in his own thoughts. No wonder the man had been so protective of Tanya since they'd arrived. Roman couldn't help feeling some relief too, that his friend clearly did not see Tanya in a sexual light. Kadin had said so before, but now Roman believed him.

He would have hated to have to maim a good man.

Fleur woke feeling more at peace than she had since before the Tutsi massacre. She ran her hand along the blanket tucked securely around her. Had she truly allowed Bennet Vincent to hold her while she cried like a broken child? And fallen asleep? On him, much less simply with someone else in the room. She had not done so, except in her daughter's presence, since she was a child.

And yet, last night . . . she had done all of that.

And it had felt good. Better than good, it had felt *safe*. Tears she had never allowed herself the luxury of shedding had cleansed her in a way she had not been able to accomplish, no matter how hard she tried.

The memories of her rape were still there, still horrible, but they now seemed a step away from her present reality. It was not quite as if they had happened to someone else, but close. She knew it had been her, how could she not? But in the years since, she had grown and become someone other than the naïve, rather spoiled girl she had been fifteen years ago. Someone other than the woman whose feminine power had been ripped from her with such brutality that she had not wanted anyone to touch her in more than a decade.

How could this man, this American, help her heal when others had been unable to? The answer lay within her. She had told him a truth she'd hidden from almost everyone else.

It didn't matter why, not really; all that mattered was that she had opened up and in doing so lanced the wound so poison could drain away in her tears.

"Mama, will you fix my braids for school? They are not so neat," Johari called from her room across the hall.

Smiling, Fleur got up from her bed. A quick look down at her rumpled clothes made her smile grow. Ben had maintained her modesty. "I will be right there, child. Be patient."

"I'm always patient, Mama. Tanna says so. She say I am the most patient little girl she know."

"She *says* and she *knows*," Fleur corrected her as she quickly changed her turban and clothing for something fresher.

"I remember," Johari assured her.

Fleur shook her head with a small chuckle as she headed for her daughter's room. Johari always said she remembered, even when she didn't. Tanya's door was still shut. The other woman must still be sleeping. For her to do so despite Johari's morning chatter meant she must be very tired. They were not so busy today that she could not be allowed a small ly-in; Tanya put in long hours.

*   *   *

Ben was already in the dining hall when Fleur and Johari arrived to break their morning fast.

Johari ran to the man and gave him a hug in greeting, which he returned with a warm smile. "Do you like my braids? Mama made them fancy this morning."

Fleur had rebraided the ones that had gotten straggly and tied them all back with a bright ribbon. She smiled at Ben and said indulgently, "She believes ribbons to be the height of fashion."

"Aren't they? For a girl her age?"

"I think so, yes."

"Oh, they are." Johari patted her hair self-consciously, looking so pleased Fleur's heart ached. She was so different from the child that Fleur had taken into her life two years ago, traumatized by the loss of her parents to the violence of war.

"Sit down and eat your breakfast, child."

"Yes, Mama. I cannot be late for school," she told Ben. "There is an award at the end of the year."

"For not being tardy?" Ben asked.

"Yes, and for not missing any days of school either." Johari's tone left no doubt she wanted those awards.

The Mission School put a premium on timely attendance, but that did not always work for the children living in outlying villages, who often had to help care for their younger siblings before going to school in the morning. Johari's life with Fleur was easier for her in that regard. But Fleur never deceived herself into thinking that that made up for not having the rest of her family.

Fleur missed her dead sister and lost brother with a physical ache to this day.

"How does she get there?"

"Mabu has one of his men drive her in the jeep."

"Where is the school?" Ben asked.

She told him.

"We can drop her on our way to the mine this morning," he offered.

Johari's squeal of delight was not to be denied. Fleur did not even try. Instead, she said to Ben, "You are leaving early."

"Yes, a good two hours before they are expecting us," he replied with a wink, determined amusement lurking in his pale blue gaze.

The amusement was contagious, and she found herself smiling.

"Good for you."

"We all do what we must." There was a tone in his voice she did not understand, but for once such a thing did not worry her.

She trusted this man who had held her for hours in safety. "Some only do what they must, but others like you, do what is necessary."

"Isn't that the same thing?" Johari asked, sounding confused.

"No, sweet one, often the two are far apart, but Ben will make sure they overlap in his job." Fleur allowed all the admiration she felt for him to show in her eyes.

His widened and then darkened with that tender desire she found so intriguing.

"His job is important, isn't it, Mama?" Johari asked.

"Yes, child." Fleur gave Ben a warm smile she usually reserved for the few people she called friend. After last night, she could give him that moniker and perhaps even more.

"I will do what is necessary on all fronts." He gritted his teeth, but a small yawn escaped. He shook his head. "Sorry."

"You are tired?"

"I did not find my bed until dawn."

She had to process what that meant. First, that he had gotten almost no sleep, considering dawn had only been a couple of hours ago. But second, it meant he had not left her for almost the whole night. He had held her while she slept. And done nothing to compromise her safety or privacy.

She reached out in a rare act and laid her hand over his. "Thank you."

"It was my pleasure." Eyes the color of the summer sky warmed and he turned his hand over, holding hers.

Johari gasped. "Mama, you're holding hands with him. Are you going to be my papa?" Johari gave Ben an earnest look that was wholly adorable. "Mama said I would never have a papa, but sometimes even moms are wrong."

Even as embarrassment at her daughter's words filled her, Fleur had no desire to remove her hand. Or look away from Ben.

He winked at Fleur and then grinned at Johari. "Holding hands is not quite an expression of intent to marry, princess, but I do enjoy holding your mom's hand. Do you mind?"

"Oh, no. I like you lots. You can call me a princess any time you like to," she offered with childish graciousness.

Ben nodded solemnly. "Thank you."

Fleur swore her hand tingled from the touch all through her morning clinic.

* * *

Tanya woke well after her normal time. She stretched her body, reveling in the unfamiliar aches. She was going to use every single one of her allotted minutes to shower this morning. After she got up. Later. She rolled over and buried her face in her pillow.

She was dozing, snuggled into her bed when her satellite phone rang. The sound so jarred her, she jumped from the bed, diving for the clunky black device, which looked more like a long-range walkie-talkie than a phone. She pressed the connect button and waited a few seconds before the buzzing air indicated there was another person on the other end of the call.

"Beau?"

"It's Mom."

"Mom?" Tanya squeaked, her heart jolting in shock. Her mother never called between their once-a-month scheduled calls. "Is something wrong?"

"It's your father."

"Dad? What happened?" She sent up a silent prayer for her father's health as fear took hold and she waited with trepidation for her mother's answer.

"He's been shot."

"Shot?" Her legs giving way, Tanya fell back on the bed. She couldn't have heard right. "Mom, you didn't say *shot.*"

"I did." Instead of the tears she expected in her mother's voice, there was an almost bemused shock.

"But—"

"He's going to be fine. The ER doctor said he was lucky the carjacker used a small-caliber pistol and didn't have the best aim."

"He was *carjacked*?"

"Yes, and you know how much he loves that stupid car." Tears laced her mom's voice now. "He wasn't about to give it up. He didn't either. He tasered the guy as he tried to drag him from the driver's seat."

"He fought the carjacker?"

"He did. And he won." The confused shock in her mom's voice made a lot more sense now. "Listen, monkey, I'm calling to tell you about what happened, but it's also made me realize how easily one of us could be gone tomorrow."

Tanya was having the same revelation, so she didn't even balk at the wave of guilt that rushed over her. Nor did she chide her mom for calling her that awful nickname from her childhood. So she'd liked to climb and had been caught on top of the refrigerator more than once before her second birthday. That was no excuse for calling her "monkey."

Pushing aside the old mental argument, she said, "I know, Mom, I'm so sorry."

"Me too." Her mom's voice broke a little. "Your dad is not a good patient. He's going to be a bear."

"I wish I was there," slipped out before Tanya could bite the words back.

She waited for her mom's "I told you so," but got a soft sigh instead. "I wish you were here too. You don't know how much. I could really use a hug from my daughter right now."

Tanya's need to be there for just that thing was so strong, it was a physical ache in the muscles of her arms. "Close your eyes and pretend I'm hugging you."

For once, her mom didn't argue practicality or semantics. After a beat of silence, she said, "Done. Thank you, monkey."

"I love you, Mom."

"I love you too. More than you'll ever know."

"I know you love me. I do."

"I'm proud of you too."

"You are?"

"Yes. I know I didn't want you to go to Africa the first or the second time, but that doesn't mean I can't appreciate what a special person it makes you for going."

Tanya thought she was going to start crying. "Thank you, Mom."

Silence stretched for several seconds. Tanya figured her mom was regaining her composure, just as Tanya was.

"So, your father's sixtieth birthday is coming up. I don't suppose you could make it back in time for the party? I would pay for the last-minute airfare."

Her father's birthday was the last day of the month, about three weeks away.

"I'll talk to Fleur," Tanya found herself rashly promising.

But she meant it. Sure, she usually planned her trips home months in advance, but sometimes a woman had to take action.

Besides, she had a feeling that once Roman was gone, a trip home to her family might be the best way to find comfort for the heartbreak she was headed toward.

CHAPTER EIGHT

"I've modified it so all you have to do is press here and power is engaged. It stays on until you press it again." Neil handed Roman the hand-held scanner.

Roman turned the small black object over in his hand. "How close does it have to be to her chip?"

"I don't know. My guess is pretty damn close, or the soldiers wouldn't have demanded a strip search."

"Maybe." Those bastards could have had their own ugly reasons for wanting to strip Tanya.

"Two of our men were with the Zimbabwe soldiers." Neil's certainty that American soldiers would never be party to rape was laudable, but Roman didn't share it.

There were bad apples in the American military too.

"We don't know if they were there on orders," Roman reminded Neil. "All we do know is that they got called to heel when Corbin put a leash on their superiors."

Unfortunately, their presence did verify that the

Americans were on active duty, though. Which led Roman to believe Colonel Idiot had something to do with the roadblock.

"Just because the American soldiers were with the Zimbabweans, that doesn't mean they knew about the hand-held scanner," Neil said, showing how close to Roman's train of thought his own was running.

"For all we know, the American soldiers intended to search Tanya, looking for a USB storage device."

"Or they planned to prick her with something that would lead to death during the search."

Roman had thought of that and it left a cold spot inside him he'd been unable to shake.

"Someone at the roadblock knew about the chip though."

"Which means we've got to neutralize this situation sooner than later."

"Right."

"You're going to have to get the reader as close to her chip as you can."

"And let me guess, you have no idea how long the transfer will take?"

"Oh, ye of little faith. I can't tell you how close you have to be to her chip because I don't know what kind of transceiver it's got. For spies, these people are cheap. The wireless receiver on their hand-held is one generation old."

"So, how long?"

"*Well,*" Neil drew the word out. "The JCAT is sophisticated software. It will be upwards of twenty gigs."

"So, not an instant transfer."

"No, but it's not going to take hours either. Assuming the transceiver is the same generation as the receiver, even twenty gigabytes should only take six-point-two minutes. If it's the generation before, you're looking at more like thirty."

"Shit."

"Don't tell me you can't stretch it out for thirty minutes, man. I'll lose all respect for you."

"Ass."

Neil just grinned. "That's Spazz. You need to work on your diction, chief."

Roman whapped him on the back of his head, not too hard, but not like he was hitting a girl either. "My dick is just fine."

"Well, you were the one worried about keeping her occupied for half an hour."

"And keeping the damn reader near the chip."

"That's a small consideration for a man who plans terrorist-level black ops before breakfast," Neil mocked.

"Staying up all night planning an operation does not count as doing it before breakfast."

"Sure it does; it's all in how you look at it."

"I'd call you an idiot, but you'd know I was lying."

"Yep. I got me some heavy IQ points there, Geronimo."

"Sometimes I wonder if you didn't fake your tests."

"And if I did? Wouldn't that make my real numbers even higher?"

Roman rolled his eyes. "Yeah, and that's what worries me."

"Don't worry, it's an old fallacy that genius drives insanity."

"So you say." It was his turn to taunt.

"Just think about all the nice little gizmos I make you."

"I guess it's just a good thing you're on our side."

"Yeah, my plans to take over the world bored me."

"The scary thing is, I don't think he's kidding," Drew said as he came into the room.

Neil gave the other man a sour look. "You're the one more likely to have delusions of grandeur like that, Face."

"For me they would not be delusions." Drew smoothed his camo shirt.

He was the only man Roman knew who could make fatigues look like they should be a three-piece suit.

"Right," Roman drawled the word out. Drew was one scary son of a bitch when it came to manipulating people on any scale.

Drew gave a superior look. "Hey, some men like me become dictators; others fight the good fight."

"You'd make a lousy dictator," Neil said.

"Yeah?"

"Yes. You're too squeamish about blood."

Roman had to agree. Drew wasn't a bad soldier, but he wasn't like Kadin or Roman either.

"So you think," Drew said with a look that implied that was just another one of his cons and that he had them all fooled.

"What the hell are you ladies gossiping about?" Kadin asked, coming in. "We've got things to do."

"Is Ben ready to leave?"

"Yep. He's going in the first jeep with the baby grunts. They're dropping Johari off at school."

"And you two are going to ride with Drew," Roman said to Neil and Kadin.

"Right, he'll drop us two clicks out. Then we'll double back. I'll go looking for sign of our watchers and Neil will sneak back into the compound."

"Enter it covertly," Neil corrected him in an unctuous voice that earned him another head smack. "What? We're covert operatives, not teenagers sneaking out to go partying with our friends." But his eyes were laughing at both Roman and Kadin's less than amused expressions.

"Okay. So, the plan is for me to entice Tanna back here and keep her occupied long enough to transfer the data on her chip. Kadin will track whoever was watching the compound last night and Neil will get himself back into our hut without being seen, and keep himself scarce in the other bedroom.

"Face, Ben seems pretty serious about doing the mining audit too," Roman added. "Help him get the information he needs today. We don't know how long we have here, but he's doing a good thing."

"Damn right," Kadin said.

Drew nodded, his expression going to mission mode. "I'm on it, chief."

"Kadin, I want you checking in with Neil every thirty minutes."

Kadin scowled. "I don't need a babysitter."

"Save it. We all know you MARSOC soldiers can fight our wars single-handedly, but you'll just have to deal with following procedure."

Kadin's scowl did not lessen, but he nodded. Of all of them, he had probably had the hardest time adjusting to working on a team. Prior to joining the Atrati, Kadin had done most of his work for MARSOC on his own. He wasn't used to relying on

others to have his back, but Roman wasn't losing a
man to stubbornness or independence. Or just
plain misplaced pride either.

Roman went looking for Tanya as soon as both
jeeps had cleared the compound gate. Dr. Andikan informed him that Tanya was sleeping late this
morning.

He found her sitting on the edge of her bunk,
her sat-phone dangling from one hand, her expression one of dazed shock.

"Tanna, *liúba* . . . are you okay?"

She looked up. "*Roman.* What are you doing
here?"

"After last night you need to ask?"

"I . . . I'm supposed to be working."

"Not according to Dr. Andikan. She said you
were having a rare ly-in. Want some company?" He
let his desire for her show on his face.

These types of operations were always easier
when an agent actually felt some desire for the
woman he was seducing. Roman felt plenty for the
sweet woman looking so lost. He wanted Tanya
with a strength that was damn abnormal, but useful all the same.

"I . . . my dad, he was shot."

"What?" He wasn't one of those soldiers who believed real violence only happened in the field,
but the news still stunned him.

She shook her head, as if trying to clear it. Obviously, it didn't work because she didn't look any
more focused. "In a carjacking. He refused to leave
his car and the guy shot him."

"Is he okay?"

"Mom said he was going to be fine. He kept a taser in his car. Even shot, he tasered the guy, called nine-one-one and saved his car."

"He must really like it." Or the man had lost his mind, but Mr. Ruston had not struck Roman as a man on the edge.

"He got it the year Beau was born. It's a Plymouth Satellite Sebring. He's kept it in pristine condition all these years. Mom gets a new yuppie car every two years; she leases, but Dad's totally attached to his baby."

"Did they get the carjacker?"

"You know, I didn't even ask, but I think my mom would have been a lot more upset if he'd gotten away."

"I'm sure she was plenty upset as it was."

"Yeah. She wants me to come home for his birthday."

"When is that?"

"In a few weeks."

"You going?"

"Yeah, I think I am."

"What about Dr. Andikan?"

"She'll probably grumble, but in the end, Fleur will approve the trip."

"You sound pretty sure about that."

"I am." Tanya was sounding better, less shocky. "Family is important to her."

"Good."

She smiled, but she was still pale. He wanted to see her back to her indomitable self. For some reason that was really important to him. He moved into the room with a predator's stride.

It was time to get her thinking about something else. He'd brought the hand-held device with him, just in case plans changed. Good thing too, because there was no reason he couldn't have sex with her here instead of his own hut. Also, there was the added benefit of knowing Neil wouldn't be showing up in the second bedroom at some point.

Tanya looked up at him, her gaze still a little fuzzy around the edges. "I need a shower."

"You sure about that?"

"If you want to touch me, I'm sure." She stood up, looking determined.

He almost laughed, but he didn't. "I don't mind."

Her nose wrinkled. "Not going to happen, Mr. Super-soldier. I want a shower and I'm getting one."

"You'll come back?" He did not want to lose her to work.

"I should work."

Ah, he had her. "But you'll come back?"

"Yeah, I will."

And she did. Less than fifteen minutes later, she returned. Her hair wet, she wore a sleep tank top and light cotton pajama pants. Definitely not work-wear.

It shouldn't be a sexy outfit either, but as he'd told her the night before, he didn't need satin and lace to get turned on. The way the lightweight fabric of her top clung to her erect nipples, exposing the shadow of their raspberry pink through the white had his semi going fully hard in seconds. The look in her eyes was damn enticing as well. The pretty hazel depths ate him up.

"You put the time to good use, I see." Her eyes traveled up and down his fully naked form.

Not only had he stripped off his clothes, but

he'd taken the opportunity to put the scanner under her pillow for easy access. "I did."

The way her breathing went shallow from one second to the next had his cock jumping as it curved up toward his stomach.

She shut her door and leaned against it. "I like this."

"It gets better." He patted the bed beside him. "Come here."

She shook her head. "Today, I want to taste you all over."

Oh, shit. He couldn't afford to lose his focus, but he wasn't about to turn down that offer either. He'd never enjoyed another woman's touch as much as he did the feel of Tanya's fingers against his skin.

"Feel free." He lay back on the bed, stretching his body out for her.

Her gaze darkened and her breath hitched. "You are beautiful."

"Men are not beautiful, sweetheart."

"So you say. I know what I'm looking at and it's pure beauty."

Damn, if he couldn't feel heat surging into his face. He couldn't remember the last time he'd blushed. Hell, he wasn't sure he ever had before.

She peeled off her top and tossed it away. "Should I leave my pants on like you did last night?"

He bit out, *"No."*

"Oh, that sounds certain."

"That's because I know what I want."

"And what is that?" she asked as she brushed her palms over her turgid nipples.

Damn, they were beautiful, perfect confections

tipping the sweetly rounded mounds that were neither too small nor overly generous. "I want to taste those."

"What? These?" She plucked them, a small sound coming from her throat as she did so.

"Yes," he growled. "Damn it, get over here."

"You're awfully bossy in the bedroom."

"We weren't in a bedroom last night."

"No, you were *in me.*"

The sweet teasing made him ache to hold her, but he could wait. He *would* wait. "That I was, and it felt damn fine."

"Did it?"

"Oh, yeah."

"For me too."

"We fit." The truth of that statement made the breath in his chest catch.

"Yes, we do," she said, looking like the knowledge was just as disturbing for her. "Better than we should, maybe, for what this is."

"You sure about that?"

She turned her head to the side as if that was one question she did not want to answer. "I don't usually do casual."

"This may not be permanent, but it's not casual either." No matter what else was going on, the way their bodies reacted to one another was anything but casual.

She nodded and then looked back at him. "So, no pants for me?"

"Right."

Her lips curved in a smirk, but she didn't make him wait too long, sliding the cotton pants down her legs and stepping out of them to reveal she hadn't worn anything underneath.

Her pretty brown curls were a shade darker than the hair on her head, but still had a golden tone he hadn't seen in the deepening twilight last night.

"I could look at you for hours." As he said the words, words meant to seduce, the truth of them slammed into him like an armor-piercing bullet. Shit.

"Maybe later. Right now I want to have my way with you." She approached the bed, her hips swaying with unconscious feminine allure.

If he didn't get a handle on his need, he was never going to last. The slightest brush against his cock was going to have him exploding like a teenager seeing his first naked woman.

She stopped at the end of the bed and dropped gracefully to her knees. "I really did mean I want to touch you all over."

"I don't know if I'll survive it." And the scary part was, he wasn't kidding. The sight of her on her knees rocked through him like a mortar blast.

And the thought of never seeing her like this again made that cold spot inside him grow until he felt hollow.

"Trust me, you'll survive. I have plans for after." Her tone was filled with sultry promise.

"You'd better get started then."

And she did.

She spent what felt like hours, but was probably only minutes, on his legs, caressing, kissing each spot that she discovered was sensitive. She whispered things against his skin he could not understand, but still managed to drive him wild. When her lips pressed to his inner thigh, her rapidly drying hair brushed against his balls and pre-cum leaked onto his stomach. She seemed to sense the effect she'd had because she turned to kiss his scrotum, licking and gently tugging on his sack with her lips.

He groaned, holding on to the sheets with white-knuckle intensity to stop himself from reaching out and forcefully guiding her mouth to his cock.

Damn, for a woman who didn't do casual often, which implied long bouts of celibacy, Tanya was incredibly good at this.

"Vidsokchy mih khuj," he ground out.

She looked up at him, her eyes heavy lidded, her lips swollen from kissing his flesh with just the right amount of suction. "English, Roman. If you want me to do something, you've got to tell me in a language I understand."

How the hell was she speaking so clearly when he'd reverted to guttural Ukrainian? It was a defense mechanism all the Chernichenko kids had learned early in life. Doing so had kept them from getting in trouble at school more than once.

" 'Suck me.' Put my cock in your mouth," he demanded, even as he continued to force his hands to stay by his sides, his fingers curved into fists around the sheets.

He would not try to direct her head where he wanted, but if she didn't do something soon, he was going to have her under him.

Only, damned if he didn't want to feel the wet heat of her mouth on him.

"I'm not done tasting the rest of your body." She said it like they had all the time in the world.

"Later," he ground out between clenched teeth

as his hands cramped with the need to reach out and guide.

Her smile was as sensual as an incubus's. "Okay." Then she leaned forward and licked him from the bottom of his dick right up to the head, where she tasted his pre-cum. She licked her lips. "Sweet."

"I drink lots of juice." It was a good source of electrolytes, but it was common knowledge that the side benefit was less bitter ejaculate.

"Lucky me." She licked his head like a lollipop, over and over again.

"No . . ." he groaned out. *"Lucky me."*

"Pre-cum is sweeter than ejaculate in most men," she whispered seductively, her breath blowing over his now spit-slick penis tip.

"Can honestly say I didn't know that." And wasn't sure he cared.

"No one's told you before?"

Shit. Did she really want to have this conversation right now? "Doesn't usually come up."

"Hmmm . . ." She hummed as she took him into her mouth until he pressed against the back of her throat.

Oh, damn. Shit . . . he didn't want to say anything. He so didn't, but he wasn't an asshole. "Condom. Should probably use a condom."

She slowly released his aching hard-on and met his gaze with moist lips, her expression fully carnal. "Are you clean?"

He was going to cream before she even got him back in her mouth. "On my last test," he managed to grind out.

"Which was?"

"A month ago."

"Anything to put you at risk since then?"

"No."

"Are you worried about me?" She gave him this look from beneath her lashes that would have killed a lesser man with an overdose of lust.

Hell, he felt ready to have a heart attack right now.

"No."

"Then we'll save the condoms for intercourse." In her mouth the word *intercourse* sounded as dirty as slang did in another woman's.

"Okay," he agreed, even as he knew he should take her to task for trusting his word. He wasn't lying, but she had no way of knowing that.

It was only his gut-level certainty that she wouldn't be so trusting with another man that kept Roman silent.

She shook her head, a smile playing at her lips. "You look like you're arguing with yourself about lecturing me on acceptable risk."

"I am."

She laughed, the sensual sound going straight to his dick. "Even if you don't think I have reason to trust you on this level, you have to admit you're not an idiot."

"No, I'm not."

"Nor are you an asshole."

"How can you know that?"

"I know your family." She shook her head when he opened his mouth to speak. "If you were stupid, you might risk giving me something, knowing I would tell my brother and he would tell your *baba* before hunting your ass down and trying to kick it."

"He's no wimp."

"Nope." She ran her hand up and down his rigid dick. "Now, can I get back to what I was doing?"

"Oh, yeah."

This time when she took him in her mouth, he closed his eyes and concentrated on the sensation of soft lips stretched around his shaft, and her wet tongue caressing him.

It was apparent she enjoyed what she was doing and she kept at it until he felt on the brink of coming.

"Stop," he ordered.

She took a last suck and swipe with her tongue that damn near sent him over the edge before complying. A question in her eyes, she looked up at him without taking her mouth completely off his aching hard-on.

"I'm going to come."

She pulled back and gave him a Cheshire grin that made his cock jump. "Want to find out if that juice sweetens your ejaculate too?"

Was he a eunuch? Of course he did. "The question is, do you?"

Her answer was to put her mouth back on him. Oh, hell. He didn't have a chance. He let her take him over the edge, knowing it would make it easier for him to stay hard later. He clenched his jaw to stop from shouting when he came down her throat.

She took it all and licked him completely clean after. That was such a turn-on, his cock barely softened, maintaining enough erection that he could have ridden her right then, but he had other plans.

She took a drink from the bottled water on the table by the bed. "I don't have a lot to compare it to—Quinton wasn't big on oral—but you were just a little salty."

He knew enough about chemistry to know his juice drinking wasn't the only reason his cum wasn't as bitter and salty as it could have been. He limited his red meat intake for health reasons, but that would affect it too, as well as the amount of water he drank and his exercise routine.

The human body was governed by a series of complex chemical reactions and he probably understood that better than most men. Even scientists, because Roman had an earthy bent to his thoughts that had always instigated curiosity in areas others dismissed as unimportant.

Okay, no matter how fine that blowjob had been, it was time to do his thing.

He sat up in one fluid movement. "Your turn."

She took another drink of water, clearly rinsing her mouth before trading places with him on the bed. He arranged her so the chip embedded in her back was closest to where he'd tucked the hand-held scanner under the pillow. He slid his hand forward and unobtrusively turned it on. Then he kissed her, not minding the telltale taste of his pleasure that remained in her mouth.

It was an earthy intimacy that worked for him. He'd never wanted to share it with another woman though, but everything with her was good. He touched her body as they kissed, caressing the pleasure spots he'd discovered during their hours of play the night before and looking for more.

She made the sexy little sounds that he'd learned drove him to distraction, and he wanted more. Keeping her in place was secondary as he sought more and more proof of her pleasure. He moved down her body, paying homage to the sweet little curves tipped by such luscious nipples. The night before, he'd been delighted to discover that she was ultra-sensitive there and he made full use of that knowledge now.

She whimpered and moaned as he suckled and nibbled, and then pinched and rolled the tender buds between his fingertips. Before long, she was thrashing under him, biting her lip to keep from crying out.

He kept it up until she started begging him. "*Please*, Roman. Make love to me. I want you inside." Her hips arched upward, her thighs spread in blatant invitation.

But he held back. "Not yet, *moyá liúba.*"

"Please. I'm so close."

"The longer I keep you there, the better it will be when I take you over the edge."

Her eyes went wide and then narrowed. "You are evil."

"No. I am a man who knows how to please a woman into oblivion."

"So, take me there, already."

"I will," he promised and went down her body with his mouth, keeping his hands busy with her lovely breasts.

She keened; she moaned; she said "please" over and over again. He nearly lost track of time in her amazing response. He'd never been with a woman who made him feel so much more than a mere man. He felt like a sex god, and he'd never been a slouch as a lover. But she reacted with so much intensity, he wanted to give her more and more pleasure. Hell, he just wanted to give her more, period.

He dismissed the thought and concentrated on taking her where he wanted her to go.

CHAPTER NINE

When his lips found her mound, she sobbed out her pleasure. He delved between her lips with his tongue, finding the swollen nerve-centric bud and flicking it with short little strokes.

Her whole body bucked under him and she squirmed against the bed sheets. Then her cries were muffled and his head jerked up.

She'd grabbed the pillow, not even noticing the small scanner so close to her shoulder.

Shit. He surged up and yanked the pillow away as he covered her mouth with his own.

While their tongues battled for dominance, he readjusted the pillow under her head and once again covered the scanner. He scrabbled through his clothes beside the bed until his hand landed on the camouflage bandana he carried in his pocket for times he needed to cover his head in the field. It was clean.

One-handed, he twisted it into a makeshift gag. Then he leaned back and showed it to her. "Better than suffocating yourself with a pillow."

She blushed, her breath sawing in and out. "The huts are not exactly soundproof."

"I understand." He cupped her face and then indicated the twisted bandana. "You okay with this?"

Her pupils expanded and her mouth opened and closed without sound, but there was no doubt her reaction was one of desire rather than rejection. She had a kinky bone to rub alongside his.

Damn, he'd never been with a woman so perfectly matched to him. And he probably never would be again, the small voice inside him taunted.

She nodded, without speaking and helped him tie the bandana in place. "Now you can scream all you need to without having anyone showing up ready to do emergency CPR, yeah?"

She nodded, her smile easy to see despite the gag.

He went back to the apex of her thighs, his tongue quickly returning to its easy torment of her most sensitive flesh. He continued to play with her breasts with one hand, but used the other to finger her.

Every time she started to contract around his fingers in preparation to climax, he backed off the intensity. He kept it up for the full half hour that might be needed to transfer the files before he finally let her tip over into orgasmic pleasure.

Her entire body convulsed in wave after wave of pleasure and he continued ministering with his tongue all through them. When her stifled cries turned to sharp whimpers, he backed off, not wanting to overstimulate her super-sensitized flesh.

He took the makeshift gag from her mouth, untwisted it and used it to wipe the wetness from his face. "You ready for me?"

The only indication she'd heard him was a small flicker of one eyelid.

He smiled. "Don't worry, sweetheart, we'll take it slow and easy."

"I know," she croaked out.

He didn't ask how she knew. Her sexual trust was something that touched him in places he didn't want to think about.

He was careful to inch inside her with slow and careful movements and he held his body back so nothing stimulated her clitoris. He kept up a steady, gentle thrusting for long, pleasure-filled minutes before she fluttered her eyes open and smiled at him.

"You're a master."

"You're amazingly responsive."

"Only with you."

Part of him did not want to hear that, but another part swelled with pride and possessive satisfaction at her words. "You liked the gag."

"Yes." Her body clutched around him in involuntary response to whatever she was thinking.

He grinned. "Me too."

"You like to get bossy too."

"You enjoy it when I do."

"Yes," she affirmed without hesitation.

"I think people would call us kinky."

"What we do in our moments of privacy isn't anyone else's business."

"No, sweetheart, you are right. It's not."

Her face twisted in pleasure. "Oh, do that again."

"What? This?" he asked as he adjusted the roll of his hips.

"Yes, that."

The pleasure and his pace built slowly until he was pounding into her and she was kissing him to stifle more screams of delight. She went over first, but he was only nanoseconds behind her as their kiss swallowed feminine and masculine shouts of satisfaction.

Dismissing the sensation of guilt the action caused, he slid the scanner from beneath the pillow and into the pocket of his fatigues as they wallowed in post-coital bliss.

After giving Tanya a sponge bath that made her both sigh and giggle, Roman left her at the medical hut before returning to quarters.

He was unsurprised to find Neil in the common area.

"Kadin checking in on time?" Roman asked.

"So far, so good. I take it the plan worked out better in her quarters than here."

Roman nodded, fishing the scanner from his pocket. "Check it out."

"Will do."

"Leave your radio with me. I'll track Kadin's check-ins."

"Sounds good, chief."

An hour later, Kadin had checked in twice and was due for his third when Neil came out of the bedroom. "It worked."

"She's got the JCAT on her chip?"

Neil nodded.

"We've got to get it out of her and destroy it before someone else with a scanner gets near her."

"Agreed."

"You think Face is right—we should ask Dr. Andikan to do the honors?"

"Yeah. She might be connected, she might not, but if she had access to a scanner she would have figured out a better way to get the JCAT than sending Tanya toward a roadblock."

"She didn't send Tanya, she just didn't insist Tanya go back to Tikikima. Not that I blame her. Tanya is stubborn," Roman said.

"Good match for you then, huh?"

"Tanya may not be the guilty one, but that just makes her an asset, not something else." Not his match.

"If you say so."

Roman did say so. He didn't have a match. He'd known that was the way it had to be for a long time. He'd seen too many good relationships destroyed by the separations required by a soldier's life. Being a member of the Atrati just made it that much worse.

And he never forgot that every separation might be permanent. Death was a reasonable outcome on too many assignments for Roman to dismiss that risk. If a man loved a woman, he didn't put her through the turmoil of wondering if this was the time her boyfriend, lover, or husband was not going to come home. It wasn't fair. And it made women do things they wouldn't otherwise do. Like trying to seduce their husband's best friend.

Old memories had no place in the current discussion, so Roman shoved them deep into the recesses of his mind and heart where they belonged.

"You're starting to sound like Kadin."

Neil put his hand over his heart. "Say it ain't so. I'm no grunt."

"Neither is he."

"No, we're both Atrati and I'm usually really proud of that."

"But not now?"

Neil frowned. "Tanya is a nice woman. She deserves better than to be used."

"Hell, if it'll make you feel better, the truth is, she and I would have had sex even if Dr. Andikan had been the mark." It had just worked out better this way.

The shock on Neil's face would have been funny if it weren't so annoying. "You never fool around on a job."

"No, I don't."

"She really gets to you, doesn't she?"

"Yes," Roman answered in a clipped voice.

"You think that's bad, but maybe it's not."

"Don't start with that sentimental shit. You know as well as I do that there isn't room for long-term in an Atrati agent's life." Why did he have to keep explaining that to his men?

"That doesn't mean you can't enjoy what you've got as long as you've got it."

"On that, we are agreed."

Neil nodded, his eyes knowing, his expression tinged with both resignation and something that almost looked like unhappiness.

Both men dropped the conversation and turned to discussing where they needed to go with the assignment.

Kadin returned an hour later. "I found evidence of where our watchers have been, but not where they are now," he announced without preamble.

"There was a Hummer parked five clicks north-west."

"Our guys then?"

"The tire tracks weren't clear enough to tell if they were military issued."

Roman nodded. "I've got a call in to Corbin. Maybe he can find out if orders have been issued."

The sound of a jeep entering the compound shocked all of them and Roman double-timed it to the front door. The others weren't due back for another hour or more and Mabu had told them the compound rarely got visitors in vehicles. Roman swung the door open in time to see Ben and one of the Marine privates helping the other one, clearly injured, into the clinic.

Muttering a Ukrainian curse as he went, he jogged to the clinic. "What's going on?" he demanded.

Face came around the jeep to Roman. "Someone took shots at them after we left the mine. A sniper, but not a good one. They got the grunt sitting next to Ben in the back."

"How bad?"

"His shoulder. He was wearing his vest, but the sniper was using a Dragonuv, or the equivalent, with armor-piercing rounds. The other private has his evasive driving maneuvers down. He managed to get out of there with only damage to the jeep. They radioed me to pick them up, but he kept the jeep moving on two blown tires until they reached me."

Roman made a mental note to commend the soldier for his effectiveness under fire later. "You seem to think the snipers were locals." When guessing the identity of the sniper's rifle, Drew

had mentioned the Dragonuv, which was an older
Soviet weapon.

"We found indisputable evidence of human
rights violations at the mine. The overseer tried to
buy Ben off. When that didn't work, he threatened
Ben and then any Americans in the area, including Tanya. That's when Vincent sent the guy whim-
pering to his knees."

Roman wasn't surprised. Elle had told him how
broad the training for TGP agents was. Bennet
Vincent might look like a bean counter from the
State Department, but he could probably kill with
his bare hands without breaking a sweat.

"So, they called in a sniper?" Roman guessed.

"That's what it looks like. Lucky for our people,
not a good one."

"Right." Roman didn't even try to stifle his growl
of irritaton as he took the steps up to the clinic in
one leap.

Roman didn't exactly storm into the exam room,
but the fury rolling off him in waves was almost
palpable.

Tanya was assisting Fleur in prepping the soldier for surgery, but she couldn't miss his entrance. The bullet had pierced the Marine's vest
and made it into his shoulder, but without enough
velocity to exit the other side. The wound was a
mess of blood and torn tissue.

Roman didn't demand status or in any way try
to distract Tanya and Fleur's attention from their
task. And for that Tanya was grateful. He seemed
to realize the only way Fleur would allow him to re-

main in the room was if he stayed out of the way and silent.

For her part, Fleur appeared to be equally aware it wasn't worth her energy to try to kick the commanding officer out. He stayed clear, didn't touch anything, but his eyes were everywhere, assessing each minute movement of both Tanya and Fleur's gloved hands.

Tanya did not relish arbitrating things between them, so she was very glad neither pushed it.

They worked on the soldier for two hours and shot him full of antibiotics when they were done.

"He shouldn't be moved for twenty-four hours, but then I recommend transporting him to a U.S. military hospital," Fleur said as she peeled off her gloves and tossed them in the container for items that had touched bodily fluids.

Roman nodded. "He going to regain full mobility?"

"He was pretty torn up." Fleur gave the noncommittal shrug that said she just didn't know. "I did what I could, but this may well earn him a medical discharge."

The sound of the other Marine private swearing in the other room showed that he had heard the exchange.

Roman nodded and left to speak to the other soldier. He didn't come back, but Tanya didn't mind. She didn't need the distraction while she and Fleur sanitized the space around their patient, changing his bedding with practiced movements while he remained sedated.

He started to wake, moaning as they finished. Fleur administered pain medication as the other Marine hovered in the doorway.

"Can I stay with him?" the man asked.

"Don't tire him," Fleur warned.

"I won't."

"Come get us in the office if he shows any signs of taking a negative turn."

The young soldier nodded, looking perfectly capable of watching over his buddy.

"Good." Tanya gave him a reassuring smile. "One of the interns will be in to watch over him as soon as they finish the wellness clinic, but I can stay in here now if you're worried."

"You wouldn't leave if he wasn't stable, would you?"

"Absolutely not. The fact we had to sedate rather than put him under general anesthesia, which he would have gotten in a hospital, means his recovery will have fewer potential complications." The potential for complications mid-procedure had been exponentially higher, but there was no reason to share that information with the Marine now.

"Go ahead, Doc," the man in the bed said. "Tommy has my back."

Tommy nodded firmly.

"Okay then. Our office is the room in the southwest corner of the chalet."

"I'll yell loud enough for you to hear me in the latrine if he needs you."

"Sounds good."

She left and went to join Fleur in the office. The compound's doctor was already writing up the paperwork for the procedure they'd just done, but she looked upset.

"Are you okay?" Tanya asked, leaning back on Fleur's desk rather than sitting at her own.

Fleur looked up with haunted eyes. "They were shooting at Ben."

"Whoever it was missed him."

"But he could have been hit."

"Yes." She wasn't sure what Fleur's point was. They lived in a dangerous part of the world. No getting past that and Ben Vincent's job painted a big red target on his forehead.

"I don't want him hurt."

Tanya felt her entire Fleur–paradigm shift. "You're falling for him."

"Yes."

The quick agreement without even an attempt at denial scared Tanya to her toes. "He's leaving—you know that, don't you?"

"Nothing says I have to stay here."

The air came and went in Tanya's lungs, but she still felt she was growing lightheaded. "You'd leave Sympa-Med?"

"If it meant I could have a family again, a real life with Ben and Johari? Yes, I would leave."

Tanya was glad she was leaning against the desk because she wasn't sure her legs would have held her otherwise. "I thought—"

"That I would give up my life to serve others as you have done?"

"Well, um . . . yeah."

"I have and did, but this thing with Ben, it was something I thought I would never have and now I think it might be possible."

"And it's worth changing the dreams driving your heart."

"Yes, I think it is." Fleur sounded even more astonished than Tanya felt.

"For what it's worth, I think a chance at that

kind of happiness is worth some sacrifice. You've given so much already, but you deserve happiness too and if that means leaving Africa, then you go."

Fleur stood up and grabbed Tanya in a hug that shocked her even more than the conversation.

Tanya wasn't an idiot though and she hugged her friend back, trying to share her own strength with the other woman. Tanya had a feeling Fleur was going to need it.

"You think he will want me?"

"I think if he doesn't, he's a fool and he hasn't struck me as the stupid type."

Fleur's laugh was choked and Tanya pretended not to notice.

They broke apart and Tanya said, "I'm not sure this is the best time to do this, but I need to go back to the States in a few weeks. For my father's sixtieth birthday."

Then she explained about the call from her mom that morning.

Fleur said, "I'm sure we can do without you for a couple of weeks. You're not going to want to make the trip to turn right around and come back again."

"I suppose not, but what about you and Ben?"

"Don't worry about that. I'm not going to run away in the night. These things take time."

"True."

"You know I'll be recommending you for my job when I leave."

"I'm not a doctor, just an EMT."

Fleur shrugged. "I didn't say they'd give it to you, but you deserve it."

Tanya grinned, though her eyes burned with emotion at the thought of losing Fleur.

For something like, oh, the second time in their friendship, Fleur pulled Tanya into another hug. "I'm sorry about your father."

"Me too." Tanya stepped back, leaning on Fleur's desk again. "Mom said he should be fine, but I have this terrible sick feeling in my stomach. My dad could have died."

"I cannot believe he fought a carjacker." The disbelief in Fleur's tone matched the feeling still most prominent in Tanya whenever she thought of what her father had done.

"I know, right? I mean, yes, he loves that car, but arguing with a man holding a gun? That's crazy."

"They think you're crazy for working here."

"True."

"So, maybe you come by it more naturally than you thought."

Tanya laughed. She'd never once thought she was like her parents, but maybe she was . . . just a little.

"Everything okay with my wounded soldier?" Roman asked from the doorway.

Fleur turned around and met his gaze unflinchingly. "*Your* soldier?"

"He's on my team. I'm responsible for him." And the fact the other man had been shot was not sitting well with Roman's highly developed sense of responsibility. That was obvious.

Tanya wanted to comfort him, but right now, the best she could do was send him mental waves of strength and understanding. She had no idea if that kind of stuff worked, or not, but it made her feel better.

"He woke from sedation fine and is responding well to the pain meds."

"Good." Roman looked between Fleur and Tanya, an unreadable expression on his arresting features.

"Did you need something else?" Fleur asked.

"An Army helicopter will be here tomorrow early afternoon. It will transport our wounded private to the closest military hospital."

"It's not quite twenty-four hours, but that should be fine."

Roman nodded, but didn't leave.

If he'd been looking at Tanya, she would have thought he was hoping to talk, maybe even go to the dining hall together, but his gaze was fixed on Fleur.

Finally, the other woman asked, "Was there something else?"

"I need you to perform another small surgical procedure."

Fleur frowned. "On who?" Then she flinched as if struck. "Is it Ben? Was he hit after all?"

"No, I'm fine, Fleur." Ben came into the small office, his face set in serious lines.

Roman's gaze flicked to Tanya and then back to Fleur again. "It's Tanya."

"Me?" Tanya demanded in shock, the sensation of having dropped down the rabbit hole washing over her. The phone call from her mom had been disconcerting enough, but this was just plain outrageous. "I do not need surgery."

Another man came into the rapidly filling office. She thought his name was Drew, but she couldn't remember for sure. The attractive black man smiled in a way that made her feel like everything was going to be okay.

His words quickly dispelled that sense of peace though. "Please, hear us out."

So far, no one had been speaking to her.

And Roman didn't change that when he said to Fleur, "She's got that chip from Sympa-Med in her back. It has to come out."

Fleur narrowed her eyes while Tanya felt her mouth fall open like a gaping fish. "Why?" they both asked at the same time.

Roman's gaze slid over to Tanya, this time staying. "It's a matter of national security. That's all I can tell you."

"No." Fleur shook her head for emphasis.

Tanya crossed her arms, absolutely refusing to accept such a lame statement. "Bull-pucky."

Once again the women spoke in unison, and with the same intent if different words.

Roman looked at Fleur, his expression set in stone. "Either you do it, or Drew does."

Fleur stepped up to Roman, getting in his personal space in a way she never did with people, her eyes snapping. "Now you listen to me, Mr. Soldier-Man. You are not cutting into my friend's body without a sound explanation why."

"He's not cutting into me at all."

Fleur turned to meet Tanya's gaze. "He doesn't strike me as a frivolous man."

"I'm not," Roman said.

Tanya remained silent.

"If he comes in here demanding this absurd thing, he has his reasons. If they are good enough, no soldier-butcher is cutting into my dear friend's flesh. I'll do it."

"It's my body. My chip. I'll say what happens here," Tanya said, feeling the situation spiraling away from her with no hope of holding on to control.

It was not a pleasant feeling and she was sorely tempted to kick Roman in the kneecap. She moved to sit at her desk, landing on her chair with a frustrated thump.

"You don't want to claim what's on that chip, trust me," one of the other soldiers said from the doorway. Tanya thought this one was Neil.

What was this? Some kind of Soldiers-R-Us convention in her and Fleur's office? She'd missed her invitation and she had a feeling she would rather have skipped the party too.

"The only thing on it is my medical information," she said, trying to figure out where all of this was coming from, much less where it was supposed to be going.

"No." That's all Roman said. One word and no frickin' explanation.

His kneecap was looking less and less appealing as she considered spots farther north.

"Then what is?" she demanded of the man standing behind him, figuring that for whatever reason, Roman was back to his annoying habit of ignoring her questions when he didn't want to answer them.

"Stolen military software." This time it was Drew speaking again, and he watched both her and Fleur closely as he did it.

Roman was giving him the glare of death, but the other man seemed immune. "This was the plan, remember?" he said to Roman.

His words only half-registered with Tanya as she reacted to his first statement.

"What? No way! Not possible. Even if something like that was put on the chip before it was embedded, the information would be more than three years out of date." She was actually due to have the battery replaced on the GPS unit soon, but the chip hadn't been fiddled with since its initial insertion when she came to work for Sympa-Med.

"It's new and dangerous technology," Roman deigned to clarify.

"Not possible." It just wasn't.

Neil frowned at Roman and then offered, "Your chip doesn't just have a GPS tracker; it has a wireless transceiver."

"What does that mean?" She'd never pretended she was up on all the latest computer stuff.

"It means someone has been using you as a mule to carry stolen information probably since the chip was installed." Roman's voice had zero inflection and that bothered her. A lot.

Shouldn't he be upset on her behalf if all this was true? They might not be in love, but he'd said their sex wasn't casual. And they were friends, at least. Weren't they?

For reasons she'd rather not face, his indifference bothered her more than the knowledge that someone had somehow put some kind of government secret on the medical information storage chip in her body.

And she wasn't sure she was convinced it had happened anyway. In fact, she was pretty sure she wasn't convinced at all. "I don't believe it."

"Believe it." There was no room for doubt in Roman's tone.

Suddenly, it was too much. Everything they were

saying, Roman's attitude, it was all overwhelming. She couldn't . . . didn't want to believe it.

Yet if she accepted it, what did that mean about last night and today?

Tanya jumped up from her desk and rushed toward the doorway, shoving both Roman and the other men aside in her need to be out of there. "I want some air."

Roman grabbed her arm before she could make it out of the room. "The chip needs to be destroyed before anyone else downloads the information on it."

"Anyone *else*?" She stopped and swung around to face him. "Who has already downloaded it?"

"Me."

"How?"

He held up a small, black hand-held device of some kind. For all she knew it was a game controller, but the look on his face said otherwise.

"What is that?"

"A wireless receiver with a storage device."

"You used it to download information from my security chip?"

He nodded.

"When?"

His look was not forthcoming, but suddenly she knew exactly *when*. Bile rose in her throat. She yanked her arm from his grasp and ran for the washroom.

CHAPTER TEN

The pain rolling through Tanya was so intense, expelling the contents of her stomach wasn't going to purge it. That didn't stop her stomach from heaving until the painful cramps produced nothing but dry heaves. She couldn't help doing so.

She'd never felt so used, so betrayed. Not even when Quinton told her she wasn't the kind of woman he wanted to build his future with. They'd gotten together their first week on the project, stayed together when they re-upped for another two years in the Peace Corps and remained a couple for four years. They vacationed together, met each other's families and he'd been the first man she'd ever taken into her body. He'd told her he loved her. She'd said the same.

She'd felt the same, but the night they discussed what they were going to do once their current commitment to the Corps was over, it had ended.

He'd told her that she'd been good for him, that she'd made his time in the Peace Corps better, but he was moving on. He'd seen her as a con-

venient friend and bed partner for four years,
even though he'd said he loved her. He'd played
her and she hadn't even known it.

He said he wanted a normal life. He wanted to
go into politics and his time in the Peace Corps
was going to score him major points with the vot-
ers. It was almost as good as a military record and
he didn't have to risk killing anyone, or being shot
just for wearing a uniform.

The thing that had hurt the most, that had almost destroyed her, was that he had admitted he'd
known she wasn't the right woman from the beginning. And four years as her lover had not changed
his mind.

She hadn't believed Roman loved her, as she
had Quinton, but she'd thought her super-soldier
respected her. No way did he.

If he had, he simply would have asked her to let
him scan the chip. He wouldn't have tricked her
into letting him do it while he used her body and
violated her trust. The worst part was this awful
feeling that she'd brought it on herself. She'd
thought she'd learned something about men after
Quinton, but she'd still assumed that Roman
would not hurt her sexually. She'd absolutely believed that, to the point she'd followed his carnal
directions without hesitation.

She hated feeling as if she'd brought this violation on herself, by trusting the wrong person, by
believing too easily in his sexual honor. Not only
that, but she'd believed they were friends. They
weren't. No, a friend would have *told* her why he
was here.

Which was actually still kind of cloudy in her

mind. *Why had* Roman and the others come to Zimbabwe?

It wasn't to protect Ben, that was for sure. Ben was here to audit human rights violations at the mine. That had nothing to do with military secrets, did it? Why had Ben been with Roman when he'd made the demand to remove Tanya's security chip?

Was everyone lying to her?

A fist pounded on the door. "Tanya, open up!"

The sound of Roman's voice sent another wave of nausea through her. "Go away!"

"I'm not going anywhere."

She didn't deign to answer. The truth was, she couldn't. Everything inside her was all messed up. She didn't know what words to say to make him leave if, "Go away," didn't do it. She didn't know what words to use on herself to make it stop hurting.

She'd known falling in love with Roman would lead to heartbreak, but she hadn't known the agony would come so quickly. Even after Quinton, the idea that one human being could use another so callously was anathema to her.

The knowledge that Ben and the others were not what they appeared only added to the maelstrom ripping apart her insides. If she had discovered their duplicity in other circumstances, she probably would have understood it, but right now, it just felt like one more nail in the coffin of her belief in honor and integrity.

On top of it all was the certainty that if what Roman said was true, then the organization she had believed in and given her dedication to for almost four years had used her every bit as heartlessly as Roman.

Someone had put that stolen data on her chip. Who else could have done it but someone working for Sympa-Med?

Tanya had been used with no regard to her safety, her feelings or her hopes, dreams and beliefs. She had unwittingly betrayed her country and that sat heavily on her. She would never have done so willingly and, even though she had not known anything about it, she still felt a terrible guilt at her part in the espionage.

How incredibly unfortunate that the very day her mother told Tanya she was proud of her choices was the same day Tanya seriously considered the possibility that her parents and Quinton had been right. There was something wrong with her. There had to be for her to have been the one both the spies and Roman chose to use.

Another devastating and chilling thought flashed through Tanya's mind. Was Fleur in on it? No, she couldn't be. Fleur wasn't just Tanya's boss, the doctor was her best friend. The only friend she really counted as such since coming to work for Sympa-Med. Since Tanya did most of her work with the interns, the people she saw on a daily basis changed every few months, which made building lasting friendships tough. So, there had been Fleur. The Tutsi doctor simply could not be in on the espionage. Tanya could not handle it.

Not with everything else.

Fleur had been as adamant as headquarters that Tanya follow the dictated schedule for the traveling clinic.

Tanya might not know all the latest computer

gizmos, but she was smart enough to figure out that if she had some super-secret military technology on her security chip, it had gotten there while she was en route for the traveling clinic. And whoever was supposed to get it off had been in Tikikima. So, the schedule was important and Fleur made sure it got followed. But did she do that because it was her job as administrator, or did she have darker reasons behind her insistence that Tanya not break protocol?

No matter what her heart told her to be true, Tanya couldn't afford to trust it. Trusting had gotten her into a world of agony and she didn't see a short path out.

"Damn it, Tanya, you cannot hide in there all day. We need to talk," Roman demanded through the door.

She didn't want to talk. She didn't want to see him. She didn't want to deal with the thoughts swirling through her brain and tormenting her heart.

Muffled voices sounded on the other side of the door. Fleur's unmistakable tones were raised in anger. Tanya had never heard the other woman raise her voice. She was doing it now though, yelling at Roman so loudly Tanya could make out some of the words and they weren't pretty.

That, more than anything, had her standing and turning to face the door.

A lighter knock sounded. "Tanna, dear one, please let me in. I am worried about you."

Was that the voice of a woman who would sell out her friend's safety? Tanya didn't think so, but then if anyone had asked her if Roman was thinking about anything but mind-blowing pleasure when they made love . . . *had sex* earlier, she would have said no then too.

"Please, Tanya, unlock the door." Fleur's voice was filled with tears and worry, not the voice of a betrayer.

No matter what others had done, Tanya refused to doubt her friend without better proof.

The sound of Roman's saying something harsh was muffled by the door, but she thought she could guess pretty accurately what it was. He'd force his way in, just like he'd taken what he wanted from her. Oh, not her body—she'd offered that. The information on the chip. All he'd had to do was ask, but he'd chosen to take instead. Her thoughts kept circling back to that reality over and over again.

At least the first time had been about their mutual passion. She tried to comfort herself, only to have a flashback of the moment he had paused over the scar on her back. *He'd had sex with her to look for the chip.* But if he'd known it was there, why not just ask to see it? So much of this did not make sense to her, but then she was looking at it from the perspective of someone who thought hurting other people should be avoided.

Regardless, there were still too many holes in her knowledge of what was going on. Only one thing was certain. Roman Chernichenko was indeed an asshole.

And she might be a fool, but she wasn't fragile. She wasn't weak.

She rinsed out her mouth and then washed her face, patting it dry as she unlocked the door.

It slowly pushed forward. Fleur was coming in

then. Not Roman. Relief bolstered Tanya's intention to be strong.

She stood resolute, determined to reclaim some measure of her dignity. Fleur came into the small washroom and shut the door firmly behind her.

The Tutsi woman's eyes swirled with a maelstrom of emotion. Anger, compassion, fear, determination and uncertainty all flickered in her espresso-brown gaze. She didn't say anything, but simply put her arms out. And Tanya's determination to stand firm and stand alone crumbled. Just like that.

She walked into the third hug in her relationship with the other woman, all of them in one day.

Fleur held her tight. "I will not abandon you."

That was her friend, honest even in compassion. She did not promise everything would be okay. She did not assure Tanya no one else would hurt her. Fleur made the one promise she could make: not to abandon Tanya.

"I don't want to cry anymore," Tanya said, unable to give voice to any of the other thoughts or feelings beating at her heart and mind.

"Then don't."

Tanya laughed, a short cracked sound that held not one ounce of joy, but conveyed her dark amusement at her friend's advice. She took a deep breath and let it out. "Okay, I won't."

Fleur let go and stepped back. "We cannot change what others do to us, but we can control our reaction to those events."

"Can we?"

"Yes."

If anyone else had told her that, Tanya would

have called her a liar, but Fleur had survived un-speakable pain.

Tanya nodded. "I'm not giving in."

"That is right."

"I have to talk to him."

"Yes, you do. You deserve as much understand-ing of this unacceptable situation as you can get."

"Will it help?"

"Alleviate the pain?" Fleur asked.

"Yes."

"Maybe."

"Did it help you? To understand what drove the massacre?"

"To know the reasons and to understand them are not the same thing, but to answer your ques-tion, no, it made it worse. To know so much cruel evil existed in the world in the guise of political maneuvering only destroyed more of my illusions regarding the humane nature of man."

"I'm sorry."

Fleur nodded her acknowledgment of the words, then gave Tanya an ultra-serious look. "We cannot change the past, but we need not let others control our present."

Again, if those words had been spoken by some-one else, Tanya would not have given them much credence. It certainly felt as though others were controlling her present. Fleur's eyes acknowl-edged that reality while demanding that Tanya still accept the higher truth of her statement.

"Right." She didn't know how she would take back control of her life, but somehow, she would.

"Right."

They gave each other mirroring looks of deter-mination. If Tanya's was tinged with recent pain and Fleur's was touched by her past, neither commented on it.

Roman wasn't alone when the women came out of the bathroom. She couldn't help wondering what the interns or security personnel would make of the congregation of soldiers in the hallway, but it looked like right now that they still had the main medical hut to themselves.

The wellness clinic was being held in an outdoor tent just as it would have been on the road. It wasn't bad training for the interns, despite the no-travel order from Sympa-Med.

The order took on more sinister connotations that added to the tension inside her as she surveyed the soldiers congregated around the washroom door.

All the men who had been in the office were there, as well as Kadin. His face was set in lines of unhidden fury and the looks he kept giving Roman were laced with censure.

She approached him. "Will you tell me the truth?"

Kadin jerked, as if surprised she'd talk to him. "Yes."

She nodded. She looked at the rest of them. "I'm going to the office with Kadin."

He followed her without a word.

Roman gave orders for two of the others to secure the premises, whatever the heck that meant. He, Ben and Fleur followed Tanya and Kadin into the office.

Tanya sat at her desk. Fleur dragged her chair over to sit beside her, giving visual proof of their solidarity. Ben leaned against the side of Fleur's desk closest to Tanya's, but Kadin stood in front of Tanya's desk in the classic military at-ease pose.

Roman leaned against the wall beside her desk, his gaze fixed on her.

Tanya ignored the bastard and turned to Fleur. "How is the Marine private doing?"

Fleur's eyes widened. "You are worried about him? Of course you are. I will go check on him. Wait to ask your questions until I return?"

Tanya nodded and then did just that. Fleur was only gone a few minutes, but her expression showed no worry for the patient when she returned to the office. "He's doing well. Tommy is watching over him quite closely."

"You don't think we should call an intern in?"

"Not until this conversation has run its course," Fleur said.

"Okay." Tanya met Kadin's gaze. "Why are you in Zimbabwe?"

One of his eyes twitched, indicating he had expected her questions to start somewhere else. Too bad. She wanted to understand what was happening and if that required asking what size and style underwear he wore, she'd ask it.

"We were sent to eliminate an information leak."

" 'Information leak'? What does that mean?"

"Someone has been taking advantage of the U.S. military presence in Africa, culling information and dispersing it for profit," Ben said from his spot at Fleur's desk. "It's one of the unfortunate side effects of trading military training for access to natural resources."

"And these *information thieves* just now decided to use my security chip to transport the data?"

"No." Ben looked uncomfortable.

Tanya asked Kadin, "What does he mean, *no*?"

"Your movements have been matched with the information leakage for quite some time."

"I see." What weren't they saying? The weight of something no one wanted to say sat heavily in the air around them. What could they consider worse than what had already been revealed?

"You believed *Tanya* was the leak," Fleur said, her voice filled with angry disbelief.

"The *Army* believes she's the leak," Kadin corrected. "We thought the evidence was too circumstantial."

"Did you?" But this time her question wasn't directed at Kadin. She was looking at Roman when she spoke and she didn't miss the tightening of his jaw.

"*You* didn't," she said, meaning Roman. "You came here to . . . what? Get my chip one way or another?"

But that didn't make sense either. An important piece of the puzzle was still missing. She just didn't know what it was, or what it was supposed to look like so she could find it.

"We didn't know about the chip," Kadin offered.

"So, you thought I was carrying the information some other way." That made more sense, especially if someone had believed she was the information leak. "That's why you stopped the strip search. You didn't want it falling in the wrong hands."

Again she'd directed her words at Roman, and his very lack of expression confirmed her suspicions.

Another lead rock dropped to the bottom of her still queasy stomach. "Last night was you conducting your own strip search."

Fleur's gasp of anger fell into the unnatural quiet that came over the room. She swiveled to face Ben. "Did you know about this?"

"Not that, no."

Fleur glared, but Tanya didn't think her friend's hopes for the future were in serious danger, not with the way Ben was looking at the doctor. As if he would say whatever needed saying, promise whatever needed promising, in order to keep the Tutsi woman's good opinion.

At least someone would find some happiness out of all this. Regardless of her own pain and still reeling psyche, a shard of happiness for her friend, pierced Tanya's soul.

"Okay, so you came here to find whatever is on my chip."

"Not exactly," Kadin said.

"What then?"

"They came to eliminate the information leak," Fleur said in a furious tone, laced with just enough hesitation to imply she'd just worked it all out. "They came to kill you, Tanya."

Well, wasn't that just one more lollipop in the suck that was becoming her life? Tanya didn't doubt Fleur's deduction for a single second. It made more sense than any other scenario she had tried to work out.

She looked at Roman, the shattered pieces of her heart ground into dust by this new revelation. Not that she would let it show.

On pure principle, she was determined to keep the pain from her expression. "No wonder you didn't tell Beau you were going to be seeing me. It could put a real cramp in family holidays afterward to have him know you'd assassinated his only sibling."

Roman didn't say anything; she hadn't really expected him to.

"So, something made you decide to look further than me for the information," she said to Kadin, doing her best to pretend Roman had dropped off the face of the earth.

"Nothing added up. You didn't fit the profile, and for us, taking orders from idiot brass just goes against the grain."

In other circumstances, she would have smiled at his attitude. "Do you know who put the information on my security chip?"

"We have our suspicions."

"I'm sure you do," Fleur said dryly.

"Who?" Tanya asked.

Kadin's gaze skated to his superior and then back to Tanya. "Who else knows about the chip?"

"Sympa-Med, the supplier of the chips, the doctor who inserted it, but probably not many others. We aren't supposed to tell anyone. So, if we're kidnapped for human trafficking, the bad guys don't know to cut the chip out." She saw what he was driving at though. The list wasn't very long.

"Sympa-Med controls your travel itinerary," Fleur said.

Tanya nodded, her muscles stiff from holding her emotions in check. "They're very controlling about it too."

"So, you think they are involved?" Ben asked.

Fleur and Tanya both shrugged, but Fleur was the one who spoke. "It would seem the most obvious conclusion, but the situation with Tanya acts as a warning against accepting the obvious without investigating further."

Ben nodded. "I agree." The look he gave Roman said he wasn't impressed with the initial conclusions drawn by the Army.

Kadin asked, "Who else could it be?"

"Tanya already told you," Ben replied before she could. "Whoever supplies the chips to Sympa-Med, or the doctor who inserts them."

"Is it always the same doctor?" Roman asked.

Tanya ignored him.

But Fleur chose to answer. "Yes. His clinic is in Lyon, near Sympa-Med's headquarters. He does all the physicals for new recruits as well before they are assigned to one of Sympa-Med's field offices."

"You don't happen to know the name of the supplier for the chips, do you?" Ben asked.

"No," Fleur said. "But the representatives from the head office should be here any day. We can get that information from them."

"What if they're coming to retrieve the information themselves?"

"There's no reason to believe the entire Sympa-Med board is in on the espionage," Ben said.

Fleur added, "It could be just one person working for Sympa-Med, or one board member."

Tanya was glad Fleur was carrying the conversation for both of them because she was too busy trying to rein in the agony of learning Roman had come to Africa to kill her. This was one of those days that made her wish do-overs were possible.

"It would have to be someone fairly high up to influence Tanya's traveling itinerary," Ben replied.

"What is on the chip in my body?" Tanya asked

Kadin, no longer interested in speculation about who was using her since they had no way of knowing the person's identity for sure. And the guessing just added to her pain.

Kadin sent Roman another one of those "Can I tell her?" looks. Whatever he saw in the other man's face must have given the go ahead because he said, "A high-level Army JCAT."

"What's a JCAT?" she asked, not caring if she sounded stupid.

"Military training software."

"Highly effective, complex, military-training software that the government paid millions to develop, but the money isn't nearly as important as not allowing our military strategies to get into the wrong hands," Ben further clarified.

That awful sense of guilt she'd been feeling earlier came back, but Tanya tried to ignore it, reminding herself that she had not done anything. It had all been done to her.

Her conscience wouldn't be fully appeased though. She had been used to betray her country and she wasn't sure she was ever going to fully come to terms with that.

"If Roman"—the rat bastard—"has already downloaded the software, why do you have to remove the chip?" she asked, trying to focus on the issue at hand, not unearned guilt she couldn't do anything about.

"The hand-held scanner is probably a lot less sophisticated than what they usually use. It has no erase function from what Neil could tell," Kadin replied.

"For all we know whoever is using you as a mule doesn't erase the information at all," Ben added.

"They may simply overwrite it when they put new information on the chip."

"So, if anyone found out about what Tanya had stored on her security chip, she would be in terrible danger," Fleur said with obvious disgust and renewed anger.

"Yes." Ben's flat lack of denial was as chilling as anything Tanya had found out so far.

"You see why it has to come out?" Kadin asked, sounding concerned himself.

And that shocked her. "You're worried about me. Why?"

Kadin looked at her like he didn't understand the question, while Fleur made a sad sound and Ben uttered an ugly curse.

"You remind him of his sister," Roman drawled. "Can we get to removing the chip now?"

Did he have to be such a jerk?

"What's your hurry? We all know the only thing you're worried about is someone else downloading the data. That's not going to happen in the next ten minutes, so just be quiet. Your input isn't needed for this conversation," Tanya said.

She ignored his and everyone else's reaction to her words and focused her attention back on Kadin. "If you remove the chip, how are you going to figure out who is behind the information leak?"

"The same way we would if it was left in."

"How is that?"

"Without compromising your safety."

"My safety has already been compromised." She swallowed down the urge to be sick again. "If you don't find out who is behind this, I'm going to continue being at risk." And she was going to keep feeling this horrible sense of culpability for something she had neither agreed to, nor invited.

He opened his mouth to speak, but she forestalled him. "Look, I know your assignment *isn't* to protect me, but in this situation our objectives are served by the same purpose. You want to eliminate the leak and I want to know someone isn't going to come after me for information stored in my body."

"Getting rid of the chip would do that."

"Like you said, they won't know it's gone."

"So, tell the head office you had to remove it because of a malfunction that was causing you pain, or something."

"That's a good idea," Fleur agreed.

"But it won't help catch whoever is selling my country's secrets. And frankly, it won't undo the damage I did, even if I didn't know I was doing it. I want these monsters caught before they compromise my country's defenses any more than they already have. They used me and I want to fight back." Tanya might not be a poster child for patriotism, but she loved her country and wasn't going to stand by while its military secrets were being sold to the highest bidder.

Fleur gasped. "You are not at fault for any of this."

"I know, I do, but I carried the information."

"If you hadn't, they would have had someone else do it."

"It doesn't matter."

"We can't risk your being captured with the JCAT information on the chip," Roman said, his expression set.

She'd like to keep ignoring him, but his point

was a valid one. She wanted to help, not make the situation worse. "So, run a magnet over the chip. That'll erase it, right?" Even she knew that.

"That's not a bad idea," Ben said.

"No." Roman looked about as movable as a stone monolith.

She glared at him.

"The transceiver would still be active. Anyone with information on its signal could track you."

"So?"

"So, the chip is coming out."

CHAPTER ELEVEN

"**Y**ou don't think the magnet will work."
He didn't reply, just gave her this immovable expression that she would smack if she was a violent person. Which she wasn't, she reminded herself.

"I don't like the idea of using you as bait," Fleur said. "Please let me take that thing out of your back."

Tanya sighed and shook her head. "You never liked the security chips."

"Does that mean you don't have one?" Ben asked.

"I refused." Fleur's austere expression showed only the tiniest flicker of the disgust she felt toward the chips. "I do not trust anyone having that kind of control of my movements."

"No one controls where I go with the chip," Tanya denied. Though they had certainly used the presence of the chip to control what she did without knowing it. So, maybe Fleur's argument had more going for it than Tanya had ever supposed.

"But they always knew where you were. The

head office called, complaining you'd gone off course hours before you made it back to the compound without visiting Tikikima."

Knowing what she'd been carrying in her body at the time, this reminder that she had always been under some level of surveillance was really creepy and more than a little scary. "Okay, so we take the chip out, but I think we should do it in secret."

"You still want to set yourself up as bait?" Fleur demanded.

"It makes sense." Right now the prospect didn't even scare her. Much. There was too much pain inside her for fear to find room. "I need to do this."

Fleur finally nodded. "We can do it in our chalet. If we do it here in the medical chalet, there are too many people who might figure it out, or who would at least wonder why you were having a procedure."

"I agree."

"I will be there," Roman declared.

"You suspect Fleur of being in league with the spies? What do you think she's going to do, keep the chip or something?"

Roman didn't answer.

Typical.

"If I were him, I would doubt me." Fleur shrugged. "If I were you, I would doubt me."

"I did," Tanya admitted in a small, shame-filled voice.

But Fleur did not look hurt or offended. "You don't any longer."

"No, I don't." She just could not make herself believe Fleur would use someone else like that. It wasn't in her nature.

"Good." Fleur turned to Roman. "As much as

you no doubt want me to remove the chip this very minute, it is better to wait until later when Tanya and I would normally return to our chalet. We should go on as if nothing has happened. While I am not involved in this espionage, we can't be certain no one else in the compound is."

Roman nodded. "Kadin, you stay with Tanya. No one gets near her."

"I'm on it."

"Ben, you and Neil need to find out what you can about the doctor Fleur mentioned. Do we know exactly who from the head office is coming here?" Roman asked Fleur.

"There are three people coming, the Director of Operations for Africa, his assistant and one of the men who is on the team that determines the routes our traveling clinics take in Africa and Asia." She grabbed a sheet of paper from Tanya's desk and wrote on it, before handing the paper to Ben. "These are their names and titles, as well as how long they've worked for Sympa-Med."

He smiled. "Thank you, Fleur."

"I also wrote down the name of the French doctor and his clinic."

The door opened and Neil peeked his head in. "Geronimo? You've got a sat-phone call. It's Headquarters."

Roman pushed away from the wall and turned to leave.

"I thought you might want to know that we had to discourage the security man assigned to the clinic from coming back here, not once but three times," she heard him say to Roman as they walked away.

*   *   *

Roman took the sat-phone into an empty exam room before lifting it to his ear and saying, "Chernichenko."

"Roman, the reception on this call is sketchy."

"Yes, sir."

"Good man." A beat of silence and then. "Orders for Tanya Ruston's elimination have come from the highest level."

"I'm not sure I heard you. The connection isn't good."

"Right."

"Did you get my report?"

"I did."

"It wasn't enough?" Roman asked.

"No."

Which meant it had gotten political. In his experience, it was usually politicians (both civilian and military), who got so stubborn they ignored evidence in favor of action. "Has another team been called in?" he asked.

"Affirmative."

Damn it. "When?"

"Officially, today."

"Unofficially?"

"It wouldn't surprise me if they were already in Zimbabwe."

The watchers. "Special Forces?" Not that it mattered; his team was the best of the best, but Special Forces would make it more difficult to make a clean extraction.

"Probable."

"Understood." They had to get Tanya out of the compound. He and his team could protect her, but the potential for collateral damage here was too great. "Sir, the call is about to drop. I'm not sure I got your message."

"See that you don't."

That was more than he'd expected Corbin to say. The man had to be livid with the powers that be to undermine orders so blatantly. Roman was pretty pissed himself. He hung up without another word, evidence, if anyone needed it, that the call had dropped.

This assignment had been garbage since the beginning, but now it was starting to stink.

Tanya was so pissed at him that she wasn't going to take the news they had to leave with her very well. Especially, when she found out that they were leaving her friend Fleur behind.

Tanya ignored Roman's orders not to get near anyone and joined the interns at the open clinic. She worked the rest of the afternoon, giving children vaccinations and instructing parents on nutrition and how to avoid illness outside the parameters of calling on their ancestors for protection.

She never belittled traditional beliefs, but she encouraged patients to seek medical care beyond a visit from the local medium.

When she finally returned to her and Fleur's hut, Roman and Ben were already there. At least the other two had made themselves scarce. The communal room of their hut still felt crowded.

"Where do you want to do this?" she asked Fleur.

"It would be easiest here at the table." Fleur had already set up for a field-medic-style procedure.

Tanya nodded, but looked around the small but fully open communal living area and frowned at the soldiers. "I'm not taking my top off in front of all of you."

"They will turn their backs," Roman said.

"I'm especially not removing my clothing in front of you," she said, ignoring his wholly inadequate suggestion.

"Why not?"

"You did not really just ask me that."

"I did. I have seen you naked, Tanya. There is no need for modesty." Both his tone and expression indicated he seriously believed what he was saying.

Could he really be that clueless?

Apparently, he could.

She grudgingly offered, "If you want someone to watch and make sure Fleur doesn't do anything suspicious with the chip, Ben can do it."

"No." Roman's steel-gray gaze flared with something that looked like anger and his hands crossed over his chest, while his stance said he wasn't going anywhere, even to turn around.

She could be stubborn too and she so wasn't giving space in her thoughts to whatever anger he had going on. She crossed her own arms and glared. "Yes."

"Not happening, *liúba*."

"Don't call me that, you rat bastard."

Instead of being offended, he laughed. "Interesting term of endearment."

"It's not, but I'm sure you've heard it before anyway."

"Ben is not watching you undress."

"Seriously? You're going to play jealous Neanderthal here?"

"I'm not jealous and I'm not playing anything. This is my operation and I'm watching that chip."

And her.

"It's my operation too," Ben said in what should have been a mild voice, but the thread of steel behind his quietly spoken words could not be missed.

"Your job was to discover the source of the leak," Roman said to him.

"My job is to protect our country's proprietary technology."

Fleur shook her head. "Tanya, go put on a tank top with spaghetti straps. Leave off your bra. I can work with that and maintain your modesty."

Tanya nodded and headed to her bedroom. Kadin went to follow her, only to get stopped short by a barked order from Roman, who walked into her room right behind her.

"Turn your back while I change," she ordered, wanting to limit her contact with him.

He did, surprisingly, and without argument.

Tanya made quick work of removing the top of her scrubs and her bra, and then donned a dark green tank that would not show the shadow of her nipples through the thin fabric. She scooted around Roman and left the room without a word.

He tried to stop her, putting a gentle hand on her arm and saying her name, but she shook him off and went back into the communal room.

Whatever he had to say, she was positive she did not want to hear it.

Fleur nodded her approval of the tank top before indicating Tanya should sit down at the table. "Johari will be here soon. I want to be done before she arrives."

Definitely.

Fleur pushed one strap of Tanya's top down her arm until the fabric was well away from where she had to make the incision. Fleur took more time numbing the area than extracting the chip. A few pokes and tugs and Tanya knew the stitches were in place. Fleur cleansed and then bandaged the area before sliding the strap back into place. "Done."

Tanya turned around in time to see Roman take the small dish with the bloody mess. He held something over the dish.

"What are you doing?" Fleur asked what Tanya wanted to ask.

Only she'd decided somewhere between her bedroom and getting her back sliced into that dealing with Roman on any level right now was more than she could handle.

"Erasing the chip."

Fleur looked confused. "I thought you were going to destroy it."

"The plan has changed."

That did not sound good.

Tanya looked at Kadin. "What changed?"

He shrugged and gave Roman a look with raised brows.

"A kill order came in for Tanya."

Tanya didn't understand. "I thought you were already under orders to kill me."

Saying it didn't feel any less horrible than hearing it the first time, and she'd spoken to him, darn it. She snapped her mouth shut and looked at Kadin, hoping he would answer.

Roman made a sound that in an animal she would have called a warning. "We were under orders to plug the leak. Someone went over my boss's head to get a directed kill order."

"That's not good." Tanya looked around the room, feeling as if everything should have gone black and white or something.

Life couldn't just go on as normal. Dust motes danced on the sun's rays as they came in through the window.

"Didn't he get your report?" Kadin asked.

"He did."

"And he couldn't squash the kill order?"

"No."

"Well, shit."

"Exactly."

"We've got to get Tanya out of here."

"What?" Tanya demanded. "You want me to leave, *with you?*" The "with you," she directed at Roman with as much sarcasm as she could infuse into two words.

He didn't hesitate. "Yes."

"You figure the watchers are another kill team," Kadin said.

Roman just nodded.

What were they talking about? Who was watching? Who were they watching? Her? Her emotions were so overloaded right now, she couldn't even work up a good sense of alarm.

Kadin scowled. "We should have moved already."

"We'll leave the compound at full dark—I won't risk a sniper attack."

"Snipers have night-vision goggles." Tanya watched movies when she got the chance.

"They have their limits and full dark will give us some cover."

Roman had answered, even though Tanya had
been talking to Kadin, which was probably taking
the avoid-Roman effort into the realm of ridicu-
lousness. She didn't want to be silly; she was just
really, really, really angry.

"But—"

"No kill team is going to see you as a high risk
for flight. They have no reason to believe you are
aware of the danger you are in, so while they might
be watching at night, the risk of leaving the compound during the day is much higher. We'll take
you out through a hole in the fence."

"There is no hole."

He just looked at her.

Okay, they were going to make a hole.

"Drew will cover all signs of our exit."

"So, he's not coming?" she asked, realizing
there was no real chance she was going to refuse to
leave.

Roman shook his head.

"Drew and Ben will stay here with the chip. The
only people who should be able to track it are
Sympa-Med folks and whoever has made her their
information mule."

"So, you *are* setting a trap." She was relieved that
even if she could not play a part, at least the chip
that had caused so much trouble would be useful
in identifying the culprits.

"And buying some time to get you out of here
safely."

"I've contacted my agency and they're sending
in a team of independents, as well as another TGP
agent," Ben added. "She'll pretend to be you and
carry the chip with her."

"No one in the compound is going to believe she's me."

"She'll keep her distance from the locals. Fleur will tell everyone you've come down with something. Your time in the washroom will give credence to the story."

Well, at least that humiliating moment would be worth something. Though how anyone was supposed to know about it since no one besides the soldiers and she and Fleur had been in the building at the time, she couldn't guess.

And then she remembered the security guard. He'd gone to the dining hall for food during the surgery on the Marine and returned sometime later. The story of her "illness" was probably already spreading around the compound, despite the fact she'd spent the afternoon giving children vaccinations.

Gritting her teeth against the annoying reality that right now the only person with the answers she needed was Roman, Tanya turned back to him. "Where are you taking me?"

"We'll hike south toward Zimbabwe's border with South Africa. I have contacts there who can get us transportation home. If I can get them to come across the border, we'll arrange a meet. Otherwise, we'll have to make our own way and connect with them in South Africa. As long as the kill order is in place, regular military or government channels aren't safe."

"I've always wanted to see more of South Africa." Though the idea of walking there was pretty daunting. She liked to camp as much as the next person, but this was serious travel without so much as a pack mule.

Kadin smiled at her, his eyes warm with approval. Roman's were filled with something else entirely and it wasn't anything she wanted to acknowledge, so she turned away from him toward Fleur.

"Are you going to be okay?"

Fleur shook her head and laughed in patent disbelief, but very little humor. "I'm not in danger of a sniper's bullet."

"But they'll come here, looking for me." That's what Roman and Ben were counting on, wasn't it?

"I'll keep Fleur safe," Ben promised with an expression that cheered Tanya despite the hellacious day she'd had.

She met him square in the eye. "You better do right by her."

"I plan on it."

Fleur made a *pfft* sound, but Tanya saw the happiness glowing in the other woman's eyes, regardless of the danger and the day's revelations.

"You keep her safe," Fleur said to Roman, her expression devoid of all the warmth it had had a second ago.

"That's the plan."

Tanya wanted to ask why he was set on protecting her, but she wasn't sure she wanted the answer, so she didn't say anything at all.

"Take a nap. You'll need your energy tonight," he said to her.

She nodded and turned to leave the room, feeling that her entire life was on the verge of irrevocable change. And not for the better.

They left the compound in the small hours of the morning, after the moon had set. Tanya had insisted on carrying her own light pack on her back, despite the now sore incision below her shoulder blade.

Roman had grumbled, but in the end he had allowed it. He, Kadin and Neil carried bigger packs, and they were fully armed.

The three men had blackened their faces, and then Kadin had helped her do hers. Roman had been watching the whole time, his expression one she couldn't begin to read. And frankly, right now, she didn't really want to.

It was hard to believe how quietly the men moved, considering their size, and the amount of weapons they carried, not to mention their packs. They also never tripped, no matter how dark it was.

She couldn't say the same, but she never fell. Not once. Every time she tripped, Roman's hand was there, steadying her. He'd directed Kadin to take the lead and Neil was somewhere behind them. She hadn't actually seen them since they'd left the compound.

She didn't know how long they'd been walking when Roman handed her a water bottle. She drank just enough to rehydrate a little and then handed it back to him. He took a drink and then slid it into the net on the side of his pack without making a sound. He repeated the action at regular intervals. He seemed to know just when she needed hydration, but he also showed an uncanny sense for timing their bio breaks to just before she had to break down and ask. Twice he gave her half of an energy bar with her water, which she ate while walking.

They walked until almost dawn when Kadin led

them to a rock outcropping. Roman quietly told her that now was time for her bio break before bed. She didn't demur, but went where he indicated, finding a spot where she would have relative privacy. She'd been camping with the traveling clinic too long to worry about someone hearing her pee on the ground, but visual confirmation was something else. The men had put up two tents and thrown a camouflage net over them by the time she returned to their resting spot. They'd used the natural long grasses to add to their concealment and she felt as safe as she considered was possible under the circumstances.

Kadin climbed into one of the tents and Roman indicated with his hand she should get into the other. She didn't know who was taking first watch, or where the others were sleeping, and she didn't care. She was exhausted physically, emotionally and mentally. She simply had no reserves left to worry about the mundane. She wasn't even sure she'd notice if an assassin walked right into camp and pointed a gun at her.

More than ready for a break after the day's revelations, having her security chip removed and their long trek, she dropped to her knees and climbed inside the tent. She didn't worry about the black gunk on her face, the mild hunger pangs cramping her stomach or anything else for that matter. She just stripped off everything but her tank top and panties before lying down on the lightweight sleeping bag that had been spread out on the floor of the small pup tent. She was asleep a few seconds later. The sensation of warmth pressing along one side came some time later, but she was too out of it to even try to determine what that meant.

She figured it out pretty darn quickly when she woke up, though. Roman was there, already awake and watching her.

She glared, but she didn't speak. She knew sound could carry and she wasn't jeopardizing the men trying to save her life with a fit of pique. But when they got to a safe place? Roman Chernichenko was going down. How dare he think it was okay to sleep with her after everything he'd done? If he needed a place to bed down, he could have shared Kadin's tent. It might have been a little crowded, but she was sure they'd done it before. They were super-soldiers, after all. Or something anyway.

She was no longer convinced Roman was even in the Army as he told his family. But his duplicity with them wasn't her problem. She had enough to deal with on her own.

She grabbed her clothes and yanked them on, determined to be anywhere but in that confined space with the man who had shattered her heart. When she exited the tent, Neil was waiting with a whole energy bar and some water. She ate her breakfast and then took care of her morning ablutions while the others broke down and packed away the tents.

It was still light out when they started walking this time. When they stopped that night, sometime after midnight, they had reached a small river, but she was not sure which one it was. Geography had never been her strong suit. If it wasn't on the traveling clinic's itinerary, there was little chance of her getting her bearings. And since all her itineraries had taken her north, this was completely unknown territory for her.

Roman and Kadin agreed on a campsite in a stand of trees near another outcropping of rock about a hundred yards from the river. The men spoke quietly, but they did speak. Tanya hoped that meant they'd made it out of the compound without anyone following them. They had MRE rations and Tanya ate hers without complaint.

"You used to bad food?" Neil asked her.

She shrugged. "You don't want to know some of the things I've eaten in my years in Africa. Offending the villagers when they open their homes and kitchens in hospitality isn't an option."

Neil grinned. "I can just imagine. I've eaten a few bugs in my time."

"Bugs are better than grub worms."

"Don't ruin my dinner," Kadin whined.

A small smile curved Tanya's lips. "Don't be a baby."

Kadin mock growled, while Neil said something scathing about his soldiering abilities. It was a well-earned light moment that ended, for her anyway, the moment she met Roman's eyes.

Her smile disappeared and she broke gazes with him immediately. Though not before she'd seen how taut his jaw went.

Was he irritated she and the others were joking around?

"Are you going to come back?" Kadin asked her.

Tanya had been asking herself that very question on their long walk. There wasn't much to do besides try to avoid falling, or tripping, rather. Roman was just as adept that night at keeping her from falling as he had been the night before. And she'd even said thank you once. Go her.

Not that she wanted to say anything else to him, but she wasn't the asshole.

The upshot, though, was that she'd had plenty of time to think. Too much time. Her mom would have called it brooding, and she might have been right. Tanya didn't care what she called it. All she knew was that the shock she'd felt the day before when she'd learned Roman had used her sexual trust in him as a weapon had worn off. What was left behind was the constant throb of pain in her heart and lots of questions she didn't have the answers for.

Why her? How could he? Who had used her as an information mule? What a terrible label, but then being one wasn't so great either. *Was she coming back to Africa?*

"Tanya?" Kadin prompted.

"Sorry, I spaced out there for a second."

"Are you?"

What? Oh, coming back to Africa. "I don't know."

Kadin nodded, like he understood and maybe he did. Something had led him from soldiering to joining whatever group Roman was with. Had he been disillusioned too?

"How did you end up here anyway?" Neil asked.

"I'm sure it was in my file."

"That you were in the Peace Corps, yeah. On a soil reclamation project, right?"

"Yes. It was important work. It still is, but I saw a greater need."

"For medical workers," Kadin said.

"That's right. There are medical schools in most

of Africa's countries, but the graduates often don't stick around to practice here. I've read that the most costly export to the U.S. for Nigeria is medical doctors. That there are actually more Nigerian doctors in the state of Illinois than in the country of Nigeria. It's crazy, right?"

The two men made noises of assent, but Roman remained quiet. If she didn't know better, she'd say he was brooding. Probably he was planning how best to use other people to accomplish his goals.

Right. She needed some sleep maybe.

"Fleur trained in Nigeria, didn't she?" Neil asked.

"She did, but she stuck around, trying to make a difference." In Africa, if not the country of Nigeria. But then Rwanda had been her homeland and that was the one place she had vowed never to return to.

Kadin finished his energy bar and tucked the wrapper into his pack. "She has made a difference and so have you."

"Maybe, but as much as I love Africa, as important as the work we're doing is, it might be time to go home." She'd known that someday she would return to the States, just not when. After the phone call from her mom and learning she'd been used to transport military secrets, she couldn't help feeling that maybe God or the universe, or her own subconscious was trying to tell her something. It was time to make a change.

"The fact you still see America as your home says a lot about what you are doing in Africa," Roman said, his tone strangely subdued.

Tanya shrugged, but she wanted to ask what he meant.

His lips twisted as if he knew she was biting back a question. "You came to help, not to make a life for yourself. There's a difference."

"Yes, there is." Not that Quinton had thought she could see that difference. He'd dumped her without even giving her the chance to try to make a life back home, to be part of that normal couple he was so certain he wanted.

She could admit now that a big part of the reason she'd returned to Africa had been because she'd needed a purpose, something to keep her going. She'd been hurting so much from Quinton's rejection, the EMT training and making plans to return had given her something to dull the pain. What would dull the pain of Roman's betrayal, of learning she had been nothing but a disposable pawn to be used by people bent on stealing and selling her country's secrets?

CHAPTER TWELVE

Beyond ready for some serious rest, Tanya stood up and went to where the sleep shelters had been pitched. She looked back at Roman. "Stay out of my tent."

"The closer I am to you, the safer I can keep you."

"I'll risk it."

"I won't."

"It's not your decision."

"It is."

"You're an autocrat."

"If you say so."

"If someone has to sleep with me, then it can be Kadin."

Kadin made a sound that could have been a hastily smothered laugh, though what he found amusing about this situation, Tanya couldn't begin to say. Neil whistled under his breath and then leaned back to watch, like it was a prize fight or something.

Tanya frowned at him. "What?"

"Nothing." The man did not do innocent well. "Just relaxing."

Kadin muttered something under his breath that sounded like, "Relaxing, my ass."

"Kadin, if you don't want to sleep in my tent, I understand." She hadn't considered he'd be opposed to the idea. It wasn't as if she was going to jump him.

The idea of sex with anyone but Roman felt like trying to run with her shoes on the wrong feet. The idea of sex *with* Roman carried a whole host of emotions she'd rather not dig into, since not all of them were negative.

And if that didn't make her a world-class idiot, she wasn't sure what would.

"If that's what you really want, it's no problem," Kadin said, giving Roman an indecipherable look.

"That is not going to happen." Roman's voice cracked like a whip in the air between them.

His reaction was a little over the top, in her opinion. That scowl probably scared terrorists, but she didn't care.

She wasn't about to let him intimidate her. "It's my tent, I say who goes in it."

"Actually, it's my tent."

"Then I'll sleep in the other one."

"No."

"Stop being so unreasonable."

"I'm not the one being unreasonable."

Oh, that so was not going to fly with her, not even if it had jumbo jet engines. She used one of the really coarse Ukrainian phrases she'd learned from Elle.

His scowl went nuclear.

She glared back. "Kadin is just as capable as you of protecting me in my sleep."

"No. He is not."

She shot a glance at Kadin, but the man did not seem offended by Roman's arrogance. If it weren't beyond the realm of probability, she would think he looked more than passing amused.

"I don't care if you are the top super-soldier here, I prefer to sleep with Kadin." As the words left her mouth, she realized how they sounded. She just didn't care.

They knew what she meant.

Both Neil and Kadin snickered anyway, but Roman looked ready to kill someone. Or at least how she thought a man would look just before doing grievous bodily harm. And the look wasn't directed at her.

She'd worry about his friends if she thought Roman had any intention of acting on his expression.

"It's my operation, I say who plays what role," he gritted out, delivering each word with deliberate emphasis.

"Like you assigned yourself the task of using sex to get information out of me?" Darn it. She did not want to get into this right now. Not in front of Neil and Kadin, but nothing could un-say the words. And part of her wanted the confrontation, no matter where they were or who was with them.

"National security takes precedence over hurt feelings."

"Is that in your super-soldier manual?" she derided.

"It's the truth."

"Your truth."

He shrugged, but he didn't look as if he was feeling even sort of casual about their conversation. That was the only thing stopping her from screaming at him.

"You could have just asked."

His expression said that had not been an option he had even considered. "I wasn't one-hundred percent convinced you were not part of the espionage."

She really hadn't believed he could hurt her more than he already had, but she'd been wrong. Knowing that when he'd had sex with her, he'd still been unsure about whether or not she was guilty was every bit as devastating as discovering he'd had sex with her to find out information in the first place.

"If our country's security is in the hands of men like you, I've got to worry, because your instincts suck." Going on the offensive felt a lot better than giving in to fresh pain.

Both Kadin and Neil made more stifled sounds of amusement, but Roman just glared at them.

He looked back at her, his expression an odd mix of things she didn't want to believe. "I made the mistake of putting personal feelings ahead of the assignment once. I lost my best friend and two other good agents. I'll never do that again."

"Bully for you." She hated, absolutely hated, that his words had elicited understanding and sympathy. "You're still not sleeping in my tent."

He surged to his feet and crossed the twenty feet between them before she even thought of reacting. He grabbed her arms, holding her in front of him. Though his grip wasn't near anything tight enough to hurt, she wasn't going anywhere.

"My team and I put our jobs on the line to keep you from getting killed. If I think it's necessary to share your tent to keep you safe, that's exactly what I'm going to do."

She stared up at him, his insistence making her feel safe instead of angrier. What did that make her? She'd already opted into the world-class idiot's club. What was left?

"I can't stand the thought of you touching me, even just to brush against me in sleep," she admitted, tugging against his hold.

He flinched, his jaw going tight. "I never hurt you in bed."

"But you *did* hurt me."

"You knew the sex couldn't lead to anything more."

Like that mattered. "I trusted you completely on an intimate level. You violated that trust." And she didn't know how to get past that reality.

He looked away. And it shocked her. She'd expected another comment along the theme of the ends justifying the means. "That was not my intention," he finally said.

A sound of disbelief escaped her. "How could it be anything else?"

"I wanted you. You wanted me." He shifted his head so their gazes met again. "Sex was inevitable."

"You think so?" Frustratingly, part of her had to agree with him.

"Yes."

"So, you decided to use it?" To use her.

"Yes."

"Damn you."

This time the flinch only registered in his eyes, but it was still there.

"You should have trusted me," she insisted. This all would have been so much better if he had trusted her, even a little.

"I don't trust anyone but my team."

"Not even your family?"

"I don't put myself in situations where that comes to the test."

She believed him. They all thought he was still an Army scientist after all. "You should tell them the truth."

"I'll take it under advisement." His tone and expression belied the words though.

His relationship with his family wasn't her problem, but she could not help feeling sorry for him. The Chernichenkos were really great people, but Roman's reticence about the truth of his life created an impenetrable, if invisible, wall between them.

She should be happy about that, but she was not the vindictive sort. It just wasn't in her nature.

"Everything I thought I could believe in is in jeopardy."

Suddenly, instead of holding her arms, he was holding her, tucking her up against him in an unexpected hug that felt way too comforting. "I know."

"You can't know. You don't trust people anyway."

"How do you think I got this way?" he asked dryly. "I know I betrayed your trust too, and asking you to believe in me again is asking a lot, but I know what I'm doing."

"I never said you didn't."

"You don't approve of my methods. In anything."

She felt an urge to say that wasn't true, because the almost defeated tone in his voice bothered her more than she wanted to admit. Only it was true. In her estimation, he'd screwed up and in doing so, he'd shredded her heart.

So, no, she wasn't going to tell him it was all okay, but she couldn't get rid of the desire to do so either.

He sighed against her hair. "I can keep you alive, but you need to let me do my job."

"I'm not stopping you."

"You're trying, but I'm going to do it my way."

"Your arrogance isn't really endearing right now."

"I didn't think you ever found it anything but annoying."

She shrugged. "Why can't Kadin be my night-time guard?" she asked.

The rigid lines of Roman's body answered without words. He'd used her sexual desire for him, but his for her had been real. Even now, with everything between them, he was at least semi-hard. She could feel his sex pressing against her stomach.

"That is not going to happen," he said again. Like that response was all he could come up with.

Maybe it was. Sexual possessiveness was probably new for him, especially toward someone he'd considered a possible spy.

"I haven't forgiven you."

"That doesn't matter."

She was sure that for him, that was true. For her? Not so much. She wanted to stop hurting and she knew forgiving him was a step she'd have to take in that direction, but it wasn't a step she could take right now.

He let her go and stepped back. "You might want to consider sleeping in the bag rather than on top of it, if you're going to strip down to your panties again."

She didn't bother to respond, just turned and dropped to her haunches to crawl inside the small tent.

Instead of the anger she should feel at losing the argument, she was just tired. As much hiking as she did for the traveling clinic, she had never put in the hours walking she had tonight and the night before.

Roman settled beside Tanya in the small tent, surprised to find her exactly as he had the night before. But then maybe he shouldn't be. She was probably delighted to ignore any instruction of his she could get away with.

He wished he could take her semi-clothed body as an invitation, but he doubted she would ever be offering one of those again. Acknowledgment of the loss sent an unexpected shard through what he almost believed was his heart. He still wanted her with a hunger that was both ever present and insatiable.

The prospect of never again burying himself inside her made his entire body clench with frustrated need.

That had definitely not been part of the plan.

With a sense of reality and fantasy converging, Fleur stared at the woman who was supposed to pretend to be Tanya. The agent had parachuted in somewhere over the savannah. She'd managed to sneak into the compound and then into Fleur and Tanya's chalet without security being the wiser.

Rachel Gannon looked so much like Tanya, Fleur wasn't sure they would have noticed if the agent had walked in through the front gate.

"From a distance, no one would know you are not Tanna. Anyone who does not know her well, would not guess even face-to-face, I think."

Rachel shrugged, exactly as Tanya would have done. "My training in theater comes in handy sometimes. The videos you have of her on your blog were very helpful. I studied them on the flight over."

"You're amazing."

"Thank you." Rachel smiled. "Coming from you, that is quite a compliment as you seem to know Tanya better than anyone else."

"She is my closest friend. I consider her the sister I lost."

Profound grief shadowed Rachel's eyes for a brief moment, then she was back to projecting Tanya-like warmth. "You're very lucky."

Fleur looked sideways at Ben and then back to Rachel. "I agree."

She had always vacillated between feeling blessed and cursed to have survived her family's deaths in the massacre, but she'd finally come down firmly on the blessed side. She had Johari. She had Tanya. She had Ben.

He had held her again as she slept the night before. His calm presence had settled her as nothing else could have after her best friend's disappearance into the African night.

He handed Rachel the cleaned and still functioning security chip. "I have installed a nice surprise for anyone who downloads what they think is the JCAT software. It's a virus that will destroy the hard drive of whatever system it is uploaded to, as well as any systems connected to it. They'll have to have a firewall as sophisticated as the one at TGP to detect it."

"Oh, good job." Rachel grinned. "I love surprise presents like that."

Fleur frowned. "I thought you were going to try to catch the spies in the act."

"There's no reason to let them know we're on to them here at the compound," Ben said. "Too much risk for collateral damage. We'll wait until they are on the isolated road between here and Harare before springing the jaws of the final trap."

"So, you're going to let them make the download? Isn't that risky? What if they realize Rachel isn't Tanya?"

"You said it yourself, only those who know her well would be able to tell the difference. And the only one in the compound who could easily get close enough to download the file is you." And he clearly did not suspect her.

"But what about the medical part of her job?"

Rachel shrugged that uncanny Tanya-like shrug again. "I'm trained in field medicine like all TGP operatives. I don't have her expertise, but I think I can keep up the pretense for as long as it takes to lure our perps into making their move. They've got to be getting desperate by now. She was scheduled to stop in Tikikima over two weeks ago. If they have buyers or an auction lined up, her deviation from her itinerary has to have them in a tizzy."

"Well, the home office certainly is in one," Fleur said.

Rachel agreed. "Yeah. My gut says it's someone in Sympa-Med, but I know Ben's been researching the doctor and supplier too."

Fleur turned to Ben. "You found out who the supplier is?"

"It was just a matter of hacking into financial records. It usually is. Follow the money. The payments for the chips led right to the supplier. It's a wholesale distributor, not the manufacturer. One thing I found interesting was that the invoices clearly state the chips have transceivers, not GPS. Now, not all people are technically savvy enough to make the distinction, but it's still worth noting."

"Yes, I'm sure you're right."

Rachel asked, "Did you get an e-mail from Alan?"

"I did. He's our top researcher and information gatherer," Ben said, making sure to include Fleur in the conversation. "He found a family connection between the supplier and a board member at Sympa-Med. Since that board member is not on this trip, we're not sure what to make of it."

"Which board member?" Fleur asked.

Ben named a man who had always struck Fleur as too self-centered to be on the board of an organization like Sympa-Med.

"If company gossip is accurate, he's dating the Director of African Operation's personal assistant," Fleur said.

Ben's face creased in a satisfied grin. "Now, that *is* interesting."

"You can never be sure of the accuracy of gossip," Fleur warned.

But both Ben and Rachel looked too happy to have heeded the warning.

"I'll ask Alan to look into it. He's got informants all over the world," Ben said.

"Is this board member married?" Rachel asked.

"Separated," Fleur supplied. With the exception of tonight, she never repeated gossip, but she kept abreast of it.

"Okay." Rachel nodded, as if she'd filed the information away, and then looked at Ben. "If you don't have anything else, I'll hit the sack. I want to get these contacts out—they're starting to irritate."

Only by looking closely could Fleur see the other woman wore a pair of contacts that enhanced the color of her eyes. "What is your natural eye color?" she asked with curiosity.

"They're a pale green. It's always been convenient for getting the best look with colored contacts."

"I don't think mine would take another color so easily," Fleur said in agreement. The brown of her eyes was so dark it looked black in certain lights.

"You'd be surprised what they can do with the right medium, but yeah, it's easier to get a natural-looking change with light irises." Rachel stifled a yawn. "Okay, enough talking. I'm off to bed."

Ben gave Fleur a questioning look after the other woman left the room. Knowing what his silence was asking, she nodded and led the way into her bedroom.

Once there, she stopped at the foot of the bed and turned to face him. "You treat me like you do not suspect me of involvement in the espionage."

"I don't."

"But you did," she guessed.

"Yes."

"Why?"

"You aren't American. Selling our secrets to provide future financial security for Johari might appear a rational choice to you."

"And you were okay with that?"

"Okay as in thought it was a good thing to do, or okay as in still wanted to bring you into my life?"

"Either?"

"I've spent my entire adult life protecting my country's security. Yet, before I realized you were innocent of any part of the espionage, my mind was as busy working out a way to change my life so you could be in it as it was trying to determine who was behind the technology thefts."

That amazed her. How could he give her equal weight with a patriotism so deeply ingrained in him? "Why?"

"Because my instincts tell me I will never react to another woman the way I do to you. The moment I saw you, something inside me settled. I had found the other half of my soul." He spoke as if making such claims was perfectly reasonable, though a shadow in his expression showed how important and different this conversation was for him.

"I thought love at first sight was for books and cheesy movies."

"It's clearly also for a federal agent who has spent big chunks of time pretending to be someone else in order to protect national security."

"You are not pretending to be anyone else with me."

"No, I'm not. I haven't since the moment we said hello."

"I know." She did. Just as she knew that for this man, to be willing to change his life so he could have her in it—especially if she'd been guilty of espionage against his country—was almost a miracle. "I did not believe I would ever meet a man like you. I did not believe a man like you existed."

"I'm glad you aren't part of this mess," he said.

"Me too. For your information, I would do almost anything to protect my daughter, but selling another country's secrets would never strike me as a reasonable way to ensure her future safety."

"That makes me very happy."

She laughed. "I think, Bennet Vincent, that life with you will be a very good one."

He went perfectly still, as if she had said something incredibly important. "So, you feel it too?"

"Yes." There was no use denying it. She didn't even want to, not really. As frightening as this might be, she wanted it.

"You don't think we are going too fast?"

"Does it matter? I would not retreat from you if I could."

"No, you're right. . . . This is not something either of us can control."

"So, we trust it. We trust each other."

"That is my deepest hope."

She knew what he meant. He wanted her trust, but he would never demand it or even ask for it. He would wait until she could give it to him of her own volition.

"Is a platonic marriage even possible?"

"For us, it will be." And he didn't even look bothered by the possibility, just confident that one day they would have it all.

"I want to try."

He didn't ask if she was sure. That was one of the things she loved about him. He trusted her to know her own mind and did not attempt to influence it.

"I know exactly where to target a body to maximize pain," he said in the same way he would have told her they were having *sadza* for dinner again.

"What does that mean? Is that supposed to inspire trust?" she wondered aloud.

"It means I also know how to touch your body and maximize the pleasure. More importantly, I know every touch that hurts and I will never inadvertently use one on you."

"I believe you." Maybe he really was her miracle. "I'm going to undress now."

"All right. I'll stay here."

How had he known that was exactly what she needed? Did it matter? This connection they had went beyond rational comprehension.

She pulled off her turban, revealing her closely cropped curls. Unlike her daughter, Fleur had no desire to spend her mornings fighting her hair into stylish submission. Her sari skirt came next and then her blouse, until all that remained was the serviceable bra and panties she wore beneath her clothes.

Taking a deep breath, she unhooked her bra and dropped it to the floor, and then pushed her panties down her thighs, leaving her completely naked.

That heated tenderness she found so appealing was very much evident in Ben's eyes as he looked at her.

"I have not been unclothed with another person since I left Rwanda," she admitted.

He nodded, his eyes never leaving her as he

slowly undressed, once again seeming to know exactly what she needed him to do next.

Ben was not a large man, being about the same height as she, one hundred and seventy-eight centimeters. Tanya always wanted to know feet and inches, so Fleur did an automatic translation to five-feet-nine inches. He might be a few centimeters taller, but not more than three. Which was tall for a woman, but not more than average for a man. However, he was not in any way effeminate. Each of his muscles was solidly defined, the small patch of hair on his chest only emphasizing the strength of his pectorals.

"I like that," he said.

"What?"

"The way you look at me."

"You drew me to you with your gentleness and your consideration, so different from other men who desire a woman, but I am happy to say I find your body very pleasing as well." She had not believed she would ever say such a thing to a man. She had been absolutely certain she would never feel the sexual arousal coursing through her right now.

"That's a good thing."

"Yes, I do think it is."

Fleur walked forward, feeling a type of feminine power she had thought lost to her. His eyes traveled over her, touching her with his controlled desire as if his hands had followed the path his eyes took.

She shuddered as unfamiliar but welcome feelings surged through her. "I want you," she said with wonder.

"You have me. For this. For everything you need or desire."

"For a life built on something besides loneliness?" she asked, not quite believing it could be possible.

"Especially for that."

She reached out and his hand met hers, the touch electric. She closed the distance between them, her breath catching as her hardened nipples brushed his chest.

He cupped her cheek with his other hand. "This right now, this is your first time making love."

"Oh, yes."

"Thank you."

She repeated the words to him, her voice barely above a whisper.

"I'm going to touch you now."

"Yes."

While his one hand held hers, anchoring her to the present, the other traveled down her neck, over her shoulder and down her arm. But instead of taking her other hand, he moved it to her waist, holding her with careful intimacy. "You feel so good, my sweet flower."

"I *am* yours."

"I know."

"This moment, it cannot be undone for me."

"Not for me either. Trust me, beautiful." The intensity glowing in his gaze told her he knew exactly what fears plagued her and he would meet and conquer them.

She smiled. "I can do nothing else."

"That's right." He caressed her side, and then slid his hand around to touch her back. "This is right."

For another woman, that would probably be an easy, casual touch, but for Fleur it was different, intimate, *amazing*. He caressed everywhere his hands could reach, bringing a wash of pleasure over her.

He hadn't been overstating the case when he said he knew how to bring the most pleasure possible to her body. He had not touched any of the accepted erogenous zones, but Fleur was already shaking with the need to go to the next level.

"Please," she whispered.

He nodded and then bent to lift her. They were close to the same height, but he had no problem carrying her to the bed. This reminder of his masculine strength filled her with delight rather than the fear she'd trained herself to expect at any show of physical power in a man.

But Ben was not other men and he would not hurt her. Not even a little.

He laid her on the bed and then lay down beside her, his body touching hers all along her side.

"So beautiful." He trailed a path from her collar bone to a just barely there caress over her breast and then down her stomach, dipping between her legs to tease the curls covering her most private flesh. The sight of his pale skin against her espresso darkness only added to the magical sensations surrounding this incredible moment. They were from different worlds, but were still complements for each other.

Was that not a miracle?

He played a soft tattoo with his fingertips on her inner thigh, humming something with it.

"What is that?"

He tipped his head up from where he'd been watching himself touch her. "What is what?"

"The music you were humming?"

He jolted as if he hadn't realized he'd been doing it and then he gave her an embarrassed smile. " 'Pretty Woman.' "

She laughed softly. "You really think I am beautiful."

"I do. So do others, but I am the only one who gets to act on it. Do you know how special that is?"

"Yes." She actually did.

His finger slipped between the slick flesh at her core and she gasped.

"Too much?" he asked, without moving his finger away.

"No. *More.*"

He smiled and went back to humming and touching. When she realized he was touching her in tempo with his humming, she laughed, but the sound broke on a gasp as one finger slid inside her.

Oh, my . . . that was so different from what she remembered. No pain. No sense of violation, only a true intimacy she could not help enjoying with this man.

"Is that good?" he asked.

"Oh, yes."

"And this?" He slid a second finger into her.

"It's tight," she gasped. "But good."

He nodded, as if that was exactly what he expected to hear. He caressed her like that for a long time, bringing her pleasure and helping her body adjust to the unfamiliar invasion.

A sensation unlike anything she had ever known began to build inside her. Tension pulled her muscles taut, but she didn't know what to do about that.

"Ben?"

He pressed his mouth to hers in a kiss that both gentled and claimed. Some of the tension drained, while a new sense of need spiraled inside her.

"Give me your pleasure, beautiful."

"What?"

"I want you to come before I penetrate you for the first time. It will relax you and you deserve all the pleasure I can give you."

She'd never had an orgasm. After the rapes, she'd shut off that part of herself. When she'd gotten old enough to have been willing to explore it, she'd allowed her ignorance of her own body to dissuade her.

Now, she wished she knew something other than the clinical location of her body parts she'd learned in medical school.

"I've never . . ." She could not admit the level of her ignorance out loud.

"I'll guide you through it. You can trust me."

She looked at him, English words too far away to grasp, and simply nodded.

A look of the most profound tenderness came over his features. "Thank you."

She was sure it should be she expressing gratitude for the amazing sensations he was causing in her body, but she was no more able to speak those words than any others.

He kissed her so softly, his lips a benediction on her, on the feelings he elicited in her, on this moment when she'd finally reclaimed a part of her femininity lost to her for fifteen years.

The gentle ministrations of his hand between her legs guided her body on a journey she had never undertaken. It was exhilarating. It was rawly beautiful. It was terrifying.

But all she had to do was open her eyes and see him and the fear receded to be replaced by anticipation. Ben would not take her to a place it would hurt to go.

He leaned forward, capturing her lips again, this time deepening the kiss as his tongue slipped easily inside her mouth. Their eyes remained open for the intimate kiss, the silent communication between them every bit as intense as that of their bodies.

And suddenly a cataclysm of pleasure washed over her, sending her body into rigid convulsions as he kissed the scream of ecstasy right from her lips.

The physical joy lasted forever and no time at all. He rubbed her lower belly as she relaxed back onto the bed in boneless trust.

He lifted his head, his smile filled with pure masculine satisfaction.

She smiled back. "Fantastic."

"Me or the orgasm?"

"Both."

He kissed her again, this time closing his eyes in happy bliss. She let hers slide shut too and enjoyed the communion of their mouths as he kissed with the attitude of a man who was in no hurry.

She could feel the hardness of his erection against her hip though. The heat and strength of it should be driving him to impatience, but he just kept kissing her until the sense that her body was not her own began to recede.

He seemed to know the moment it happened and broke the kiss. "Are you ready to join your body with mine?"

"Are you real? How can you be?" He knew exactly what she needed and how could any man be *that* intuitive?

He winked. "When you spend as many years as I have working undercover, you learn to read people. My motivation for assessing your reactions and feelings is stronger than it has been in any other situation I have faced."

"You don't mean that." He was Mr. Patriotic. He could not consider her feelings more important than his job.

"Oh, I do. One of those thoughts I had about building a life with you when I thought you might be a spy included my leaving TGP."

"You would have left your job for me?"

"Yes."

"But . . ." She broke off.

"We barely know each other? It's too soon? It doesn't make any sense?"

"Yes, all of that." And more.

"What can I say? I believe in the connection of souls, even if I've never known such a thing before. My soul *longs* for yours."

Her heart swelled. "You are going to make me cry."

"If that is what you need."

She shook her head decisively. "What I need is to be one with you in body as our souls have already joined."

She didn't care if it made sense or if someone else would understand. This thing between them went beyond the rational into the mystical and she was finished questioning it.

He came over her and it did not bring back any bad memories, but rather washed them clean as his body blanketed hers with pleasure-filled safety.

He paused with his hardness poised at the entrance to her body. "I stretched you with my fingers, but I'm going to go slow. If you feel—"

She pressed her fingers against his lips. "Shh . . . you will stop if I show any discomfort. Of this, I am most certain."

He nodded, kissing her fingers before sucking one into the heat of his mouth.

Oh, my . . . that felt . . . well, it felt simply lovely.

As he began to breach her body, she concentrated on the foreign feelings coursing through her. There was pleasure, yes, but a sense of profundity too. This moment between them, this first joining, would only happen once. Her body seemed to know it as a sense of anticipation held her thoughts and even her breath suspended.

Despite his efforts with his fingers, his hardness stretched her intimate flesh farther, but there was no sense he would not fit, rather that the fit was exactly perfect.

Once he was fully seated within her, he stopped and looked down at her, his expression filled with an emotion she was afraid to give name to.

He wasn't. "I love you, Fleur Andikan."

She repeated the words to him in Shona, the language of her childhood, the language of love to her, the words ripped from her throat. She could no more hold back this outpouring of emotion than she could rewrite her history.

And for the first time in her life, she did not mind that she could not. For her past had brought her to her present and it was a present worth living.

She would never forget her family, but perhaps now the pain of their loss would not be such an acute grief in her every waking moment.

"Can I move?" he asked.

"You know you can."

He smiled, that male satisfaction flashing in his eyes again. "I thought, but in this, I want to be absolutely sure."

"Be assured."

And he started to move, showing her that the pleasure had only begun. He swiveled his hips on each downward thrust, rubbing his pelvic bone against her most sensitive flesh. The now familiar tension started building inside her again until she was on the verge of another inner explosion.

"Together," he said.

She didn't know what he meant, but then the pleasure burst inside her as he ground down against her, groaning out his own satisfaction.

Heat filled her and she realized he had found the ultimate pleasure inside her body. The knowledge she had finally been able to give that pleasure made tears come to her eyes.

He smiled down at her. "It was inconceivably wonderful, wasn't it?"

She nodded, not even laughing at his superlatives. He kissed the tears from her cheeks before carefully pulling out of her and taking his spot at her side again.

"I didn't use a condom," he said, not sounding particularly worried.

"Johari would make a wonderful big sister."

He hugged her and kissed her temple. "You are so perfect for me."

"It is the same for me."

"Of course, it is. We're soul mates."

"Yes." She really believed they were.

* * *

"Tell me how your best friend died." They'd gotten up fairly early in the day and had been walking for two hours when Tanya decided she needed a break from the thoughts chasing each other in her head.

Kadin was in the lead, as he had been since they'd snuck out of the compound. About twenty yards ahead of her and Roman, he was not a candidate for talking to. Neil wasn't an option either. Once again, he was following, but she had no idea where he was as she hadn't seen him since they broke camp.

"I don't like to talk about it."

"I don't like knowing the sex we had was all about you checking me out for stolen technology. Sometimes, life sucks. Deal with it."

"It wasn't all about the JCAT." Oh, somebody was growly about that topic.

Good. Misery might not love company in her heart, but it didn't want to be flying completely solo either. "Right."

"Hell, Tanna, how could you think that after what we did?"

"How could I *not* considering what came after?"

He growled. Honest to goodness made a sound just like an angry wolf, or something.

She smiled. Getting under his skin felt good. Maybe misery *did* love company. "Your friend?"

"We were in the Rangers together," he said, as if making some big concession.

When he didn't add anything for several seconds, she prompted, "And?"

"And we were given a kill order."

"I guess you get a lot of those, huh?"

"More than most people realize, yes."

She'd been mocking; he wasn't. Oh. Wow. Not sure she wanted that confirmation. "Who were you supposed to kill?"

"A four-star general's daughter."

"My gosh, why? Was he being punished for not falling in with some despicable plot?"

Roman actually laughed at that, like she wanted him to, though the sound was dry and lacking real humor. "It wasn't some Hollywood movie."

"You were ordered to kill a child. That's pretty out there."

"K.B. was no child. She was suspected of exposing military secrets to Filipino terrorists."

Just like Tanya, except for the *Filipino* terrorist part. If she had to guess, she would say whatever intel she was supposed to have sold had gone to Middle Eastern terrorists. Though she had no idea if that were true.

Regardless, Tanya didn't like the tone of voice he used when he said the woman's name. Not at all. It was too . . . intimate. "K.B.?"

"Yes. She was beautiful, full of life, a real flirt and only a couple of years younger than me. She knew her way around men, but I didn't realize it at the time."

"You had sex with her."

"Yes."

"Wow, this situation is sounding more and more familiar." And less and less like something she really wanted to know.

"I didn't have sex with you until after I was told you were a spy," he said in a clipped tone.

Wholly derisive of his attempt to split hairs, she replied, "I see. That makes all the difference."

"It shouldn't have, but it did. I couldn't believe K.B. would do what they'd accused her of. Not on purpose. Not even by accident." For a moment he sounded lost and that bothered Tanya in a way that surprised her.

"So, you disobeyed the kill order?" she guessed.

"I told her about it." He went silent again.

This time, in shock, Tanya just waited to see if he would speak again. She could not reconcile the Roman she knew with a man who would reveal his orders to the enemy. Not even the enemy he was sleeping with.

Finally, after a few minutes of walking, he sighed. "I warned her about the operation, assuming she would go to her father and get the order rescinded."

That made a little more sense. "She didn't."

"She couldn't. She *was* guilty. She knew if she went to her father, he'd figure it out. He was a tough man, maybe too harsh, but his honor and country came first and she knew it."

Tanya could almost feel sorry for this K.B. person, but she sensed there was more to Roman's story than the woman going on the run because of what he'd revealed to her.

"He wouldn't have covered for treason and the treason she was guilty of would have gotten her the death penalty," Roman said, as if speaking to himself.

"What happened?" Tanya asked, reminding him she was there.

She was pretty sure she didn't want to know any longer, but they'd come too far along this conversational path for Roman to turn back.

"Her terrorist connections were there waiting

for us. One of them, the man she really loved, killed Teddy. Two other Rangers were killed as well before I managed to take him and the others out." He said it as if single-handedly doing all that was nothing.

"And her?"

"I used one of the terrorists' guns to make it look like she'd gotten caught in the crossfire."

It was harsh justice, not something Tanya could even imagine doing. But Roman was that man, the one who knew how to follow through on his duty, even when it tore him apart on the inside. No one would hear his screams; they were all in his soul. She wondered if he even heard them anymore.

"You were protecting her family."

"Yes. Her mom loved K.B. so much, and her little brother looked up to her like she was his hero. They deserved to keep their illusions."

Especially when their husband and father was the hard-assed general. "You weren't court-martialed?" Tanya didn't doubt for a minute he'd admitted to his mistake.

"The Atrati recruited me before proceedings could be started. I was due to re-up soon; my new boss arranged for me to be honorably discharged early."

"The Atrati?" she asked delicately, knowing for a certainty that this man did not let things slip anymore.

"Super-Soldiers-R-Us."

She smiled at his using her term to describe the group, but then grew serious again. "I'm sorry about Teddy."

"Me too." There was a wealth of pain in those two words.

"You tried to act with honor, you just chose the wrong person to protect." He knew that already. He had to know that.

"I vowed never to make the same error."

That made sense of a few things, even if it didn't make them hurt any less. "So, you were prepared to kill me."

Again silence fell and once again she was pretty sure this time she didn't want it broken.

"No," he said too firmly for her doubt, but in a subdued voice nonetheless.

"You were going to go against orders?" she prodded. "Again?" This she did have a hard time believing, no matter how sincere he sounded.

"My orders were to plug the leak. My team wasn't convinced you were the leak. Hell, neither was I, but emotional shit got in the way when I was determined not to let it."

"How can you say that when you didn't let your emotions guide your actions?"

"You're so sure I didn't? I wanted you to be innocent, so I ignored my gut when it told me you were."

"You still had no problem using me."

"I didn't see it the way you do."

"Right. You figured that since we were going to have sex anyway, why not use *the opportunity?*" Sheesh. The man could really be clueless, but she thought just maybe he had some reason to be. And maybe, just maybe . . . it wasn't as bad as she'd thought at first.

Oh, he'd used her all right, but he'd seen it more as using the situation. For a man like him, that distinction could be crucial. She still had this really strong desire to kick him in the kneecap though.

"I don't have recreational sex while doing a job."

Was that some kind of admission, a warning, what? "Then the sex was *not* inevitable."

"It was."

Okay, seriously. What was he trying to say? Because she was not getting it. Unfortunately, his body language said in no uncertain terms that the subject was closed, so she didn't bother to ask.

The sound of distant traffic carried across the still air. "How far are we from the road?" she asked, knowing sounds could be deceptive this far from major civilization.

"A couple of clicks. Our route is parallel to the road, but we're keeping to cover for obvious reasons."

There wasn't a lot of cover in the savannah, but Kadin had done a good job of leading them on a path that utilized what there was: bamboo, rocks, trees. She was just glad he didn't have them crawling on their bellies across the grassland.

They stopped in the late afternoon and she was so grateful for the respite from walking, she didn't ask why.

Kadin and Roman conferred quietly before Roman came to her. "Get down here, in the rocks."

She noticed they'd stopped near an outcropping about twice as tall as she was and about as wide. Some of the boulders were stacked haphazardly in front of the main outcropping, creating a sort of shallow recess. It was the only defensible position they'd seen for hours, she realized. She didn't ask what was going on. Roman's manner indicated that whatever was happening was serious. Deadly so, and she wasn't about to get in his way.

But she couldn't help wondering if they'd been followed from the compound. Only, why would the other kill team take so long to make a move? She didn't get much opportunity to think about it before Roman was in front of her, shoving her back against the huge rock behind her with his body.

"Don't speak," he warned.

She didn't, but she did try to look around him to figure out what he was protecting her from. A wild animal, maybe?

A second later, they were surrounded by several armed and disreputable-looking African men. Well, crap. *That* was not what she was expecting.

"Give her to us, and we will let you live," a tall, cruel-looking man in the center of the group said in Shona.

She didn't bother to translate.

"English," Roman barked.

"We want woman," the man answered, anger creasing his brow.

Roman didn't bother saying no. He flicked his wrist and a few seconds later the man who had spoken fell forward, a knife protruding from his chest. Two other men fell in the same way, telling her that both Kadin and Neil were there, protecting her too. Only they weren't standing in front of her like a human wall.

Roman raised the submachine gun he wore on a strap over his shoulder. "Drop your weapons," he ordered.

Wanting to avoid more bloodshed, she repeated the order in Shona in case the men did not understand. Three were already dead, or at least grievously wounded. Maybe the others would see the futility of going up against men like the Atrati.

At least one decided he'd rather take his chances.

Gunfire sounded and rock chips started flying with the bullets. Roman returned fire, his body a living barrier between her and the bullets spitting out of the African men's guns.

A few seconds later, the gunfire stopped. Men littered the ground around them. Tanya scooted past Roman, intending to give first aid where she could.

He grabbed her arm. "Don't bother. We don't shoot to wound."

Sure enough, none of the bodies on the ground were moving, not even to breathe.

She turned away from the sight only to be caught by a new one. Blood on Roman's fatigues.

"You've been hit," she exclaimed.

"It will have to wait." He turned to Neil. "Was this all of them?"

"They left a guard back with the truck."

"You take care of him?"

"Naturally."

"Who were these men?" she asked, with a sick feeling she knew.

"Slavers. Their truck has seven young boys incarcerated in the back," Neil replied, sounding disgusted.

"You didn't let them go?" she demanded.

"I thought you'd want to look at them and make sure they're okay." He looked at Roman. "Thought we could return them to their villages before we take the truck south again."

"You don't think they'll make it on their own?"

"They're kids, Geronimo."

Tanya felt bile rise, but refused to give in to the nausea. "The slavers probably intended to sell them as farm workers in South Africa." Or worse.

"Shit," Kadin said. "Kids are not commodities."

"So, what do we do, chief?" Neil asked.

"We get the truck and haul ass out of here. The gunfire could have drawn attention and that's one thing we can't afford." Even as he spoke, he was leading her at a rapid pace toward the sound of traffic and the road.

"Is that why you killed the leader with your knife?" she asked.

"Yes."

He'd been willing to avoid further deaths too, but the slavers had not allowed it.

They reached the truck faster than she expected. The slavers had driven it off the road and tucked it behind a large stand of trees. She ignored their fallen comrade to jump into the back and get her first look at the boys who had been kidnapped, some perhaps even sold from their villages.

"You are safe now. These men will not hurt you. Please do not run. We will help you return to your families," she said in Shona as she began to untie the ropes that bound their hands and linked the children together so they could not escape.

They stared at her and then one asked, "Do you have any food?"

Tears sprang to her eyes. These children had been starved to the point that their first thought was for food rather than getting home. "Yes, we'll feed you. And we'll take you home too," she promised again.

A couple of the boys brightened at this, but the others continued to watch her warily.

Roman joined her in the back. "Status?"

She figured that meant he wanted to know what had been said, so she told him.

"Spazz, we need food for the kids. I don't think their systems are going to like the energy bars."

"They might do okay with the MREs," she suggested.

"That'll do for now, but we're going to have to stock up."

Water and MREs were passed around even as the truck started moving. One intrepid boy, who looked like he couldn't be more than eight, asked, "Where are we going, lady?"

"We're getting away from the slavers," she told them, not bothering to mention the men were dead.

This made sense to the children, though it was clear they were reserving judgment. She asked each one what village he had come from. As she suspected, five of them had been stolen. But two had been sold: the little guy who'd asked her where they were going and an older boy whose eyes were dull with hopelessness.

"My family is all gone," the older boy said. "My village did not want me. I am bad luck family now."

Tanya reached out and touched his arm. "You're not bad luck. What is your name?"

"Mbari." His gaze lifted to meet hers. "My uncle, he went to the city and never came back. Maybe our family is bad luck like the medium say."

"No," she said firmly.

"Can you speak English?" Roman asked the boy, clearly wanting to participate in the conversation.

The boy nodded, his fear of Roman palpable.

"His name is Mbari," Tanya said.

Roman nodded. "Good to meet you, Mbari. I'm glad you speak English. Then you will understand when I promise I will not let you be hurt."

The boy jolted as if shocked. "You not mean it."

"I do." Roman sighed, as if accepting a burden no one else could see, and looked at Tanya. "We'll start with the nearest boy's village."

"Sounds good, but right now, I'm cleaning that wound." She pulled her utility tool from her pack and used the scissors to cut his sleeve off. She let out a heavy breath of relief. "It looks like you got hit by a flying rock, not one of the bullets."

"That's good?" he asked in an amusement-tinged voice.

"Rocks are cleaner than bullets." Especially here where ammunition could be stored anywhere and exposed to pretty much anything.

"Good to know."

It didn't take long to remove the bits of debris and cleanse the wounded area before bandaging his arm. "Neil and Kadin are okay?" she asked, feeling bad for not checking herself.

"Not a scratch."

"That's a relief."

He looked down at her, his mind clearly not on his friends' lack of wounds.

She ducked her head. "Where are we going to get something besides MREs to feed the boys?"

"We'll buy some food from the village we're headed to now."

She nodded. She should have thought of that. "You stood in front of me, when they were shooting."

"They didn't want to kill you. They wanted to kidnap you."

"So, then you should have crouched down to minimize the target you made."

He didn't even deign to respond to that and his expression said he didn't think her observation worth a reply.

For some strange reason, that made her smile.

CHAPTER THIRTEEN

Tanya's smile was still playing over in Roman's mind as the truck slowed to a stop alongside the road an hour later.

Neil hopped out, came around to where Roman leaned against the side of the bed and handed the sat-phone to him. "Call from Face."

Roman took the phone. "Report."

"The Sympa-Med people showed up today. So did that pissant government guy who met us in Harare."

"What is he doing there?"

"Ibeamaka said he came in response to our Marine private getting shot. Thing is, we didn't report the incident to official Zimbabwe channels."

So, either Ibeamaka had something to do with the attempt on Ben's life, or he had an informant in the compound.

"Did the wounded private and his buddy make it out of the compound okay?"

"Yep, two more were sent to replace them too."

"Are they a kill team?"

"Nah, these babies are greener than my grandma's

backyard in the spring. They're not MARSOC, but they're good soldiers."

"I don't want them becoming collateral damage."

"No way, Geronimo. I know my job."

"You do. So, the government stiff, did he try to see Tanya?"

"He tried, but she's taking a sick day in her room," Drew replied, speaking of Rachel, who was masquerading as the medical relief worker.

"That works."

"She's a ringer for our girl," Drew said with admiration.

"Good. This plan might work after all."

"That's the hope, chief."

"What about the Sympa-Med suits? They showing any particular interest in seeing Tanya?"

"Hard to say if it's particular. The director has got a bug up his ass to talk to every single employee in the compound. He didn't show any particular annoyance that he had to start with security staff."

"You listening in on these interviews?"

"You know it. Spazz left me some fun toys to play with while you are all out there on safari."

Roman looked around the dusty bed of the beat-up truck, filled with young boys rescued from slavery. "Some safari."

"I sense sarcasm in your voice, chief."

"I'll tell you about it Stateside."

"Roger that. I'll hold you to it too."

Roman would expect nothing less. "How is Dr. Andikan holding up?"

"She's doing real fine, yep, real fine indeed."

"What the hell?"

"She's practically glowing."

"Her and Ben?" Roman asked, not able to wrap his mind around the idea of the Tutsi woman glowing.

"Looks that way. He's got his own glow on, though it's harder to tell with that guy. He's the shit, you know?"

"TGP hired my sister; of course, they get the best."

Face laughed.

"Keep me informed."

"Roger that."

Roman disconnected the call.

"How's Fleur doing?" Tanya asked immediately.

"According to Face, she's glowing."

Tanya's expression softened. "She and Ben got together."

"You think that's a good thing?"

"Absolutely."

"What happens when he goes home?"

"She'll go with him."

For a brief moment, Roman found himself completely speechless. "She told you she planned to leave Africa?"

"Yes."

"And you think Ben will want her to follow him?"

"I think if she didn't, Ben would leave his job and relocate to Zimbabwe."

"No way."

"You can't look at everyone else's situations through your own cynical gaze."

"I'm not cynical."

"Whatever you say." But her tone said she thought otherwise.

"Even if he wants her to follow, do you really

think she'll be happy in a long-term relationship with an agent?" Could any woman?

"I think she'll be deliriously happy married to Bennet Vincent."

"You've got a romantic streak, don't you?"

He couldn't be sure, but he thought she was blushing under the remaining black face paint. "Maybe."

Oh, it was more than a maybe. This woman had a romantic streak as wide as a sumo wrestler's waistline. Roman wished he'd realized that before they'd had sex. He'd taken her acknowledgment of the temporary nature of their liaison at face value, and she'd ended up hurt because of it.

He didn't like that at all.

The worst part was knowing that he could not be absolutely certain he would have avoided the sex, even if he'd been aware of her romantic bent.

They reached the first kidnapped boy's village near nightfall. The villagers congregated around the truck and Tanya explained in Shona what they were doing there.

The sleepy boy was pulled from the back of the truck right into his weeping mother's arms. Other family members crowded around, rejoicing in the child's return.

An impromptu celebration was soon underway, traditional dancing breaking out around a village bonfire while all the children were plied with food and questions.

Roman bought extra supplies of water and food from the villagers, who were thrilled to sell their goods without having to transport them to the nearest market.

The boys were given beds in several huts, but Roman insisted on his team staying in the bed of the truck, each of the men taking turns at watch throughout the night.

Tanya didn't argue when Roman put her sleeping bag between his and Neil's. Kadin was taking first watch.

She slept surprisingly well, considering the circumstances. They woke to a meal of pumpkin *sadza* and chicken prepared by the lost boy's family.

After another round of gratitude, they gathered up the other children and were on their way. Neil drove the truck, while Kadin kept watch in the front. Tanya rode in the back with the children again because she spoke Shona and she hoped that would make them feel more comfortable. The boys were more hopeful today, having seen their fellow almost-slave returned to his family.

They managed to get three of the remaining boys back to their villages that day, two of them coming from the same place and another not far away.

That night followed the previous one's pattern, though it was clear to Tanya that Roman would prefer not to be spending another overnight in a village.

"Why are we staying here?" she asked him, as she settled into her sleeping bag beside him. Neil had opted to sleep on the truck's front seat that night. He said he'd seen some of the men eyeing the truck thoughtfully. He didn't want to leave the cab unprotected.

"The boys deserve to sleep in homes, even if

they aren't *their* homes." Roman lay on top of his bag as he had the night before.

It was probably so he could react to a threat faster, super-soldier that he was.

"What are we going to do about the boys whose villages sold them?"

"I don't know."

"We can't take them back to their villages. They'll just get sold again."

"Agreed."

"So, what—"

Roman laid his hand over her mouth. "I don't know. I'm thinking on it."

"Oh," she breathed against his hand.

His eyes closed, as if he was in pain, and then opened again, dark with unmistakable desire. "I want to kiss you."

"No." But she didn't mean it. She wanted his kisses. She just didn't want the pain that came afterward.

"You say no, but your lips part as if waiting for my claim."

"Please, Roman."

"Please what?" He leaned forward, his lips only millimeters from hers. "Please kiss you?"

She couldn't deny him again, but she couldn't give him verbal permission either. She didn't move away though and that was probably what cinched it for him. He completed the connection, his mouth claiming hers just as he'd suggested she wanted him to. And it felt wonderful.

She let her sense of the present melt away, getting lost in the kiss and refusing to be bothered by that fact.

His hand cupped her neck and he deepened the kiss, sweeping her mouth with his tongue.

The sound of a child's laugh from nearby had them breaking apart.

He sighed heavily. "I wish we were in our tent."

She agreed, but managed to stop herself from saying so out loud. She took several restoring breaths before saying, "That would only lead to more temptation."

"It would lead to me buried as deep in you as it is possible to go."

"No."

"Tanna."

"No, Roman. Just, no."

He didn't get mad; he just put one arm over her middle and tugged her into his body, sleeping bag and all. And once again, she fell asleep feeling safe and protected.

They had dropped the last kidnapped boy off at his village by noon the next day. Like the others, the people of this village had offered them a meal and much appreciation. Roman graciously accepted both through Tanya's interpretation, but he insisted on being on the road again by mid-afternoon.

The two boys left looked at Roman and Tanya as they climbed back into the bed of the truck.

"What happens to us?" the smallest one, Amadi, asked.

Tanya didn't have to repeat the question for Roman because Amadi had used English.

"What do you want?" Roman asked.

"I no want to go my village," the older boy said. The hopelessness so prevalent in Mbari since the

beginning abated some when he was with Roman.
He was doing his best to emulate the adult male,
but he was still so very sad, it broke Tanya's heart
just to look at him.

"I no too," the littler one affirmed.

"Do you have family somewhere else you want to
find?"

"My sister, she marry and go to other village."
Amadi grinned. "Her husband important man,
give many cows for her."

"How did you end up sold?" Tanya asked.

"My mama, she die. My auntie say it from the
black plague," he said, meaning the AIDS epidemic. "My auntie no want me in her hut. She say
I make her baby sick, but I no sick. My mama, she
get the sweat sickness, no the black plague."

Tanya didn't ask if the sister would accept the
boy into her home. The least they could do was
find out. "What village is your sister living in now?"

The boy said the name of a fairly prosperous village, not far from where they were. In Zimbabwe,
prosperity was a relative term, but she knew this
village had its own marketplace and government
office.

"Let's take you to your sister," Roman said, echo-
ing Tanya's thoughts.

Ben rubbed the back of his neck, forcing himself to focus on the sound feed for the interviews
between the Sympa-Med director and compound
workers. Drew had brought the receiver for the listening device he'd left in the dining hall, where
the interviews were taking place, to Fleur's chalet.
He'd wanted Ben's input on the overheard discus-

sions, and this way they could both be on hand if Rachel's role as Tanya put her into serious danger.

All Ben could think about, though, was the fact that with Drew there, Ben wasn't strictly needed in the hut.

He itched to be with Fleur. He'd never been this distracted on a job, but he hated the thought of her working in the clinic with Sympa-Med person-nel who could well be in on the espionage.

Her pointing out that if she was, she had been for some time and was none the worse for it, did nothing to alleviate his desire to watch over her.

The director's questions took the same tack they had in his previous interviews and, despite his preoccupation, Ben found himself looking at Drew to see if the other man had noticed.

"Is it just me, or does it sound to you like the di-rector has figured out something hinky is going on over here and he's trying to determine who is in-volved?" Drew asked with a thoughtful frown.

Ben nodded. "I was just thinking the same thing."

"That could get dicey."

"For him, definitely."

"I think we need one of your Marine privates as-signed to watch over him."

"They aren't my Marines."

"They think they're here to protect a State De-partment bureaucrat, and that would be you."

"I told them both to take the day off because I wasn't leaving the compound. They think I'm working on my report here because of the thing I've got going with Fleur." He'd also asked them to keep his location private, ostensibly to keep gossip down. If it looked as if someone was here with

Rachel, chances were high no one would approach her for the download.

"Does Fleur know she's your cover?"

"Yes, but she also knows she's a hell of a lot more than that." Fleur was rapidly becoming his everything.

"Good for you. Congratulations," Drew said, sounding sincere.

Ben found himself giving a rare genuine smile. "Thanks. She's pretty wonderful."

"I've got nothing but respect for her, that's the truth," Drew said.

It didn't surprise Ben. He'd gotten to know the pseudo-soldier pretty well since he'd been part of Ben's active protection detail from the beginning. Drew wasn't a career soldier, he was a career patriot, and Ben admired the attitude as much as he identified with it.

But Drew was also someone who believed in giving his all to making the world a better place. He admired all the Sympa-Med employees. Except whoever was involved with the espionage, Ben was sure.

His thoughts returned to Fleur. "She's strong and so beautiful."

"That she is," Drew said, giving Ben a wink.

The other man's blatant admiration had annoyed Ben at one time, but now he just found it amusing because Drew so clearly had no intention of acting on it.

"I'm going to check on her on my way back from asking the Marines to hang out around the dining hall until the director is done with his interviews for the day."

"How are you going to explain it to them?" Drew asked.

"I'm going to tell them I overheard something that has me concerned."

"Nice misdirection without lying."

"I do try."

"I bet you do. Not many men could give me a run for my money, but I have a feeling you're one."

"I can guarantee it." Ben had honed his skills at manipulation and covert work at an agency that required damn near perfection from its operatives.

He was careful to keep his trip from Fleur's to his quarters covert. When he got there, the Marine privates were playing a game of gin rummy and only too happy to be given an assignment. They moved their game to the dining hall and Ben walked openly from his quarters to the medical hut. Fleur was between patients, so he followed her back to her office for a moment of alone time.

He felt that it had been days rather than hours since he'd seen her last. This was love as others had described it, but Ben had never experienced the heady emotion himself. It was distracting, but he enjoyed it. Quite a bit actually.

"Anything suspicious?" he asked as he closed the door behind him.

She shook her head with a smile. "Are you always going to be this protective?"

"Yes."

"I think I like it."

That was really good, because he didn't think he could change. "So, nothing out of the ordinary?"

"No. Several people have asked after Tanya's

health, including Mabu and two members of his security force, but that's to be expected. She's well liked in the compound. The interns miss her a great deal. I'm not as understanding of training mistakes." Fleur's beautiful full lips twisted in a self-deprecating grimace.

"Rough morning?"

"I miss Tanya."

"I bet."

"Have you heard from the soldiers that took her?"

Ben tugged Fleur into his arms. "They didn't kidnap her, sweetheart. They helped her get out of the compound before she got killed."

"I know." Fleur's generous lower lip protruded adorably.

He touched it with his forefinger. "Is that a pout?"

Her eyes widened and her mouth dropped slack in shock. "I *was* pouting."

"Yes."

"I don't do that."

"You must have learned from Johari."

"Tanya had to teach *her*. Tanya said all children should have that expression in their arsenal."

He could imagine that when Johari had come to live with Fleur, she had reacted as a child who had survived trauma, not as one confident of a parent's protection and love. "Tanya helped Johari remember how to be a kid again."

"Yes, though my daughter is not a baby goat."

He just grinned, taking Fleur's criticism in stride. "She's a pistol. Do you think she will like America?"

"She's very excited at the prospect of going and

building a new life with you." At Fleur's insistence, they had spoken to Johari about the upcoming move, and having Rachel in their home and why she was there. Fleur said her daughter had survived war, and she deserved to know of the danger, regardless of how intent Ben and the others were on minimizing it. "My daughter will adjust faster than I will, I fear."

"I don't know, I have plans to help you adjust." He ran his hands down her back and leaned forward to take her lips in a gentle kiss.

When they separated, she smiled. "I like your plans, I think."

"Good."

"I need to get back to work. The interns left without supervision will probably end up blowing up the clinic."

He laughed. "Bad as all that, hmmm?"

"Yes. And that odious Ibeamaka has threatened to return today."

"I'll listen for his jeep. When he arrives, I'll make sure you don't have to be alone with him."

"I can handle the unctuous toad."

"No doubt, but I'll still be here."

"Thank you."

He just shook his head. As if she needed to thank him for doing what came naturally. "We think the director has suspicions about the situation over here. His interviews are straying from the typical, experiential surveys into waters that might get hot for him."

Fleur's expression became concerned in a heartbeat. "Will he be all right?"

"I've got my Marine guard watching over him."

"Oh, good." She frowned. "He's a good man

who has dedicated his life to making a difference
to indigent people. He should not be hurt for trying to protect Sympa-Med."

"You think that's what he's doing?"

"What else?"

"Indeed. It might be a good idea to try to find
out what raised his suspicions."

"Maybe I can talk to him, implying I have my
own."

"Good idea. If you could do it in the dining hall,
we can listen in and I'll know the privates will be
watching over you."

"You really are protective."

"Yes."

"I am not used to it."

"But you like it," he reminded her.

She smiled with feminine indulgence. "I do."

He didn't even mind the indulgent attitude. He
was so gone on this woman.

Roman was surprised by the difference between
this village and the others they had visited in the
last two days. The signs of moderate prosperity
could be seen from the bigger herds of cattle in
the fields, to the newer-looking materials used on
the huts.

There also wasn't as much interest in the bat-
tered truck's arrival. They stopped in front of a
small marketplace and Tanya went to get out, but
Roman shook his head. With a marketplace came
visitors, but the venue was too small for them to
blend in. Especially Tanya. He didn't want her exposed more than was necessary here.

"I was going to ask for directions to Amadi's sister's house," she said.

"Amadi and I will do it. I want you to stay back here." He handed her his bandana. "Cover your hair with this."

Her face was still streaked with the black grease-paint they used for night camouflage. With the bandana, it would take a family member to recognize the medical relief worker known in the Sympa-Med compound.

She stared at the bandana as if it was a snake, poised to strike.

"I remember too," he gritted out. "Apparently my memories are better ones."

She shook her head.

"Would you prefer I get Kadin's?" he asked, his own mood going south.

That had her meeting his gaze instead of staring at the bandana. "You would do that?"

"Yes." He wouldn't like it. Letting Kadin provide for her didn't sit right with Roman, but if that was what she wanted, he'd do it.

"I never let anyone do that to me before."

He nodded. He'd figured that.

"Was it just part of the . . ." She let her voice trail off.

But it didn't matter. He knew what she meant. "No."

"Give it to me." She put her hand out.

He handed her the bandana and watched while she tied it around her head, tucking all the loose strands of her hair under the fabric.

He did not know why, but he felt that he'd won a powerful battle with her distrust. Maybe he didn't deserve her faith in him, but that didn't mean he wasn't hoping for it.

A vegetable seller at the market gave him directions to Amadi's sister. Her new family lived on the outskirts of the village, so they went back to the truck and drove the boy to his sister's home.

To say she was thrilled to see her younger sibling was an understatement. She grabbed the small boy to her and hugged him fiercely, talking a mile a minute to him in Shona.

"She's telling him she went to the village to get him after learning of their mother's death. Their aunt told her that he had been sent to work on one of the large farms, but wouldn't tell her where. She was scared to death he'd been sold as a slave." Tanya smiled with satisfaction. "She's furious that that is exactly what happened. Her husband has already offered to send Amadi to one of the mission schools and accept him into their home as another son."

"That's pretty generous."

"That little boy deserves it."

Both the boy and his sister were grinning ear-to-ear as she offered to share the evening meal with them in halting English.

"I am sorry, but we must be on our way," Roman said, his hand settling on the shoulder of the remaining boy.

The quiet child looked up at him with uncertainty. Roman knew Mbari wanted to know what would happen to him, but Roman still didn't have an answer. At least not one that didn't seem crazy-nuts.

The boy stepped forward. "My name is Mbari. Is

your husband, or anyone else in the village looking for a boy to work?"

The woman's face creased with sadness as she
immediately realized this boy had no family to return to, but she shook her head. "Maybe these
men can take you to the city where work is more
plentiful."

This village might be doing better than others,
but in a country where the majority of the adult
male population was out of work, a boy had little
chance of finding employment.

Mbari's shoulders drooped, but he nodded po-
litely. "I will ask."

Roman wasn't about to leave a child alone in a
city to fend for himself, but he didn't say that. He
just settled his hand back on the boy's shoulder
and stepped closer to him.

Tanya gave him a warm look, and it was so different from the way she'd been looking at him
since finding out about the information on her security chip, he almost staggered at the impact of it.

"Let's go," he said to Mbari.

When they got back outside to the truck and
Kadin and Neil, who had stayed with it, his fellow
Atrati operatives gave identical looks of compas-
sion to the single boy left.

Kadin stepped forward. "You want to ride up
front with us?" he asked Mbari.

The boy looked up at Roman. "You go too?"

Ah, shit. The future was starting to look inevitable. "I'll drive. Kadin, you and Neil ride in the
back."

Both men nodded, but Tanya frowned. "You
shouldn't be driving with your arm."

"Ah, does your boo-boo hurt?" Neil mocked before Roman could answer.

Roman ignored him and said to Tanya, "It's not a problem. I can barely tell it's there now."

Which wasn't exactly true, but the last time he'd let such a superficial wound slow him down, he'd had training wheels on his bike.

"But I can ride in back and someone else can drive," she tried again.

He just shook his head and went to climb into the truck. He stopped with the driver's door open. "You coming?" he asked Mbari.

The boy double-timed it to the cab and climbed up, taking the middle seat with a grin that Roman knew was going to be his downfall. No way could he stand the idea of that glow of happiness turning into fear and disappointment.

"You ever wanted to go to America, kid?" he asked as he started the truck's engine.

When he didn't receive an answer, he turned his head to look down at the child. Mbari was staring at Roman as if terrified to hope. And that cinched it. Roman let his future settle over him.

This was going to change things, a lot of things, but the boy needed family and Roman had a boatload to share with him. "My *baba* is going to eat you up with a spoon."

"She a cannibal?" the boy asked with undisguised horror.

Roman didn't laugh. He just ruffled Mbari's closely shorn curls, or rather rubbed his palm over them since ruffling didn't really happen with that tight nap. "Nope. It's an American saying. It means she's going to like you."

"Who is your *baba*?"

"My grandmother."

"She still lives?" the boy asked in disbelief. In a country where the average life expectancy was forty-two years, his reaction wasn't surprising.

"You bet. And she's gotten real loud about us giving her some great-grandkids."

Mbari considered this for several moments and then asked with a trepidatious hope that squeezed Roman's heart, "You want to make Mbari *your* child?"

"I think it was meant to be, kid, but if you want something else, you just say. I'll make sure you find a family here if you'd rather stay in Zimbabwe."

"I do not want to be a slave." The terror the boy experienced at the thought was written all over him.

"We agree on that, kiddo."

The child looked sideways at Tanya. "You my mother then?"

She shook her head, suspicious moisture making her eyes glisten.

"She's a friend, not my wife," Roman explained.

Mbari gave him a strange look and then turned back to Tanya. "Maybe you wash the black stuff off your face, show you pretty. He might pay many cows for you."

She choked out a laugh. "In America, wives are not bought with cows."

"What buy them then?"

Tanya was silent for several beats before saying, "Love."

Mbari shook his head as if he could not believe such naïveté.

CHAPTER FOURTEEN

Fleur gave final instructions for the day to the interns before going to find the director. When she entered the dining hall, there were a couple of Sympa-Med employees in one corner, playing a game of *mancala*.

Though, if they were there for any reason other than to listen in on the director's discussion with their fellow workers, she would rebraid Johari's entire mass of curls every morning for a month. The Marine privates were at a table a little closer to the director, playing a card game and snacking on a plate of flat bread.

The director was alone, so Fleur approached him. "How has your day gone, sir?"

The man rubbed his eyes with his thumb and forefinger, his gray head shaking. "Tiring, Dr. Andikan, very tiring."

She respected the fact he had come to find answers, but she doubted he'd had much luck. "I'm sorry to hear that."

"Has the schedule for the interviews changed?"

he asked. "I thought I was doing medical staff to-morrow."

"Nothing has changed, but there was something I wanted to discuss with you."

The director's eyes narrowed. "What is that?"

"It's a delicate matter."

If anything, the man's expression sharpened. "Is this personal?"

"In fact, I do have something personal to discuss, but the issue I wanted to raise is related more to Sympa-Med, or rather someone who works with the organization."

"Who?"

"I don't know."

"That sounds mysterious."

Fleur sighed and leaned forward. "It is. A mystery, I mean."

"What is that?"

"You heard about the almost strip search of Tanya Ruston, I assume."

"I did."

"I found the circumstances"—she paused for effect—"questionable."

"In what way?"

"The security guard argued against the search, but made no move to actually stop it."

"You would expect something different?"

"In fact, I would. Roman Chernichenko made a call on his sat-phone, but our vehicles are all equipped with shortwave radios. The driver could have reported the incident in progress, but he didn't."

"Perhaps he feared for his own safety."

"Perhaps."

"I have always found you to be an eminently

practical woman, Dr. Andikan. I assume there is more to your concern than this incident."

"Yes, in fact. When Miss Ruston returned from her last traveling clinic, she had to miss the final stop."

"I am aware."

"Yes, of course, but your insistence that she make the trip to Tikikima surprised me somewhat."

"My *insistence*?" he asked.

"The e-mails came from your office."

"And these e-mails, they demanded Miss Ruston return to Tikikima before the next circuit of the traveling clinic?" he asked.

"Yes, sir."

"I see."

"You didn't instruct that they be sent?"

"No. I did not."

Well, there was confirmation that his assistant was part of the espionage. "Miss Ruston has always found the inclusion of that village inefficient, considering it is near a stationary clinic."

"It is? That information was not included in the data used to determine this compound's traveling clinic itinerary."

"That is disturbing, if you do not mind my saying so, director."

"I agree." He sighed, as if not just tired, but exhausted. "I noticed that some of our medical workers have been given transceivers rather than GPS locator chips."

"You found that significant?"

"I did. The chips were almost twice the cost of the ones we used for the other medical workers."

"So, these chips aren't just being used in workers from this compound?" That meant this espionage ring was bigger than she was sure Ben was expecting.

Then again, maybe not. Her secret agent man was brilliant at his job.

"No."

"Why did you begin your investigation here? That is what you are doing with these interviews, isn't it?"

"It is. I had hoped to identify outside influences manipulating the situation, or, in the best case scenario, to be wrong about the significance of the different chips. I had hoped it was simply a matter of one of our board of directors trying to engage in a little nepotism."

"But you have ruled out that possibility?"

"I hadn't entirely when I came, but I have now."

"Because of what has been going on with Tanya."

"That and the inordinate interest one of the members of the board has shown in the itineraries of our traveling clinics."

She named the board member she had heard was having an affair with the director's personal assistant.

"Yes. How did you know?"

"It's a matter of logic. If you didn't send those e-mails demanding Miss Ruston go to Tikikima, then your PA did. She's rumored to be in a liaison with that board member."

"He's a married man."

Fleur shrugged.

The director shook his head. "I am a Frenchman, but that does not mean I approve of infidelity. And there is a definite conflict of interest in having office staff involved with a board member."

"I notice she's not participating in your interviews."

"I sent her and George to Harare with Mr. Ibeamaka to glad-hand the local government officials," he said, naming the other man who had traveled in their party.

"No wonder Ibeamaka has not returned as he threatened."

"I take it you are not fond of him."

"He's a supercilious toad who thinks I would make an ideal traditional wife."

The director laughed with true amusement and Fleur found herself smiling.

"I take it he is not the reason you wished to discuss something personal."

"No, he is not."

"Mr. Vincent, the State Department official auditing the mines?"

"He's only auditing one mine and yes."

"Ah, I suspected something from the rather protective stance he took at mealtime."

"I will be joining him in America with Johari as soon as visas can be arranged."

"Are you sure that is what you want? You've dedicated your life to healing the sick."

"I can be a doctor in America too."

"True." He sighed, clearly accepting that she meant to move on from Sympa-Med. "Do you have a recommendation to fill your position?"

"I *would* recommend Tanya Ruston."

"But she is not a doctor. Do you think she would be open to attending medical school at Sympa-Med's expense?"

Fleur found herself smiling. "The woman hates school with a passion."

"That is unfortunate."

"For Sympa-Med, yes."

"Point taken." He rubbed his eyes again. "Thank you for sharing your concerns with me. I'm still not sure what all this means, but it's not going to be good for Sympa-Med."

"I'm sorry," Fleur said with genuine sadness.

"Have you noticed any other odd behavior in the security personnel?" he asked, as if it was an afterthought.

"Not really, no."

He nodded. "A couple behaved very strangely during their interviews. I cannot decide if that is because they were nervous talking to me, or if it indicates a need to hide something."

"The unemployment rate is over eighty percent," she said, giving the men the benefit of the doubt.

"There is that. We do a good thing here."

"In more ways than one, yes, we do."

"Is it naïve of me to hope greedy people aren't going to screw that up?"

"To hope? No."

"But you're worried too, aren't you?"

"Yes." She saw no reason to deny it. If the espionage ring was linked to Sympa-Med, donations were going to plummet and along with them the budget for the legitimate and necessary work the organization did.

Tanya and Mbari were starting to make dinner from the stores they had gotten at the village the day before while the men put up the tents and secured the area. Mbari kept turning to watch Kadin as he worked on the first tent.

Tanya smiled and gently nudged him. "Go help Kadin. I've got this."

The boy looked at her, his expression agonized. "Roman told me help with food."

"He won't mind. Trust me."

Kadin called, "Come on over here, Mbari. I could use your help."

"I have never put up a tent."

"I will teach you how."

Neil arrived with another load of wood for the fire a few minutes later. "Will this do for cooking?"

"Sure. I'm not making a feast and we didn't get meat because we don't have a cooler. The cornmeal will take the longest to cook."

"So, Roman's keeping the kid."

"He said so." She still couldn't quite believe it. "How is he going to arrange Mbari's move to the States?"

"Our boss has a lot of clout in high places. As soon as Face and Ben identify the real culprits for the espionage, the General will get the kill order on you rescinded and we can come in."

"Your boss is a General?" Somehow, she'd gotten the impression that the Atrati were not connected officially to the military.

"Retired. Still acts like brass though, at least the smart kind. He'll get the wheels spinning on Mbari's adoption."

"Adoption. Wow. I never would have expected Roman to adopt a child."

"I don't think he planned on it either, but sometimes you just gotta swing the bat when life throws you a curve ball."

"That's a good attitude to take."

"Yeah. Roman helped me see it that way when I didn't make it into the SEALs."

"You didn't?"

"Nope, but the Atrati wanted me anyway. I've been on Roman's team since I joined."

"You make it sound like military."

"More like paramilitary, but yeah. Technically, we're mercenaries, but most of our funding comes from Washington."

"And no one even knows you exist."

"Wouldn't be very effective if they did."

"I suppose." Roman had said this wasn't a Hollywood movie, but it was pretty intriguing to say the least. "So, how can a man who will use a woman sexually to get answers be the same guy who will adopt an orphaned Bantu boy?" she asked before she even realized the question was lurking in her thoughts.

"He puts the assignment ahead of personal considerations."

"He told me that."

Neil started peeling bananas to add to the cornmeal. "With you, that attitude is all bullshit."

"What?" Her head jerked up and she stared at the blond soldier.

He met her gaze with a serious look of his own. "Listen, I heard him tell you he would have had sex with you no matter what, right?"

"So he said."

"He wasn't lying. He reacts to you like I've never seen him react before. He was looking for excuses to break his own cardinal rule about no recreational sex while on a job."

"I don't consider sex a recreational sport."

"No, I don't imagine you do."

"He told me it wasn't casual."

"Did it feel casual to you?"

"No." Anything but. "Only . . ."

"Nothing. Listen, Tanna, I don't know what your past experience with sex is, but I'll tell you that as long as I've known Roman, no woman has gotten to him like you do."

"So, he wants me."

"He's possessive of you. You have to have noticed. He practically shits bricks when Kadin gets within spitting distance of you."

"That's ridiculous." Only it wasn't. She'd noticed.

"They got into a fight, would have torn up our quarters if I hadn't moved the furniture double-time."

"Why would they fight over me?"

"Kadin didn't want Roman having sex with you and Roman figured that meant Kadin wanted you himself."

"What a couple of knuckleheads." But it warmed her heart to think of Kadin's trying to protect her the way Beau would have done. She wasn't sure what she felt about Roman's sexual jealousy.

She was pretty sure she liked it, not another banner moment for her responses. "So, you're saying that I'm special to Roman?"

"He risked his career to keep you safe."

"He said something about that, but I don't understand. It sounds like your boss approved Roman getting me out of Sympa-Med's compound."

"Unofficially. Officially, if we're caught before the kill order is rescinded, political pressure could be brought to bear and Roman could be kicked out of the Atrati. We guarantee our clients a certain amount of loyalty, especially Uncle Sam."

"You and Kadin could lose your jobs too."

"He'll take the fall for us, say he ordered us to do what we did."

"You won't let him take the blame though."

"Nah, but he thinks we would. The man's a serious control freak. He thinks he can tell the rest of the world what to do and they'll listen."

"Arrogant."

"You think so?"

"You don't?"

"We like to call it 'fully justified confidence'." Neil winked.

She laughed. "I should have known."

"Should have known what?" Roman's voice came from behind her.

She spun to face him, surging to her feet from her crouch beside the fire. "That Neil agrees with you on the definition of arrogance."

Roman's features tightened. "Talking over my faults?"

"Don't be a drama queen, Geronimo. It's not all about you. Didn't your mama tell you as much?"

"Not lately."

"I bet." Tanya gave him a teasing smile. "I imagine she acts thrilled to see you when she gets the chance."

"She does that."

"Maybe now that you're taking on Mbari, you'll see her more."

"It's inevitable."

"You're an amazing man, Roman."

"You think so?" His tone was about ten times more serious than hers.

And just like that, the atmosphere around them changed, went deep and meaningful.

"You going to sleep in Mbari's tent tonight?" she asked.

Roman's brows rose. "You going to fuss if I say no?"

"Maybe." She looked down at her nails, as if they had a full manicure instead of ragged cuticles and blunt tips. "Maybe not."

"It looks like he and Kadin are making friends."

"Yeah, I suppose they are."

"So, *maybe* or maybe *not?*"

"Probably not," she answered, knowing what the real question was. Did she object to his sharing her tent?

Whether it was his actions with the kidnapped children and Mbari, the things Roman had said, the claims Neil had made or simply the love that refused to be denied inside her, but she was prepared to share a tent without argument. Maybe more than simply share. Heck, who was she kidding? Definitely more.

At least this time she could be sure he didn't have ulterior motives for making love.

Ben didn't wait for Fleur to come back to the chalet, but started heading toward the dining hall as soon as her conversation with the director wrapped up.

He met her outside the medical hut. "You told him."

"You look pleased, so you must be talking about me informing him that I will not be continuing as compound administrator."

He took her hand, lacing their fingers. "Yes, that."

"The sooner Sympa-Med is made aware of my imminent departure, the better."

"I like the sound of that."

"Departure?"

"Imminent."

"I do not know how long the paperwork will take to obtain, but I am ready to move as soon as it has cleared proper channels."

"I work under the aegis of the State Department. We can clear proper channels in record time."

"Nothing would make me happier." And he could tell she meant it.

He wanted to kiss her right there, but knew she was shy about public displays. The fact she'd allowed him to hold her hand was pretty amazing as it was.

"You've got that look."

"The one that says 'I want to kiss you'?"

"Is that what it means? All I know is I've never had anyone look at me so tenderly. I believe I fell in love with that expression even as I fell for you."

"I'll have to make sure I look at you like this often then. I don't want you falling out of love."

"I do not think that can happen. Not for us. We are too aware of what a miracle it is we have found each other."

"You are right. I hope you can forgive me." But he could not hold back from kissing her right then.

She didn't even ask what for, just tipped her head to make the caress of his mouth against hers easier. He didn't let it get hot and heavy; he just needed the connection.

"You are so precious," he said as he moved up to place a kiss on her forehead.

"I feel the same about you. You are an uncommon man."

"For you."

"For me."

Drew and Rachel were waiting in the hut when Ben and Fleur returned.

"We've got to try to keep Sympa-Med's name out of the espionage case," Rachel said as soon as the door shut behind Ben.

"Is that possible?" Fleur asked, her voice laced with hope.

"Probable? No. Possible? Yes." Ben shrugged. "But our agency specializes in the improbable."

Rachel grinned. "He's got that right. I remember the first case I worked with TGP. I was a DEA agent on leave then. I haven't been on an uncomplicated assignment once since joining."

"You sound like you thrive on the challenge," Drew observed.

Rachel grinned. "Yep. But don't try to tell me you don't. Super-spy, super-soldier, they're all about going beyond the norm, even when the norm is federal undercover work."

Drew nodded. "True." He looked at Fleur. "I called Roman with an update on your discussion with the director."

"You must have called him right after I left the hut," Ben said.

"I'd sent the connection before Fleur and the director were done talking. I didn't figure Roman needed deets on Fleur's move to the States."

"I imagine Tanya would not mind having them," Ben observed.

"True, but I already told Roman that you two
are glowing like a couple of camping lanterns in
the middle of the desert."

Fleur made a sound of amusement. "You have
quite the way with words, Mr. Peterson."

"I have been told," he said, with an attempt at
humility in his expression that was less than con-
vincing.

"How is Tanya?" Fleur asked without preamble.

"Doing fine. They've dropped all six boys off
with family."

"I thought there were seven."

"Roman decided to keep one."

Ben couldn't even begin to hide his shock at
that. Fleur looked well and truly stunned too.

"Say again. I thought I just heard you tell me
that your team leader has decided to adopt a
child."

"You heard right. The poor kid doesn't have any
family."

"That's true of a huge number of children in
Zimbabwe," Fleur said. "The AIDS plague and
continuing spread of malaria, not to mention malnutrition have taken their toll on family lines."

"Not all of those other kids got themselves into
Roman's bubble of protection."

"Must be a serious bubble."

"It is."

"So, Tanya really is safe with him?"

"As safe as she can be anywhere with a kill order
out on her."

"Isn't Rachel at risk right now?"

"She's pretty safe here in the hut."

"Besides, I can take care of myself."

"A sniper's bullet isn't going to bounce off your attitude alone," Ben reminded her.

"I'll wear a vest if I leave the hut, Dad."

He shook his head. "You'd better."

"Besides, Kadin checked for line of sight into the compound and there are only a couple of places she would be vulnerable to sniper fire. One is near the south-end latrines and the other is the open area between the dining hall and the medical hut."

"That's good to know," Rachel said.

"The dining hall could be an issue."

"Hopefully, the perp will act before the sick day story gets old."

"She's in Harare until tomorrow," Fleur said.

"You're convinced it's the director's PA?" Ben asked.

"I'm convinced she's connected," Fleur replied. "No one else could have sent those e-mails."

"Unless you think the director is playing a deep game."

"I think there are few people in the world who think on the manipulative levels you do."

"Why, thank you."

"Think nothing of it."

They agreed Drew would go to the dining hall early for the evening meal and leave a few minutes after Ben and Fleur arrived, sneaking back to Fleur's hut to watch over Rachel. The female TGP agent grumbled, but she'd taken her course in teamwork and didn't put up too much of a disagreement.

CHAPTER FIFTEEN

Mbari showed no visible disappointment when I told he would be sharing a tent with his new friend, Kadin. He and Tanya went to the tents together and she hugged the yawning boy goodnight. He'd had a rough few days, but from the sound of what his life was like before, none of them had been easy for a long time.

He held her back from going into her tent. "You think he really take me America?"

"Yes, I do." And it was in that moment that she realized no matter how hard she fought it, how futile it might be, she was in love with Roman.

The feeling was deeper than anything she'd experienced with Quinton, more uncontrollable than she thought love should be and she suspected irrevocable.

She hugged Mbari again. "Get some rest. Roman doesn't go back on his promises."

He might withhold the truth. He might take advantage of an undeniable attraction, but he wouldn't break his word.

Just as he'd promised to protect Tanya and had

stood between her and bullets to do it, not to mention risking the job he loved and believed in, he would do whatever it took to bring Mbari to America with him.

"I think he good man. You take him without cows."

She laughed, tears only a heartbeat away. "I'll think about it," she managed to get out with a smile.

"Yes. I like you for family. You very pretty without black stuff on your face."

"Thank you." Kadin had found them a small off-shoot of a river to camp near that night. Bamboo hid them from curious eyes, at least of the human variety and Tanya had taken the opportunity to take a thorough bath. She'd even washed her hair.

Roman had watched her and watched over her and she hadn't even made a token protest about turning his back. She'd fled when he'd started stripping for his own bath after she'd rinsed her hair, though.

She had no desire to put on a show for the others and hadn't trusted her own control if both Roman and she were naked.

Roman joined her a half hour later, the darkness in the tent almost complete. She listened to the rustle of his clothing as he undressed, and waited in silence for him to join her on top of the sleeping bags.

His big body came down beside hers, his hand closing over her hip immediately. "Please tell me this is an invitation," he whispered quietly.

She'd gone to bed completely naked. She reached out and placed her hand on his chest, burying her fingers in the masculine hair. Instead of answering verbally, she leaned forward and up so her mouth could brush the underside of his chin.

"Oh, thank God." And he said it exactly like a prayer.

She smiled against his stubble. It scratched her lips, but she didn't mind. The rasp of it against her skin later was going to feel very, very good.

"I was going insane watching you bathe. You know that, don't you?"

She didn't bother to reply, just kissed along his jaw and down his neck, inhaling the clean male musk that would haunt her dreams when they went their separate ways.

"That feels good, *liúba*. Don't stop."

She didn't, latching on to the join between his neck and shoulder and sucking gently while his big warrior's body moved against hers. His hard-on pressed hotly against her hip, letting her know that he wasn't exaggerating his level of desire.

Not that she doubted it. The one thing she could not doubt between them was the reality of their mutual passion.

If she did, she couldn't do this, no matter how much she loved him. But she believed now that he had used a convenient situation, not seduced her into thinking he wanted her when he didn't.

He wanted her all right. The increasing urgency of his movements made that undeniable.

"I want to be inside you," he gritted. "But I want to taste you too."

He sounded confused by his own conflicting desires. That was okay by her. How fair would it be if she was the only one with disconnected thoughts and feelings?

He pulled her into his body, rubbing them together with passionate purpose. She bit his chest to muffle the moan snaking out of her throat.

He grunted, but he didn't try to push her face away. Instead, she could feel pre-cum leaking onto her skin from the tip of his penis.

And then, somehow they were kissing, and not a gentle, let's-get-started kiss, but rather a demand for more and deeper and more again. His hands roamed her body while she returned the favor and did her best to stifle the sounds of passion coming from her.

He broke the kiss and whispered next to her ear. "Do you want my bandana?"

She sensed that he was asking something more, something bigger, but she wasn't sure what. One thing she did know, if she said yes, she would be legitimizing the time before, acknowledging it had not only been about the data on her security chip. She was ready to accept that it had been real passion. Perhaps she was even ready to forgive him.

She nodded against his head.

"Say the word. I need to hear it."

But she didn't want to talk. If she let words out, the wrong ones might escape.

"Come on, baby, tell me. No doubts." He tugged at her earlobe with his teeth.

"Yes," she hissed out, needing the bandana to stop her from blurting out her love as much as to keep her passionate noises muffled.

He tucked the knotted center of the bandana into her mouth and then tied it snugly behind her head. Having it in her mouth brought back the feelings she'd had that morning in her bed, leading to an arousal so intense, she was shaking with it.

They touched each other in a frenzy of need

that had her gripping his erection and tugging it, while he used his fingers to spread the wetness between her legs along her swollen lips to her clitoris. She thrashed against him and he growled with need.

This felt so primal, so intensely unique to them that she could not even consider it mere sex. Despite the level of passion flowing through them both, or maybe because of it, this felt spiritual and elemental and absolutely necessary.

"I love the gag, especially here in the dark where we can't even see each other, just feel," he said into her ear. "But I want to kiss you."

She nodded her understanding, rubbing her cheek along his.

"I'll just have to kiss you everywhere but your lips."

She moaned at the image his words presented and then moaned again when he started with her collarbone. He didn't just kiss her, or at least he made the kisses as erotic as anything they'd done with their mouths. By the time he'd reached the apex of her thighs, she was floating on a haze of eroticism that turned the dark around them into a sensual blanket of air caressing her oversensitive body with invisible fingers.

He pressed inside her with his very real, thick, long fingers while using his tongue to kiss her nether lips with powerful intimacy. He was so intent on her pleasure, showing no impatience to consummate this lovemaking. Apparently, he had decided what he wanted most was to taste her.

She reveled in the experience, her heart storing away every drop of pleasure, every emotional response for later, when she would not have his hard body to make her feel both wanted and safe.

Her climax caught her by surprise, jolting her body into rigidity before the convulsions of her womb radiated the ultimate pleasure outward into her every extremity. She was still shuddering in aftershocks when he pushed inside her body, stretching and filling her in a way she knew she would miss for the rest of her life.

The moment was so profound, so intense that she could not hold back the emotion washing over her, drowning all her inhibitions with a tidal wave of feeling. "I love you," she cried out, praying he could not understand the words through the gag.

Because she simply could not hold them back.

He untied the gag with jerky movements and then yanked it from her mouth before covering her lips with his. The kiss carried them through her second orgasm and his first.

He collapsed on top of her, but pulling out, rolled to the side all too soon. She didn't know what he did with the condom and she didn't really care right then. She just let him curve her into his body and draw her into sleep.

Ben carefully disentangled himself from Fleur's body and silently left her bed. The muffled sounds of someone coming into the hut had woken him from his light doze.

So, someone in the compound *was* working with the espionage ring.

He crept to the door in time to see one of the security guards going into Tanya's room. Ben trusted Rachel to be awake, but feigning sleep. That didn't mean he wasn't going to watch her back though.

He made his way across the hall without making a sound. The guard had left the door ajar, probably not wanting the *snick* of the tumbler to wake up the woman sleeping within.

Rachel was lying on her side with her back to the door. The guard held some kind of device near her. He checked his watch twice over the next ten minutes, his nervousness a discernible presence around him.

The tableau did not change for fifteen silent minutes, but then the guard checked his watch again and tucked the device into a pocket before backing away toward the door.

Ben melted into the shadows, following the other man when he snuck out of the hut. The guard went to the security dormitory and slipped inside.

After waiting fifteen minutes to make sure he wasn't coming right back out, Ben made his way to quarters and woke Drew to tell him what had happened.

One of the Marine privates came out of the other bedroom, weapon drawn and moving on quiet feet.

Ben nodded approval at him. "Good reflexes," he said quietly.

The private let out a breath. "Sorry, sir. I thought you were an intruder."

"Don't apologize for doing your job."

"And doing it well," Drew said, tucking his shirt in.

"Is there a problem, sir?" the private asked.

"We do have a situation, soldier, and I'd like you and your fellow private's help with it."

"I'll go get him."

"I'll stake out the guards' dormitory," Drew said as the other man left. "Send one of the privates to relieve me once you brief them on the basics of the situation."

"Will do."

When the Marines returned, Ben shared a very truncated version of what was going on. "I need you to keep a protection detail on the director and help us watch the security guard to see who his contact is."

They agreed and the one who had woken when Ben had entered the hut went to relieve Drew. Ben put in a sat-call to the Old Man, asking for more Marine backup to be on standby for the arrests. He would have enjoyed arresting the spies himself, but that wasn't the way TGP operated.

They maintained secrecy by not participating in the cleanup segment of an assignment.

When Drew returned, he made his own call to Roman, telling the team leader of the guard's involvement.

Roman waited until morning to tell Tanya about the call Neil had brought to him in the early hours of the morning.

"So, they know who the spies are?" she asked with an unreadable expression.

"They strongly suspect the PA, but they're sure of the security guard, of course. They're watching to see who he has a rendezvous with."

"Is Fleur okay?"

"She never even woke up while the guard was

downloading the data with another hand-held scanner."

"He must have gotten it from one of the Sympa-Med people."

"That's the current theory."

"So, I can return?"

"Not quite yet. I called my boss, but he wants us to lay low for the next forty-eight hours while he gets the kill order rescinded and any teams in the field recalled."

Corbin had also promised to expedite the paperwork on Mbari.

The General thought the Zimbabwe government would cooperate in order to keep another story about the human-trafficking problem within their borders out of the international media. They were already at risk for further economic sanctions; they couldn't afford a major incident right now.

"That makes sense." She hugged herself, somehow looking more vulnerable than she had when he'd told her they had to leave the compound. "Are we going to stay here and camp out until you get the all clear?"

"No."

When he didn't say anything else, she gave him a look. "Care to expand on that?"

"I thought we'd take Mbari into Harare and do some shopping for him."

"Won't they be looking for me in Harare?"

"Actually, no. Even if they knew you had left the compound, they would assume you'd made a run for a border, most likely South Africa's, just like we planned originally. There's no reason for an Army kill team to be in Harare and whoever arranged the roadblock to get to you believes you are still in the compound, so they won't be looking for you. Even if they were, they wouldn't be looking in Harare."

"But you were going to take me out of the country."

"That was before we got sidetracked returning Peter Pan's lost boys. We can stay under the radar for another two days and then return to the Sympa-Med compound."

"Sounds good by me. Are we staying in a hotel tonight?"

"We are."

She perked up at that, the first time she'd really smiled since they'd started talking. He would have thought she'd be happier to find out that the people who had used her as an information mule were going to be brought to justice.

"You want a hotel bed?"

"I want an unlimited hot shower. I haven't had one of those since the last time I was back home." She looked at him through her lashes. "I wouldn't mind sharing the water."

And just like that he was hard enough to bust a zipper. "I'll keep that in mind."

But they had things to do before that.

The drive into Harare was uneventful. They found the market and took Mbari shopping for extra clothes, paper and art supplies and a hand-held game system that Kadin insisted the kid needed. Roman wasn't inclined to disagree.

He left Tanya with Kadin and Neil in the hotel while he and Mbari went to the appointment Corbin had set up for them with the local emigration officials. The government had agreed to expedite the paperwork in exchange for being able to take credit for the takedown of the slave ring and the return of the stolen children to their villages. Corbin had also pulled strings on the U.S. side so the adoption would be recognized and Mbari would get his conferred citizenship.

Roman didn't want to know what favors his boss had had to call in to manage that one.

The appointment went without incident, Mbari getting his photo identification and traveling papers at the end of about a hundred signatures. Roman didn't like paperwork.

Afterward, the young boy looked up at Roman with wide brown eyes. "I am you son now?"

"Yes." He didn't correct Mbari's speech. That would come soon enough. Roman would have *baba* work with his new son. She would be thrilled. If she could teach *him* Ukrainian, even the good words, she could teach proper English to the Bantu youth.

Tears filled those still disbelieving eyes. "This is a sleeping picture."

Roman pulled the boy into a fierce hug. "No, it's not a dream. We are a family now."

This assignment had changed his life in important and irrevocable ways. And the funny thing was, he didn't mind. Roman had thought he would never have a family, but he'd been wrong. He'd believed he would never fall in love either, but Tanya had destroyed his illusions of solitude.

It had taken him more time than it should have to figure that out, but last night when she'd told him she loved him from behind the gag, he'd realized how very much he wanted those to be the words she said and how much he needed her to mean them. The Atrati had been his life for so long, recognizing the change hadn't come naturally to him.

But he saw it now. Tanya was as unaware as he had been of his love for her, but he'd convince her they were meant to be together. Even if he had to buy her a whole herd of cattle.

Ben watched with only slight surprise as the government official Fleur disliked so much met with the security guard. The small scanner, as well as some money, passed hands. Ben informed Drew of the handoff through the small communication ear-buds Neil had left behind.

"We'll watch him for further contact with the PA, but they spent over twenty-four hours together in Harare."

"I'll arrange his pickup after he leaves the compound. He doesn't strike me as a brave man. How about you?"

"I would concur."

"I think we can get him to roll on his partners."

"Agreed. I'll handle the interrogation."

"I bet you're good at that."

Drew just laughed.

Ben looked around the compound and realized his job here was done. He went back to Fleur's hut and called the Old Man.

"So, you think he'll name the others involved?"

"Yes."

"Your report on the mine was read with interest."

"Enough interest to take action?"

"Diplomatic talks will start next week. What they will result in is anybody's guess."

"Our government wants the minerals."

"But our President isn't the type to close his eyes to human rights violations like some in the past have been."

"I hate politics," Ben grumbled.

"You ready for a new assignment?"

"About that . . ."

"Dr. Andikan is going to change your life, isn't she?"

"Yes, sir, I do think she is."

"You sound pretty happy about that."

"I am."

"I can minimize the travel for your assignments."

"I don't want to have to leave the agency—that would be a good compromise." He was sure Fleur would agree.

Roman started his campaign with Tanya that evening in the shower. They made love and he tried to elicit the words she'd hidden behind the gag the night before, but she was stubbornly mute. Or if not silent, at least unwilling to vocalize the love he was pretty sure she returned.

A woman like her would not have let him back into her body without powerful emotional motivation, but it might be time for the cows.

When he told Mbari what he planned, the boy was ecstatic. He wanted Tanya in their family too.

* * *

Tanya dressed for dinner in a new sari she had bought at the market the day before. Roman had invited her to share a special dinner with him and Mbari in the suite. She couldn't believe they had less than a day left together. The night before had been filled with passion, every moment of which she'd recorded in her memory for later.

They'd spent the day doing touristy things around the city with the others. Mbari had been incandescent with joy as he held his new father's hand and pointed out the treasures of his former homeland's capital.

He and Roman were dressing in the suite's other bedroom, though Tanya and Roman were sharing this one for their mini-vacation.

Tanya brushed her hair until it settled silkily against her head. She rubbed lip-gloss on, but she hadn't worn any other makeup since Beau's wedding. Her sandals had a small wedge heel, making her calves look pretty good, even if it was her thinking so. The green blouse and complementary sari flattered her figure of modest curves and brought out the emerald flecks in her eyes.

Well, she wasn't going to get more ready than this.

She went into the main room of the suite and stopped short at the sight that met her. There were pictures of cows covering all the flat surfaces. Some were pretty unique, done in purples, oranges and even teal.

In the center of the room, a table set to the nines took pride of place with gleaming silver domes over the food. Standing behind it, Roman and Mbari faced her with matching Cheshire cat grins.

"There are a lot of cows in here," she observed.

Mbari's grin grew bigger, if that was possible. "I drew them all."

"Each one represents a cow purchased through World Vision for a different village in their network."

"You bought cows?" she asked faintly, her brain making an instant connection she just as quickly dismissed as impossible.

"There are thirty of them," Mbari said in awe. "That is bride price bigger than village chief pays."

"Bride price?" she asked in a weak voice.

Roman came around the table and dropped to one knee in front of her. He took her hand and met her gaze, his a swirling molten silver. "I love you, Tanya. I believe you love me too. I fu—screwed up really badly by not admitting my feelings to myself or anyone else. I hurt you and made you think I was using you, when the truth was, I can't resist you and I don't want to. Not anymore. Will you be my wife and Mbari's new mom? Help us make the kind of family every kid deserves."

Oh, he knew the buttons to push. Even if she didn't love the man to distraction, she'd want to marry him after that speech. But she did love him. With everything in her heart, and she forgave him too.

"Yes. Yes, I love you. Yes, I forgive you. Yes, I will marry you."

Mbari let out a whoop of delight and Roman surged to his feet, pulling her into his arms for a kiss that more than sealed the deal.

They broke apart and he looked down at her. "You forgive me? You're sure?"

"Positive. We had a really untraditional courtship, but I think we weathered the storm pretty nicely. That gives me lots of hope and peace about our future."

"You're right. You're everything I could ever want in a woman. I can't believe I didn't see that right away."

"You weren't looking for someone to share your life with."

"But I still found you. And Mbari." He turned and opened one arm to the boy, who came and joined in their hug.

Tanya smiled down at Mbari, holding him tightly to her side. "You are a matchmaker, you know that?"

"Is this a good thing?"

"It is. This time, anyway."

"Then I like to be this matchmaker."

"My mother is going to love you," she said.

Maybe even as much as Tanya did. She couldn't believe how all the old dreams of her heart had come true, with the one man she'd thought she could never have. Africa was a land of miracles, but she looked forward to going home again and making a life of love and joy with the two males who held her in such a loving, family embrace.

EPILOGUE

Tanya was right. Her parents both adored the Bantu youth, declaring Mbari a wonderful addition to their family. The Rustons were equally pleased that Tanya had decided to move back to the States with Roman.

The director of the Atrati needed a new assignment assessor and coordinator. Wanting to spend more time with his family, especially his new son and soon-to-be wife, Roman took the position.

Kadin was promoted to team lead; Neil and Drew took him out and got him drunk to celebrate.

Ibeamaka did roll on his partners and the espionage ring was disbanded. The risk to the U.S. military technology wasn't going to disappear though, not while it was still being used as a bartering chip for petroleum and access to raw minerals. France refused to extradite the board member and the personal assistant identified as part of the espionage ring, though they were both banned from any further connection to Sympa-Med, which also changed its supplier for GPS locator chips.

Unfortunately, the former Sympa-Med board member died of a heart attack in his sleep two months later. The PA he'd had an affair with and who had facilitated the use of medical relief workers as unwitting information mules discovered it was impossible to get another job. Rumors swirled about her, though the source of the rumors could not be discovered.

Ibeamaka traded detailed information on his partners for his freedom, but it did him little good. He was found floating in the river near his home. Local authorities speculated his clients suspected him of giving their secrets away as well.

With help from fellow agent Alan Hyatt, Ben found Fleur's brother living in America already. The reunion of brother and sister was both emotional and heartwarming. The young man was thrilled a member of his family still lived; he had believed Fleur dead for the past fifteen years. He was even happier to find out he would be an uncle in less than a year's time.

He accepted Johari with open arms, though treating her more like a treasured friend than a niece.

Have you tried the other books in Lucy's Goddard Project series?

Satisfaction Guaranteed

Anytime, anyplace, Ethan Crane's your man. An agent's agent, he's tough, smart, and fearless. Exactly the guy you want when the stuff hits the fan—and the kind Beth Whitney avoids like the plague. It took a fiancé in the business to teach her, but she's learned her lesson: Don't. Date. Agents. It's this rule that's kept her employed at the agency, doing her part for world security from behind a desk. So when a case throws the two together, Beth's determined to keep it strictly professional. So far, so good—except for the steamy kisses, the red-hot phone sex, and . . . What was that rule again?

To Ethan, Beth couldn't be less his type if her father ran the agency, which, oh yeah, he does. Still he can't help but find her work in the field a total turn on. Off the field it's even better. But hot pursuit of a notorious information broker is what they should focus on—not each other. That can wait until they've accomplished a job well done. Or can it?

Deal With This

When reporter Alan Hyatt is assigned to investigate a case of high-tech espionage in the Vancouver film industry—and meets sizzling actress Jillian Carlyle—he finds a perfect reason to work in bed. But Jillian is also his landlady—and she doesn't date her renters. When Jillian suggests he play a background actor on her sci-fi show to get closer to his suspects, Alan's not about to turn down the red-hot redhead, even if she keeps throwing him curves . . .

Alan may be six-feet-something of chiseled ruggedness, but Jillian doesn't do relationships with men who stir more than her senses. No one is getting a chance at her heart. Especially not one of her renters. Still, there's nothing wrong with enjoying Alan from afar—but not too far to appreciate his rock-hard abs. If only he didn't make her feel safe and oh so right whenever they touch . . .

The Spy Who Wants Me

Warning: May Be Too Hot To Handle

Elle Gray looks like a supermodel, thinks like a super agent, and can kill a man with her bare hands. But when she meets Dr. Beau Ruston, the brilliant scientist and ex-college football star in charge of the project she's been sent to protect, she wants more of her bare self around him than just her hands. If his muscular grace and quick wit hadn't turned her on, there would still be those big brown eyes . . . watching her suspiciously. With a man this smart and sexy questioning her cover, the bad guys are the least of her problems.

Beau Ruston knows Elle is a government spy, and he doesn't like to be spied on—or lied to, no matter how charming the liar happens to be. Wait, did he say "charming"? Damn hot is more like it. He should know, chemistry is his business, whether it's in the lab or in the bedroom, but the reaction Elle is setting off might be too much for even him to control . . .

Watch Over Me

Mission: Irresistible

Super spy Mykola Chernichenko comes from a family of geniuses, and though he's no idiot himself, he'd rather be where the action is than analyze it to death. That's why his vacation has just been cut short by a call to get two of his siblings out of some serious trouble—while protecting a nerdy scientist who's latest project could change the world . . . and get her killed.

The guy who'd rather act than think guarding an egghead in a lab coat? Myk would appreciate the irony more if he weren't so busy trying to figure out how, exactly, to get under said lab coat. Because Lana Ericson just happens to be the hottest thing working the scientific method since, well, ever. Myk has a feeling Lana's laser-like focus would translate to something equally intense in the bedroom. And if she's as curious about him, Myk might just be willing to donate his body to science—each and every night . . .

Books by Bestselling Author
Fern Michaels

___The Jury	0-8217-7878-1	$6.99US/$9.99CAN
___Sweet Revenge	0-8217-7879-X	$6.99US/$9.99CAN
___Lethal Justice	0-8217-7880-3	$6.99US/$9.99CAN
___Free Fall	0-8217-7881-1	$6.99US/$9.99CAN
___Fool Me Once	0-8217-8071-9	$7.99US/$10.99CAN
___Vegas Rich	0-8217-8112-X	$7.99US/$10.99CAN
___Hide and Seek	1-4201-0184-6	$6.99US/$9.99CAN
___Hokus Pokus	1-4201-0185-4	$6.99US/$9.99CAN
___Fast Track	1-4201-0186-2	$6.99US/$9.99CAN
___Collateral Damage	1-4201-0187-0	$6.99US/$9.99CAN
___Final Justice	1-4201-0188-9	$6.99US/$9.99CAN
___Up Close and Personal	0-8217-7956-7	$7.99US/$9.99CAN
___Under the Radar	1-4201-0683-X	$6.99US/$9.99CAN
___Razor Sharp	1-4201-0684-8	$7.99US/$10.99CAN
___Yesterday	1-4201-1494-8	$5.99US/$6.99CAN
___Vanishing Act	1-4201-0685-6	$7.99US/$10.99CAN
___Sara's Song	1-4201-1493-X	$5.99US/$6.99CAN
___Deadly Deals	1-4201-0686-4	$7.99US/$10.99CAN
___Game Over	1-4201-0687-2	$7.99US/$10.99CAN
___Sins of Omission	1-4201-1153-1	$7.99US/$10.99CAN
___Sins of the Flesh	1-4201-1154-X	$7.99US/$10.99CAN
___Cross Roads	1-4201-1192-2	$7.99US/$10.99CAN

Available Wherever Books Are Sold!
Check out our website at **www.kensingtonbooks.com**